Praise for Joseph Heywood and the Woods Cop Mystery series:

"Heywood has crafted an entertaining bunch of characters. An absorbing narrative twists and turns in a setting ripe for corruption."
—*Dallas Morning News*

"Crisp writing, great scenery, quirky characters and an absorbing plot add to the appeal. . . ."
—*Wall Street Journal*

"Heywood is a master of his form."
—*Detroit Free Press*

"Top-notch action scenes, engaging characters both major and minor, masterful dialogue, and a passionate sense of place make this a fine series."
—*Publishers Weekly*

"Joseph Heywood writes with a voice as unique and rugged as Michigan's Upper Peninsula itself."
—Steve Hamilton, Edgar® Award-winning author of *The Lock Artist*

"Well written, suspenseful, and bleakly humorous while moving as quickly as a wolf cutting through the winter woods. In addition to strong characters and . . . compelling romance, Heywood provides vivid, detailed descriptions of the wilderness and the various procedures and techniques of conservation officers and poachers. . . . Highly recommended."
—*Booklist*

"Taut and assured writing that hooked me from the start. Every word builds toward the ending, and along the way some of the writing took my breath away."
—Kirk Russell, author of *Dead Game* and *Redback*

"[A] tightly written mystery/crime novel . . . that offers a nice balance between belly laughs, head-scratching plot lines, and the real grit of modern police work."
—*Petersen's Hunting*

Praise for *The Snowfly*

"A truly wonderful, wild, funny and slightly crazy novel about fly fishing. *The Snowfly* ranks with the best this modern era has produced."
—*San Francisco Chronicle*

"A magical whirlwind of a novel, squarely in the tradition of Tim O'Brien's *Going After Cacciato* and Jim Harrison's *Legends of the Fall.*"
—Howard Frank Mosher, author of *The Fall of the Year* and others

"*The Snowfly* is as much about fishing as *Moby Dick* is about whaling."
—*Library Journal*

"Fly-fishing legend meets global adventure in Heywood's sparkling, ambitious novel . . . an engrossing *bildungsroman* . . . part Tom Robbins, part *David Copperfield.*"
—*Publishers Weekly* (starred review)

"If *The Snowfly* becomes a movie, it will blast *A River Runs Through It* out of the water."
—*Fly Angler's Online Book Review*

". . . a finely tuned plot and masterful, literary craftsmanship. It will stand with *The River Why* as the finest of its kind."
—*Riverwatch*

Praise for *Red Jacket* (A Lute Bapcat Mystery)

"Joseph Heywood has long been a red-blooded American original and an author worth reading. With *Red Jacket*—a colorful and sprawling new novel with a terrific new protagonist named Lute Bapcat—he raises the bar to soaring new heights."

—C. J. Box, *New York Times* bestselling author of *Force of Nature*

"In 1913, Theodore Roosevelt recruits former Rough Rider Lute Bapcat to become a game warden on Michigan's Upper Peninsula in Heywood's absorbing first in a new series. Outsized characters, both real (athlete George Gipp before his Notre Dame fame, union organizer Mother Jones) and fictional (randy businesswoman Jaquelle Frei; Lute's Russian companion, Pinkhus Sergeyevich Zakov), pepper the narrative."

—*Publishers Weekly*

"Joseph Heywood tells a great story, weaving real and fictional characters throughout his narrative . . . [C]risp writing with a sense of humor . . ."

—*Woods 'N Water magazine*

"Heywood mixes history—the [miners'] strike and the violence it engenders, culminating with the Christmas Eve Italian Hall Disaster in Calumet, Michigan, in which 73 died—with vivid characterizations in a . . . promising series opener."

—*Booklist*

HARDER GROUND

MORE WOODS COP STORIES

JOSEPH HEYWOOD

Guilford, Connecticut

An imprint of Rowman & Littlefield

Distributed by NATIONAL BOOK NETWORK

British Library Cataloguing in Publication Information Available

Library of Congress Cataloging-in-Publication Data

Heywood, Joseph.
   [Short stories. Selections]
   Harder ground : more woods cop stories / Joseph Heywood.
      pages ; cm
   ISBN 978-1-4930-0902-2 (softcover : acid-free paper)
   1. Game wardens—Michigan—Fiction. 2. Women—Michigan—Fiction. 3. Upper Peninsula (Mich.)—Fiction. I. Title.
   PS3558.E92A6 2015
   813'.54—dc23

                                                                                    2014043232
   ISBN 978-1-4930-1682-2 (ebook)

∞™ The paper used in this publication meets the minimum requirements of American National Standard for Information Sciences—Permanence of Paper for Printed Library Materials, ANSI/NISO Z39.48-1992.

For those women who choose to live the harder life in order to make the rest of our lives easier and richer.

CONTENTS

First Day of the Last Day of the World

Candola "Pokey" Clare had an unexpected day on the day the world ended. She was twenty-nine, and happy to remain below the threshold of thirty which would mark an entire new phase of life. Her best friend Curry Boland took her to dinner, toasted her with Cold Duck and a saucer-size birthday cake with two candles, a waxy two, and a nine. Curry said, "Isn't that the most romantic thing you ever seen, and what if our candles are the last lights left on earth?"

That's the moment the restaurant and everywhere outside went dark. Six years as a conservation officer had taught Pokey Clare that when shit hit the fan, people like her were expected to willingly dive into the spinning blades, which was clearly an unnatural act except for the most abnormal of folk. Clare fished a flashlight out of her purse. Other diners were doing the same and small light blades were swishing around the room like Star Wars light sabers.

"Laurie?" Clare called out. Laurie Pell was the restaurant's owner, a forty-year-old widow with two kids, her husband killed by a sniper in Afghanistan in 2003, the same year her youngest daughter was born. The girls were now fourteen and ten.

"*Hey*! Laurie!" the conservation officer repeated.

"For Pete's sake," Curry Boland said impatiently. "Laur's got this. This is exactly what generators are made for."

"Generators are wired to kick on automatically when the power goes down. It's still dark," Pokey Clare said. "Laurie!"

When Clare started to stand up her friend said, "Nuh-uh, you're not leaving me here alone."

"It's just a wee bit dark," the game warden teased.

"Just is a person-specific frame of reference and this person loathes the dark. I'm going with you. Most of us normal world folks don't get paid to crawl around in the night groping for trouble."

"Which means you miss most of the fun. Use your lighter on those candles."

"They're too damn small," her friend said.

Boland fumbled in her own purse and brought out a small light and clicked it on.

"Okay," Clare said. "Let's move." There had been six people in the small restaurant when the lights blew. Pokey Clare said, "Relax folks, there's a generator."

Light beams continued to dance as they made their way into the kitchen and found the back door standing open. They stepped outside and looked around. The whole area was black. The shed behind the restaurant had an open door and a flashlight beam jumping around.

Pokey Clare found Laurie Pell and her older daughter, Sudie. They had a battery-operated lantern beside a Honda generator.

The CO said, "What's the problem, Laur. Can we help?"

"I'm not sure, Pokey. This damn thing is supposed to kick on immediately with any power surge. We've got it rigged to a computer program that makes it start with even a hint of power loss or surge and it's not supposed to shut off or switch regular power back on till we tell it to do so. Now it seems dead."

"The computer fart-glitched," fourteen-year-old Sudie said. "Techno-hiccup. No biggie."

The girl's ten-year-old sister Gainey stood nearby, rolled her eyes, and mouthed "what . . . ever." The girl wore garish pink-frame glasses with lenses the size of Slurpee cups, and had her hair dyed a fiery pink.

The younger girl looked directly up at the conservation officer and said, "We should talk."

"I know," Pokey said. "And we will." What an odd damn night. First the power goes kerflooey, and then apparently the power then switches on in the girl child who never willingly talks to adults and only sparingly to other children. As personalities went, Gainey had all the animation of a beepless heart monitor, never smiled, rarely gave any indication of any awareness that she was on a planet with seven billion people, much less her own family. Kids. Gainey was typical of young folks and their blind acceptance of and allegiance to computer and sundry electronic devices. Pokey Clare felt no affinity for computers and in her experience they tended to fail at the moment you most needed them—like most of the computer-run equipment in her state-owned patrol truck. "Is there gas?" she asked Laurie.

"Tank's full. It should run seven or eight hours on what's in it. The computer alerts us to refill time."

"This ever happen before?"

"No," Laurie Pell said. "It's less than three months old and guaranteed three years. So much for goddamn sale prices and deals, but how do you pass up nine hundred instead of fourteen hundred?"

"So much for capitalist guarantees," daughter Sudie quipped.

"Businesses make computers too," Sudie's mother snapped at her.

"That's different."

"Really?" Mom said sarcastically.

Laurie stood up. She was a tall woman, five-ten, lean, long dark hair. "There's a backup starter and that won't work either. It's designed to bypass the computer in situations like this."

"It's not comforting that the manufacturer plans for moments like this," Curry Boland offered.

The restaurant owner stood with her hands on her hips. "Well, I guess we get a night off. Not the way I like to plan such things, but there it is. Sudie, get your sister. We're gonna move all our perishables into the freezers and throw all the ice from the ice machines in there too."

"What if the power doesn't come back?" Sudie asked.

"Don't be foolish. The power always comes back. This is the twenty-first century. The only question is when and how much we're gonna lose and how much I'll have to fight the dang insurance company, which no doubt will rush to declare this an act of God and wash their hands of responsibility."

"Insurance company giving you trouble?" Pokey asked.

"The company should re-name itself Not-Our-Fault Inc."

Pokey Clare walked out to her personal truck, dug out her transistor radio, which ran on batteries, and turned to emergency frequencies, expecting to hear nothing and instead heard, "This is a pre-recorded emergency message transmitted automatically in the event of any major power outage. Because you are hearing this message, you can assume there has been a major power outage, cause unknown, extent unknown. Do not call to report your outage. The outage is clearly known and you can be assured that the authorities and your power and local service providers are working on the problem and hope to have it resolved as soon as possible. People should remain calm, stay where they are, and await help."

The words gave Pokey Clare a chill. Wait for the government to help? "Yeah, how'd that work out for the Katrina folks?" she said out loud. The conservation officer turned off the radio to conserve the batteries. Stay here, or go get my work truck, find out what other cops are doing, and pitch in? Her friends would be fine. This was the moment when it hit her: "*You're* the government, stupid."

Clare told her friends she was going.

"I don't think you should leave," Curry Boland said.

"It's my job. Who I am, what I do, hello?"

"Well, what if it's not anymore?" her friend countered. "What if nothing's ever going to be the same ever again?"

"What the hell is that supposed to mean?"

"I don't know," Curry said. "Just a feeling I have."

Pokey touched her friend's arm. "How about we keep our deepest feelings private for a while. There's no sense panicking anyone."

"You're feeling it too?"

"I felt something, maybe. I don't know. I don't have words for it yet." Mostly it felt like a shitty night for cops and other first responders.

"Think Armageddon," her friend whispered.

"Don't start down that road," the game warden told Curry Boland. She had known her friend all her life, knew Boland had always been churchy, easily led, severely whipsawed by various public declarations and predictions of various cataclysms predicting world's end. "Just hush and pray to yourself."

"Ain't me needs to be hearing prayers," Boland said.

Pokey Clare said, "Assume He's listening to what's in your head."

"If He's in there, He's looking at a real mess," her friend confided. "I've had that pesky Gibb Pawlowski on my mind all night long. Wine," she concluded, as if that explained everything.

Gibb Pawlowski had been a county deputy sheriff married to their friend Paula. Curry and Gibb had been known to fool around from time to time, which her friend rationalized as okay and not immoral because their friend Paula openly declared how much she hated sex, calling it the "disgusting deed," and openly told them, "I wish I could be done with all that stuff."

Wanderings aside, Gibb was a good cop and a good guy. And Curry, despite her sense of oneandonlydom wasn't his only side dish.

Pokey Clare knew that unlike Paula, her friend Curry was far from done with "all that stuff," and every time she met with Gibb, Pokey was burdened with hearing a play-by-play after-report, and more than once she had told her friend that listening to her sex reports was like listening to a golfer playing every damn shot on some meaningless backwoods course.

"Hey," her friend would say. "Scoring is what the game's all about."

Curry was not talking about golf. Her friend's libido was in max overdrive, so severe she swore the woman could ignite charcoal by walking past a grill. Men hit on her continuously and relentlessly, and she loved the attention, and once in a while, when the mood or chemistry struck her right, she opted for more than flirting and words.

"I have to get my uniform and work truck," Pokey Clare told her friend. "Drop you at home?"

"Like hell. I'm staying with Laurie and the girls. They'll need my stability."

CO Pokey Clare drove toward home thinking a lot of strange thoughts and having feelings she'd not felt in a long time. Naturally and predictably, her mother Ione had to make a grand psychic entry with her litany of you must not, should not, cannot, will not, do not, on and on with unlimited limits and walls and ceilings and strictures, and not once an encouraging word other than a side-armed "Love you," or a sloppy verbal "kish-kish," the latter after she'd been drinking, which had not been all that often, and that was a good thing because Ione was a drooler drunk. She didn't bob or weave, but slid along on some kind of alcohol-induced carpet, leaving a trail like a slug. Ione married Number Four, an intellectual pipsqueak named Barry who had been an MP in the Army for two years and could regale himself for hours with the same two stories of arresting famous Hollywood actors who'd been drafted and not taken to Army life.

All streetlights were out, and many of them were new and solar-powered, so what the hell is that all about? And no house lights, no nothing, just stars in the sky and no moon, and many of the stars occluded by passing cloud banks, leaving the night even darker than usual. Up here in the far north, light pollution was rarely an issue, and nights tended to be far darker than farther south in the towns and cities below the bridge.

She quickly ran into her rented house, put on her uniform, climbed into her patrol truck and headed out. Five miles up the road she saw a van on its roof, wheels up, no dust in the air, meaning it had been there awhile. She turned on her emergency flashers, got out, and approached the van just as a shot sounded a couple hundred yards down the county road. Followed by a second.

Oh crap. She could almost predict this one: Some old guy with a gun had gotten spooked by the power failure, and when people from the wreck came up on his house looking for help, he'd opened up on them, seeing them as zombies, or God knows what, some sort of insidious force looking to take over the world. Get rid of all old people with old-time values and drive Jesus out of America. Her county was filled with such folks.

She drove her truck closer to the source of the shots, leaning sideways to reduce her silhouette, got to where she wanted to be, shut off the engine, and opened the door, leaving it open like a protective wing. "Hey, this is Conservation Officer Clare. What's going on? Hold your fire, repeat, hold your fire!"

"We've been shot," a female voice said weakly.

Clare unsheathed her .308 and made her way toward the voice.

"My name is Pokey, who am I talking to?"

"Renee. I'm hit in the shoulder and Frank got one in the foot."

The Fagans, Renee and Frank. They lived two hundred yards away. "You overshoot your driveway?" Clare asked.

Renee laughed painfully. "Frankie got a wee-bit over-martinied tonight, overshot the landing."

Frank was a retired Blue Goose pilot.

Pokey Clare realized where they were, stood up and yelled, "Kangas, you fucking madman, you just shot the Fagans!"

"Liberals!" Kangas shot back. "Let 'em go get Obamacared!" The man laughed maniacally. Cell phones not working, police radio silent, no help coming, up to you, sis, she told herself.

Can't believe I'm asking a civilian this question. "How many rounds has he fired?" she asked Renee Fagan.

"Six or eight, including the last two. We both got hit in the first salvo."

Which must've taken place before Clare arrived in the area.

The conservation officer made her way over to the wounded couple, assessed wounds. The foot was nasty but not critical, Renee's shoulder only a nick, more or less.

"What are we going to do?" Renee Fagan asked.

"I'm thinking on it." Training never quite prepared you for unreality, which was sometimes the job's prevailing reality. Kangas was a semi-hermit, a bigmouth drunk who loved to bully anybody he could.

"Women cops are losers," her mother used to proclaim.

"What's that make those loser cops' mothers?" she'd retort, which usually ended the discussion.

"I'm going to talk to Kangas," Clare told Renee. "Give me a few minutes and yell out that the state police are here."

"The troopers are coming?"

"Just yell it out."

By the time the yell came, the game warden was on the shooter's porch. His front door was open, only a screen between them. "Gig's up Forddy, troops are on the scene. You know they'll come in shooting."

"Fuck them," Kangas said. "And you too, you cunt cop."

CO Clare went through the screen with her flashlight in the man's face, sending him backwards with her on top of him. She heard a gun go off in her ear and then a ringing and no other sound as she roughly rolled him face down, pulled his arms back and cuffed him. "Goddamn you, Forddy, you might've killed your neighbors. Or me."

"Fuck them, fuck you," the man muttered.

Suddenly it was daylight, so white and bright that even in the man's cabin she kept blinking.

"God's here," Kangas said.

Pokey Clare got him up and walked him out into the light. There was no sun, just a massive coating of white light burying everything. She'd never seen any such thing, never even heard of it.

"It's God," Kangas said again.

She said, "With cops tied up everywhere, I guess he figured to send someone to fetch your sorry ass. It's not God."

"It ain't?"

"Does that hot sky look like fire, maybe?"

The old man said, "Uh huh." Then, "You mean?"

"You're in deep shit, moron. Shit deeper than any court."

"I ain't afraid," Kangas said.

"That just makes you a dumb ass."

At some point Deputy Gibb Pawlowski drove up in his cruiser. "You okay? I seen the girls at Laurie's place and they said you come to get your work truck, only nobody seen you since and they're all worried. Got to your house, but no you, so I nosed up this way and seen the truck."

She explained what had happened and he said, "Good grief, Pokey."

"Ain't my fault. Them people attacked my house in the dark," Forddy Kangas told the deputy. "I got proof," Kangas added.

"I bet you do," Pawlowski said and turned to Clare. "I'll run Kangas into the jail."

"I'll get the Fagans to the hospital. The jail got power?"

"No, everything's black except the sky. Any idea what the hell is happening?"

"The devil coming for Kangas," she said. "This whole thing's his fault."

• • •

The light in the sky lasted three hours and blinked out. The Fagans were at the hospital getting treatment. Pokey Clare drove back to the restaurant to check on her friends. She found them sitting at a table with candles, drinking wine.

"You see that sky?" Curry Boland asked.

"I saw," the conservation officer said. She looked over at the ten-year-old. "You wanted to talk to me, Gainey?"

"Not here," the girl said. "Outside."

Standing in the dark the girl said, "This is not the end of the world. It's a CME."

"Come again?"

"Coronal mass ejection, like a massisimus solar flare."

9

"Yeah?"

"I read about this kind of stuff all the time. Beats Facebook or dumb games. The light in the sky says this is a big deal, like an X-class flare. Geomagnetic fluctuations and disruptions, messed up GPS, all that crap. It will last nine hours and be over."

"For real?"

"Yes ma'am. I'm gonna be a geophysicist when I grow up."

"Good for you, Gainey."

"The women inside are driving me crazy with end-of-the-world wah-wah-wah," the kid said. "Will you please tell them everything will be fine, especially Ms. Boland. She's like on the verge of losing it totally."

"Okay," Pokey Clare said. "Why don't you tell them yourself?"

"Nobody listens to a kid."

The CO explained and this was met with doubt, but eventually they settled down and Clare excused herself and continued her patrol and found Gainey waiting out by her truck. "Geophysicist, eh?"

"Or dolphin trainer," the girl said. "I'm like torn, ya know?"

Pokey stuck out her pinky. "Sisters?"

The girl hooked her pinky through the adult's. "Sisters."

Pokey Clare smiled until the power came back, precisely nine hours after it had gone out.

Gravy and Bear Breath

"At ease, Graveraet."

Meanderbelle Graveraet said, "Yes Sergeant."

"That name, Graveraet, where's that come from exactly?"

"My mom and dad."

"Don't be a wiseass. I said at ease, not off the wall."

"Sorry, Indian and Dutch, Sarn't."

"You a tribal, Cadet?"

"No, Sergeant. Never signed up."

"But you qualify?"

"Yes, Sergeant."

"Listen to me Graveraet, I really mean it. At ease. This isn't commander to cadet. This is just the two of us."

"Whatever you say, Sergeant."

"Are you hardcore, Graveraet?"

"No Sarn't."

"Know what your classmates call you?"

"No, Sergeant."

"Gravy. They say everything flows easy for you. Good looks, smarts, great shape, tough. Gravy. You like that name?"

"No opinion, Sergeant."

"You know why we're here, just us two?"

"No Sarn't."

"Because I see buds of leadership qualities I want to see in full bloom. Who's the best all-around cadet in the class here, Gravy?"

"Me, Sergeant."

"Bit conceited, donchuthink?"

"No sergeant. That's how I see it."

"You're a weirdo, Gravy. Air Force Academy, third academically in your class, seven years in the Office of Special Investigations, rank of captain, and you signed up for this *abuse*?"

"Affirmative, Sergeant."

"Mind explaining? It doesn't add up for me."

"Bored. Second looey, first looey I got to work and make cases, captain they plopped me more and more in an office. I'd made major, the office is all I'd've seen. Not for me, Sergeant. I hate desks."

"Why'd you go to OSI?"

"Couldn't pass the physical for PJ school."

"Bullshit. You earned your jump wings at the academy."

"Yes, Sergeant."

"So why wouldn't the PJs make an exception?"

"Just how it is with them, Sarn't. No nuts, no can do."

"No female PJs?"

"None I know or heard of."

"Piss you off?"

"No Sergeant. Well maybe a little."

"So here you are."

"Affirmative Sergeant. Here I am."

"Who in the class beside you has the most promise?"

"Barnes," she said.

"Bear Breath?"

"Yes, Sarn't."

"Why?"

"Book smart, common sense, good emotional control."

"He was a pretty fair college football player but he can't cut the physical program here."

"He can," she said.

"Why isn't he?"

"I don't know, Sergeant."

"Don't you give a shit about your classmates?"

"To be perfectly frank, all I care is that they don't get in my way, Sergeant."

"Seems like an anti-team attitude, Cadet Graveraet."

"No, Sergeant. We become a team only after we graduate. Except in exercises where teamwork is required."

"That's cold-blooded."

"So's life, Sarn't."

"How many tours you pull in Afghanistan?"

"Two."

"Your record says Purple Heart and Bronze Star with a V."

"Yes, Sergeant."

"Spill any blood, Graveraet?"

"Yes, Sergeant."

"Like to spill mine right now?"

"I'll take the Fifth."

"This ain't a court."

"I still take the Fifth."

The sergeant stared at her and shook his head. "Bear Breath, that's really your opinion?"

"It is, Sergeant."

"Are you tightly wrapped and all business, Cadet Graveraet, a Zoomie to the core?"

"No, Sergeant."

"Way I see it, Gravy, you don't like men and class competition is some kind of personal vendetta."

She stared at him. "You're entitled to your opinion, Sergeant."

"You always in control, Gravy?"

"I try, Sarn't."

"You one of them Lebanese types, Gravy?"

"Beg your pardon, Sergeant?"

"Lebanese, carpet-muncher, like that."

"None of your business, Sergeant."

"You gonna boohoo and call your lawyer now?"

"No Sergeant. I handle my own fights."

"This a fight, is it?"

"If that's how you want it to go, Sarn't."

"The others aren't real lovey-dovey with you, are they Gravy?"

"No Sergeant, they're insecure."

"They are? Tell me three things I don't know about you."

"One, afraid to fly. Two, can't hold my liquor. Three, I love to fuck."

The sergeant laughed out loud. "Jump wings and afraid to fly?"

"Is what it is, Sarn't."

"Are numbers two and three connected?"

"They can be, but no."

"Bear Breath. *Seriously*?"

"Yes, Sarn't."

"Could he top the class?"

"It's probable."

"Top even you?"

"Yes, Sarn't."

"Good. That bother you if he finished numero uno?"

"Not if he earned it."

The sergeant stepped back. "Okay, Gravy, do that."

"Sergeant?"

"Do what you said."

"Which is?"

"Make Bear Breath compete and push you for the top slot in the class."

"Isn't that *your* job, Sergeant?"

The sergeant stiffened. "I see you as a leader, Cadet Graveraet. Prove it to me, prove it to everyone, prove it to yourself. Barnes is your test. You think that's unfair?"

"No Sergeant."

"You must think *something*."

"If I told you, I'd have to use the word asshole and I choose not to do that."

"I talked to your academy coach. You hold every physical fitness and long distance running record in academy history. All five-feet-three of you. No more dicking around, Graveraet. I think you'll be a top officer and I want you to lift Bear Breath and the rest of the class."

"How?"

"Push them until they hate your guts."

"Why would I do that?"

"Because the hate won't last. It will convert grudge to respect over time, and respect into love. You want to be loved, Gravy. We all do."

"If you say so, Sergeant."

"Twelve Mike," the sergeant said. "Focus on that. You run as far as you can in twelve minutes, carry a day pack and a .308. We want you to push the whole class to a class average record."

"Why me, Sergeant?"

"Because I can't run that far anymore. Want to know what you get out of this?"

"Satisfaction, Sergeant?"

The NCO chuckled. "You ever at a loss for words, Gravy?"

"Not so far, Sergeant."

He looked her in the eye. "I think those PJs fucked their own doggie when they passed on you. Now beat it, skedaddle. I'm all out of chittychatshit."

• • •

Barnes was in a study room. His given name was Rob. She sat in a chair next to him. "Wanna be my workout partner?" she asked.

"Why me?"

"I need a partner who can push me."

He laughed out loud. "I'd have to catch you to push you."

"I know," she said, deadpan.

"Are you serious?"

"Damn right."

"What do you have in mind?"

"Mornings before they get us up. And at our free hour every night. Aerobic, anaerobic, free weights, all of it."

"Why me?" he asked.

She put her face to his. "Kiss me."

He did and she said, "Sweet breath, not bear. Partners?"

"More kissing too?"

"Not likely."

"So I don't have to stay on top of dental hygiene?"

"I didn't say that."

"For the record, you don't taste like Gravy," Barnes said.

Graveraet punched her training partner in the bicep. It was like striking a cinderblock filled with cement. "We're gonna beat the Twelve Mike record," she said.

"You, maybe."

"You, me, all of us, the whole class." She looked him in the eye. "Trust me, Partner. You just won the lottery."

He grinned. "What did you win?"

"Nothing special," she said, knowing that she would not be treated special, which would make it special, and normal.

Working the Problem

"What the hell is going *on*?" husband Ronald threw at her seconds after rolling off her. "Used to be twice a day and now you're gone a week and you're too tired?"

"Leave it alone, Ronald. I hardly had enough strength to walk into the house."

"No damn wonder, up there in a dorm, sneaking bed to bed all night long, you got plenty of strength for all those guys, but not your own spouse."

She sat up. "Are you stupid? It's a police academy. Even if anybody had the wants, nobody has the get-go or the opportunity."

"Ah, so you *admit* there're attractions."

"We've been over this ground before," she said. "Every damn weekend they let me come home."

Ronald sat up. "How would you like it if our situations were reversed and I was up there in a dorm sleeping with twenty women?"

She sighed. How many times did they have to have this argument? Ronald Colt Bridges, she said in her mind. I want a divorce. I've had enough and I'm filing. It sounded so solid in her head but the words refused to transfer to her mouth. She'd married a tripartite name, three assholes rolled into one, more to hate. The thought made her giggle.

"Something is *funny* to you?" Ronald said with a gotcha in his voice. "Tell me his name."

"There is no him."

"Oh God," her husband said, slapping his forehead. "It's a damn woman, isn't it?"

She squinted and reached for her robe. "Yah, you got me Ronnie, we go all night long, four women and me, that's it and now you know my secret so let me sleep. I'm exhausted."

"Long as it ain't men," Ronald said. "Want to tell me about it?"

"They'll kill me," she said, spearing her slippers in the dark.

"I can keep a secret," he said. "It turns me on. Where are you *going*?"

"To the couch, Ronald. I need *sleep*."

"Work the problem!" their instructors bellowed every day, all day, every exercise, every simulation and drill. They had just come off three days of chilled ice tank drills, no exposure suits, swimsuits only, bare skin turning blue, the whole ordeal in total darkness. She had never imagined, much less experienced anything like it. Cold was a monster that didn't need teeth to take you apart. Never wanted to do it again, but knew if she was out on the job and saw someone in trouble she'd be out on the ice trying to help, the urge more in the heart than in the mind.

Just awful. Total fear, anger, frustration, disorientation and you had to stay focused, control everything, be in charge of the problem that you found, no matter what it was. Work the problem, work the problem, stay in the game, work the problem, focus, focus. Twice she'd thought she was drowning, had been right on the edge, felt it grinning, but fought her way back. Now *this* bullshit?

Yesterday, all day long, fifteen pairs of cadets running around with canoes on their shoulders, five hundred pounds of dead weight inside the aluminum craft. Back and forth across a grass field slipping in cold rain. Torture, but she knew the instructors wanted to push them past their endurance, give them a look at their breaking points. So far she had remained plastic, pushing out the breaking point, but *this*, at home, every weekend they got off, in her *sanctuary*? No way.

She'd known before leaving for the DNR academy that this was going to be a problem. Ronald Colt Bridges was a cling-on, Mr. Milquetoast Macho. If she left him, would that mean he had broken her when the academy couldn't? Corporal Holloway, in her last tank experience, had outweighed her by a hundred pounds, hauled her to the bottom like an anchor, and held her there.

She had wiggled and squirmed and finally gotten an elbow free and blasted him in the nose as hard as she could. She was sure she had heard cartilage crack but he had let loose immediately and she had hauled him to the surface and multiple hands helped both of them out of the tank. Holloway sat there with a stupid, dazed look, blood streaming from his nose, grinning for God's sake. Grinning. Out cold on his butt, and grinning. Good God!

That night after chow he'd pulled her aside. "Never hesitate to do what you have to do when you're immersed in a goat rodeo. Great job, Cadet Lungcharsky. You worked the problem."

Goat rodeo? What was this if not that?

"Ronald," she said. "You go sleep on the couch. Pack your bags in the morning and get out. I'm calling a lawyer."

"Maybe you need a lesson in who's the boss here."

"Ronald, if you so much as try to touch me, you'll be sleeping on a steel gurney in the ER tonight. Get the hell out of *my* bedroom."

Her husband lingered at the doorway and finally turned away. She closed the door behind him.

And slept peacefully and deeply, dreamlessly, the way dead souls slept in eternity.

Come morning, Ronald was sitting at the kitchen table with sunken eyes. "You look like shit," she told him.

"Because of you, I cried all night."

"Tears can be good for the soul," she said. "A cleanser."

"This cop thing makes me crazy," he said. "You *know* that."

"I do know that, but it's going to happen, Ronald. This is what I want. I'll graduate, put on my badge, and hit the field and be out all hours with partners, mostly men. That's reality."

"It doesn't have to be," he said, softening his tone. "I make enough to take care of us. Stay home, start our family." Ronald was district supervisor for a successful hardware wholesaler.

"There isn't going to be an our family," she said.

"But this was our dream."

"Your dream, never mine. I may want kids and I may not. I don't know yet."

"What are those *people* doing to your head?"

She had to think about that. "Making me whole, Ronald."

"That's crazy. You *are* whole."

"Not as long as you're in my picture. Pack your stuff and get out. I'm done talking."

"We *haven't* talked," Ronald said. "Not really."

The phrase goat rodeo formed in her mind. "Shower, pack, leave," she said. "One hour."

"Or?"

She stared at him until he broke off the eye-lock. He said, "You're unbalanced, crazy."

"I am me," she said. "Call it whatever you like."

"I get the house," he said. "And the boat. House and boat are mine."

"Take it all," she said. "Life isn't about stuff."

"You used to think it was."

"I used to not think at all," she said. "And now I do."

"Because you're gonna be a doughnut dolly in a green suit? That's rich," he said and laughed malignantly.

"Fifty-five minutes," she announced.

"This isn't right," he whined.

"Someday you'll think differently," she told him.

"I don't *want* this," Ronald said through clenched teeth. "What'll my parents say?"

"Fifty-four minutes."

"Dyke-lesbo-butch-cunt," he said with a hiss and left the kitchen.

She later watched him back his Lexus out of the driveway. He had gone through the garage putting sticky notes on tools and other things he was claiming. The notes said "MINE, not HERS." He even took phone photos.

Three years: You were married to that jerk three years? It had been an awful decision, and an even worse experience.

Sunday night back at the academy in East Lansing, her roomie Shelly Conner said, "You look peaceful."

Astute observation. "I got some quality sleep."

"With a *husband* in your bed?"

"Ronald wasn't a bother."

"Lucky you. Bengt was all over me like a second shadow. The man is relentless."

"Goat rodeo," Cadet Sidonie Lungcharsky said. "Keep that image centered in your mind and work the problem."

"You sound like an instructor."

Lungcharsky grinned.

The Roadrunner Should Make You Laugh

"I don't know who you are, I ain't your pop, and get out of my house!" Sigmund Bergson ordered in a stentorian voice. His daughter thought his brain might be melting but his voice remained fine, still loud, and, incredibly getting louder.

"I'm your daughter Calliope and this isn't your house, it's mine, Pop."

He bellowed, "Tirzah, Tirzah!"

"Your wife is not here. She left Pop, and the way you treated her, I can't blame her."

"A wife don't got no choice," the elder Bergson said.

"Only in the long ago days when Mom was alive. Things're different now."

"I don't like you," her old man said.

"Whatever floats your boat, Pop."

"I have a boat. She's called Calliope."

"You had a fishing boat with no name. I'm Calliope, your daughter. You sold the pram when I was twelve. You said it was a piece of sorry shit."

"How much?"

"I don't remember. You wouldn't tell anyone, including Mom."

"Boat is the man's business. Nobody else."

"Want to take off your coat?" she asked.

The old man looked at a sleeve. "This is *not* my coat. My coat's a horse blanket."

"That coat is long gone, Pop. You're not a game warden any more. You retired a long time ago. The coat you're wearing is yours. I know this for a fact."

He said, "You were with me when I picked this out. Tell me your name again."

"Your daughter Calliope."

"Calliope's my boat. I have a daughter?"

"Four daughters, Pop. California, Carole Ann, Camille, and me, Calliope."

The old man snorted. "What kind of fool names a kid for a state full of screwballs and queers?"

"Cal has wondered that her whole life. It was your idea, not Mom's. As eldest she thought she should have been named after Mom."

"I have a daughter named Mom?"

"Your wife, mother of your four daughters, Betty?"

"No, I don't remember no Betty."

"She got pregnant just before you shipped to Korea. You married her, and got on a train and headed west to the coast."

"Fairytales can come true," he said, apropos of nothing.

At least he's calm. That's good. She helped him out of his coat.

Now hunched over with scoliosis, slumped over like he wanted to spend his life looking at the ground, he looked old and used. But he had once been a driven physical beast, dripping self-confidence and with enough skills to do damn near anything he decided he wanted to do. Being wounded three times in Korea had not changed him, Mom said. He was always happy and in charge, bulletproof, impervious to life's vicissitudes and ill winds. Now this shell sitting at her table, empty yet still hardnosed without knowing why. He had been a fighter throughout his life, with a mind and without, as if there was a second mind in his brain, unaffected by the old timer's disorder, a second mind modern medicine had yet to identify, much less unmask.

Maybe it was his soul in control, his youngest daughter thought. Poor Tirzah, his second wife, the arm-candy spouse, loaded from hauls from four previous hubbies, all of whom she'd outlived. Not Tirzah's fault. She had been good for and with Pop until one day he awoke with his second mind fighting to take over.

"Want some lunch, Pop?"

"I hate baby food," the man said.

"I have soup," Calliope said. "Big-boy soup. Pop-soup."

"Pop-soup? Okay, I'll take that one, but no goddamn baby food, hear me?"

"I hear you, Pop." He had been in a nursing home, but she had found him strapped to a bed, soaked in urine. The facility's explanation was that he refused to stay in bed and out of other patients' rooms. She pulled him out of the place and brought him home. Still not sure of the logistics. Like him, she was a conservation officer and could flex her schedule and work split shifts some of the time, but during certain seasons she would have to be on the job for twelve hours, sometimes sixteen.

Pop had alienated Tirzah, bullied all of her sisters as well. His off-the-wallness rarely bothered her because she saw it all the time in her job and dealt with it matter-of-factly. But she knew she was going to need help when that second control center took complete control of Pop. It would make him more than a handful for anyone.

"They collected our shit, ground it up, salt and peppered it, rolled it in cracker crumbs, and gave it to us as food," her father said.

"That's disgusting," she said.

"It's true. You can't make that shit up."

She swallowed a laugh.

Calliope put a bowl of warm soup in front of him and sat beside him.

He slurped and drooled soup down his chin into his scraggly beard and his hand shook. Her father glared at her. "They usta feed me in that place. Told 'em I could do it myself."

"You're not *in* that place anymore, Pop."

"Hah," he said, resuming his slurping. "I usta kill people," he said.

"A long time ago."

He nodded vigorously. "Terrible business, killin' all them racist chinks."

"Tigers play tonight."

He made a puffing sound. "Candy asses, paid millions, they couldn't carry Al Kaline's jockstrap. Go on the disabled list with a damn pimple these youngsters. Can't pull that kind of shit in a war or when you're a game warden. They find out, they shoot your ass for cowardice." His voice went soft again. "Course we were all tempted to shirk and run, but you can't do that. Not never, hear me?"

"Loud and clear, Pop."

"Game warden's a cop nowadays, right?"

"Yes, Pop."

"You can't run neither, Cal. Coppers and soldiers got to stand the line, fight the fight."

"I'm not Cal," she said.

"*Sure* you are: You're Calliope, Cal, my youngest daughter, the one most like me."

"You call California Cal."

"Who's California?"

"Not a problem, Pop. There's a fella coming over this afternoon to meet you."

"I don't want meet nobody," the old man said.

"His name is Al Buell. He served in Afghanistan and lost a leg, roadside bomb. He's a good guy."

"He kill Chinks too?"

"You can ask him yourself."

"Ask who?"

"Al. Al Buell."

"Oh yeah," he said, and smiled. "Brain fart!"

"I've asked Al to live with us."

"He some kind of a boyfriend, this Chink-killer?"

"He is, Pop."

"He puttin' the pork to you?"

"That's none of your business."

"Usta put the old pork to Tirzah. Wowzer. I miss that. You think she misses that?"

"No way to know, Pop. You could call her and ask her."

"Nah, she's dead."

Calliope understood. "If you say so, Pop. Al will be here around three."

"For baseball?"

"To meet you."

"Okay. Did I tell you what Tirzah used to do to me?"

"Yes, Pop. A thousand times."

"Yah that's about right, she done it a thousand times, maybe a million. Boy was she a pip and a half."

She helped him to an easy chair and turned on the TV.

"Cartoons," he said. "Not that *I-Love-Lucy* shit. God what a screamy bitch. I hate redheads."

Calliope flipped through channels. "Roadrunner good?"

"It ain't no Mickey Mouse. You think Mickey schtupped Minnie?"

"Probably, Pop."

"How come Minnie Mouse is a girl and Minnie Minoso a man? Did Flash Gordon have a girlfriend with big headlights?"

"I don't know."

"I bet he played windshield wiper with her," Pop said, demonstrating.

Talking to him was exhausting and exasperating.

He said, "It's okay, you know."

"What, Pop?"

"It's okay. I like being here, with you. I know I need help. Give your Poppy a hug, Calliope."

She leaned down and hugged him, clinging.

"How come them tears?" he asked.

"I don't know."

"Roadrunners should make you laugh, not cry."

Which made her laugh. And he laughed with her and she knew they could make this work.

Bambigumbo Yumyum

It was late October. G-Lata Treat gripped the top grab iron of the boxcar, eased across the side, flattening herself as train speed and wind buffeted her. She drew one deep breath at the bottom, and swung across to the open boxcar door.

A startled voice yipped. "The Lord done sent us a shine in green!"

"Evenin', boys. How many we got in here?"

"We be six," a familiar voice said.

"Billboard, what you hawkin' these days?" She had never known the man's real name, only his road handle. Consensus said he was a king bo, a lifer, true royalty among the country's transients. The man got up and stepped toward her. He wore a lime green hooded sweatshirt that proclaimed NIKE FUEL. His arm held a dozen or more electro-plastic bands in various hues of eclectic electric, throwbacks to dayglo days.

"Knock-offs?" she asked.

"You impugn my integrity and honor, Officer Treat. These all real, fell often back of a Chinaman's truck. Retail one fitty, for you whinny fie, two go foe-tee."

"You keep track of your steps and calories, Billboard?"

"Yes-um, Damn-straight. Man got to watch his own health, even with Mr. Obama's fine gift."

"You sign up yet?"

The bo chuckled. "Wun't know where to begin and we sign up, the man be watchin's sayin'?"

G-Lata Treat had been a conservation officer in Wayne County for ten years. She'd grown up in River Rouge north of West Jeff on Victoria, been a basketball star, all-state. Got a degree in police administration from Lake Superior State. Had forty basketball full ride offers out of school but had grown up fishing with her granny-ma'am on the St. Mary's River in the Soo. They'd been up there every summer when she was a girl. Had always intended to transfer up there, but there was so much action here in Wayne she thought the U.P. would bore her and Granny-ma'am was still kicking in The Rouge.

Her partner, Brindle Brown, had just retired and was yet to be replaced, which left her alone. She didn't mind. Way more than two officers could do, much less a solo, but BB had taught her how to flip off the duty switch when she went home at night. It had been a great gift. She laughed when she heard some officers in country counties having fifty or sixty contacts a week and bemoaning the workload. She had some days pushing two thousand contacts during the silver bass runs, and hardly thought of it. You looked quick and corrected what needed addressing.

The silver bass run was almost a festival, like Mardi Gras. Thousands of brothers and sisters with cane and telescoping poles on the riprap banks while white guys in bass boats caught walleyes out in the river, a study in real-life contrasts, white versus black.

"Here's my whatfor men. I'm hearing reports some bo in rollin' stock whackin deer from the state herd, sayin'? I ain't likin' 'at shit."

"Ain't my people," Billboard said. "We stay own stray since you brung us to Jesus way back was ought nine. We want fish, game meat, we get word G-Lata, you bring, yes ma'am, too damn bad whole gov-mint so snappy with citizenry. Ain't no boxcar bo you huntin'. More like some hoosier yegg rider sneak out at night, make the shoot."

Billboard was alleging a local poacher got on trains at night for one purpose. He could be right. "You gone eat snowbaws this year?" she asked, meaning was he going to spend the winter up north.

"Could be so, I speck. Bin laid up boneyard, pin ulcers, sayin'?"

"All healed?"

"Nuh-uh, but I heard 'at black bottle make a rattle and I lit out fore I catch the westbound,sayin'?"For some reason hobos believed government and welfare hospitals had death pills in black bottles, pills reserved for eliminating the country's unwanteds.

"I seen bo croaker tell me use jigger on his sores. An I brang some them white pills over fum the boneyard eat evil one the inside, and keep the stank down. You want smell how good it work?"

"I'll take your word." Jigger was a lye-based paint acid rumored to be a street cure-all for skin problems. "You eat snowballs, you be 'round. You and your colleagues keep your ears on for me?" She passed him a business card. "Hear something, you know how to get in touch. Or call the RAP line. It's anonymous and there are rewards. You got a phone?"

"Four G," the man said. "The best, they say."

"Fall off a Chinese truck did it?"

"Wunt s'prise me none." He looked at her. "I'm thinking woodtick come D, see them deers as brown sugar lump, easy take, bambigumbo yumyum. You hear caliber spoke of?"

"Rifle, two two Henry or long probably."

"Huh, can't hide 'at in a bindle, lessen mebbe he use it for bindle stick, sayin'?"

Sticks were something the bos carried over ashoulder, all of their worldly goods in a bag suspended from the end. "You might could be right," she said.

But six months ago she'd assisted Metro to bust a gun house on the river where there was a case of USAF M-6 Scout over-under rifles made by Ithaca Gun company and packed in survival seat packs pilots and aircrews sat on. Fourteen-inch barrels, could shoot 22 Hornet and 410. Thousand bucks a copy on the black side. They'd recovered twenty-five weapons, missed a hundred more that had already gone out the door and into the streets. A little M-6 was easily hidden under a winter coat. The weapons had a greenish sheen to them. The ATF agent leading the raid told her the color was typical of weapons stored in armories and in high demand with collectors. She never understood the allure of guns. She liked to shoot and practiced regularly, but guns weren't any kind of religious experience and she'd grown up watching dumbass motherfuckers whack each other over imagined insults. Nice tools, but just that: tools.

Her parting words to Billboard and his companions. "You hear something, let me know, hear?"

Billboard saluted crisply as she took a deep breath and swung across to the handholds, but this time climbed up top and made her way back to the caboose, where she could safely dismount when the freight stopped.

Every railroad had its own cops and company management as a rule didn't like other cops prowling their properties, but she knew if she asked for and got official permission, it would take months to actually happen. If ever. Likewise, she said nothing to Sergeant Larue Bobbs, her supervisor. Bobbs was a good sergeant, kept out of the way of his officers, backed them when they needed backing. His officers never had to look to see if the sergeant had their backs. Bobbs was always *there*.

• • •

One week later she was checking a report of an illegally kept alligator in a squat-row on Livernois, and instead found T. J. Bellman, who until eighth grade promised to be the greatest ballplayer in Rouge history, but T. J. "Thunder Jumper" discovered drugs and pussy and gangs and easy money and was lost to the other life. He had been in and out of jail for twenty-five years, would never get his act together, but she had always had a soft spot for him because she saw him as a kind and generous boy who took a wrong turn and was lost. Had she not had her Granny-ma'am riding herd on her she might have gone down the same road.

"T. J."

"G-Lata," he said in a honeyed voice. "You know dude, Billboard?"

"I do. How do you know him?"

"Start hang with bos. They don't cut no slack for dope and such, good way stay clean, safe."

It sounded like he was making an effort. She had to give him credit for that, knowing deep down he was doomed. "What's Billboard want?"

"Say tell Oaf-a-sir G-Lata Treat word go round there be dude work CR marsh track to Tecumseh yard. Bambigumbo boy, Billboard say. This dude was workin' further north, yah know? Now he gone come south and Billboard he say tell the man. How a be-otch ballplayah become the man?"

T. J. asked, puzzlement on his face.

"Just fell into it," she said.

"Ah know how 'at tune go," the man said.

"How far north, T. J.?"

"Oh, I think Billboard he say that Moun' Olib grabeyard and like dat."

Rough neighborhood out by the city airport, now named for Hizzoner Coleman Young. "You done good, pass word to me, T. J. You got walk-around?"

"Man, I'm flush," he said.

She slipped him a twenty. "Give somebody a good tip."

The man stared at the bill and smiled. "Indeed," he said and she immediately hoped she had done the right thing.

"T. J.?"

"Ma'am?"

"You take that twenty, buy hash, beans, spuds, makings fo 'at Mulligan them bos like eat when it get cold. You hear me T. J.? They got your back, you give back, sayin'."

"I hoyd. God bless you G-Lata. Give my best your old Granny-ma'am. I pray she ain't gone over to the Lord yet."

"She still with us, praise God."

• • •

The reputed area was a dark track, no lights, off the beaten main-lines, a backwater flanked by fecund marshes, and deer aplenty, perfect poaching ground. She drove her truck back down a mile of tracks. To leave the truck anywhere but close to her was to invite vandals at least, theft at worst. Here in the D you learned to work close to your truck. This wasn't like some country above the bridge where you could park and walk off into the woods for four hours and still find your truck intact. In this way, Wayne County and some other counties were like different countries.

A mile or so down she stopped and opened the windows, turned off the engine to keep exhaust clouds from shrouding the darkness. Seven o'clock she heard one sharp crack, got out, locked up, and headed for the sound. She got to a place where she saw a light near some dry cattails and she stopped striding and went into creep mode, got close and switched on her own SureFire, and found herself looking into the rheumy eyes of Billboard, an Air Force survival weapon in hand, a dead doe at his feet, shot once through the head.

"Way I see dis t'ing go down," the royal bo said, "dey say I gone lose dis laig to this thang ain't got no cure. But boneyard dey got dat black bottle and I never heard about the bluebar, sayin'? So, I say you take this dead gal to my peeps and me to the hoosegow. Dis damn laig dis way I never make spring alive and I got no choice. Wid me or agin me, G-Lata?"

Here was a good man, not normal by any means, but good as best he could define such values, taking care of others like it was a sacred trust. "You been doin' some deep thinkin' on this, Billboard."

"Hab indeed. I always done planned good."

Which never helped him out of the transient, homeless life, she thought. Twenty-first century and millions of people still living day by day on the edge of disaster. When are we going to get it together as an actual country, of one people, where citizenship mattered and nothing else? Not in your lifetime, girl.

"Okay, your Majesty. I'll pull my truck closer, we'll load the meat, drop it off with your peeps and get you booked. Gonna charge you with hunt no license, illegal deer, hunt out of season, use rifle in shotgun zone, vagrancy, theft. You stole that over-under, right?"

"Oh yes ma'am, sackly where I steal it fum?"

"Fell off a Chinaman's truck."

"Yah, that 'at fo show wha' happen. I forget, but now I 'member some."

"We get enough on you they'll remand you to a head-checker before any trial. Don't plea bargain, no matter what. Make them go whole hog, spend whole damn dime. You hear me?"

"You think dey try me?"

"If I do my part and you do yours."

"My lips to God's ears. You come visit me?"

"You bet," she said.

"I get out, we have big party when warm-up come. You think they keep me through warm-up?"

G-Lata Treat smiled. The life you chose, girl. It's not great, but it could have been a lot worse.

"You ever jump outten an airplane?" the bo asked.

"No."

"I was Airborne," he said. "Eighty-Second. We always used a stack line, you know what dat is, Stack line?"

"I don't think so."

"Open your chute when you step out, so you don't gotta do it. Sure thing to be safe," he said. "Static line. I ain't never forget 'at."

"Assures the opening, but not the landing," she said.

"Speck 'at's right-own," Billboard said. "But little doubt is spice of life, sayin'?"

Leprechauns

It bothered Mary Vallier to know she had what amounted to the most common name in the country; she'd always thought of herself as unique and now she felt more like a plain brown wrapper. Fiancé Ringo Atola had told her about the name thing two weeks ago. It had quickly turned into an earworm and she was still pissed at him. What was it about him that annoyed her so damn much? More to the point, why're you marrying the jerk? Marry. God, *that* word again.

Atola was a year younger, heir to Atola Long Haul Trucking. Ringo's dad had been a drummer in a big-time Detroit band in the city's rock heyday, saved and invested his money, left the music biz and bought a small trucking business, which he had built into one of the largest trucking companies in the Midwest, the company's ads everywhere, TV, Internet, radio, you could hardly miss all the paid exposure, and Ringo was daddy's go-to guy, got paid an exorbitant salary and even had a vacation house in the non-tourist part of the Bahamas. Marriage meant the gravy train and that had seemed pretty good until he announced she would have to resign her commission as a conservation officer and become a housewife because Atola women don't work outside the house. Her future in-laws were good Republicans with family values they lived by, were proud of it, made sure everyone knew it. It was hard enough to have him rubbing on how common her name was. That same day he'd informed her his family would expect a baby within the first year, and once pregnant, his old man would pay for genetic testing to make sure the kid was perfect.

She said, "And if the baby's not normal?"

"We only have normal kids," he said.

"You call *that* a family value?"

"Hey, the bloodline for this family is important."

She had made her drive him home that night and not seen or spoken to him since. *Asshole.*

"You got the ouchies today," Vallier's partner of three years said from the passenger seat.

"I guess," she told Joe Coalwood.

"Your idiot fiancé again?" he asked.

She cringed. Ringo had several times introduced her as his fiancé because "she was gonna be high up-keep, but worth it." She had been forced to scream at him to get him to stop and he had acted mystified.

"Wha? What I do?"

What a wad.

"He still asking you to resign?"

"It's a tell, not an ask."

"You gonna be a good little wifey and do what he wants?"

"Shut up, Joe. I'm conflicted."

Vallier felt like she should defend Ringo, even though there was no ring yet. But words failed her. Good words. She had a surplus of negative ones.

"I caught a RAP call this morning," her partner said. "Complainant says there are leprechauns hunting the Manistee Dells."

The Dells were glacially carved small valleys and canyons between steep, narrow ridges. "South of Grassy Lakes?" she asked him.

"Uh huh."

"Hunting what?"

"Deer."

"With a bow?"

"Rifle," the guy claims.

"Boy oh boy," Vallier said. "Leprechauns. That's a first."

"No shit," her partner agreed.

"Shall we work our way in that direction?"

"Can't dance," she said, making Coalwood laugh; they had bandied about the old joke since they had first met. Get lunch? Can't dance. For some reason she never tired of this or her partner, who tended toward pathological quiet but who was always there for her. Unlike Ringo.

"Couple of weeks back he told me I have the most common name in the USA and I ought to feel proud to catch a husband with a unique name from such a well-off family."

Coalwood said nothing.

"He says not only do I have to resign, but he wants a baby boy like yesterday, but only if prenatal testing shows no problems. Said he has a cousin with 47 C-21 and it has been a nightmare to raise. 'It,' can you believe that?"

"A what?"

"He couldn't explain it and the whole conversation made me want to puke." She looked over at him. "You're single, Coalwood. How come you never hit on me?"

"You're too damn good with a gun."

"Be serious."

"I am serious. I feel like Murtaugh, the comic relief partner in *Lethal Weapon*. You're Riggs."

"Jesus, Joe. Riggs is a damn animal."

"There ya go," Coalwood said.

"Seriously?" she asked.

"Half serious, maybe 60 percent."

"Don't be an ass. I am not like Riggs."

"Remember that Tippy Dam salmon snagger ruckus last fall?"

"They started that, not me."

"Excuse me, but you Tarzaned off an embankment into four of them and had them all punched out and stumbling before I could even get over there. Looked like they'd fought a tiger."

"I saw an opening and took it," she said.

"You ambushed them, same as Riggs would've. Heroic, but stupid."

"I can't be too scary a partner if you're telling me this."

"I've got my seatbelt off and one hand on the door handle."

"Jesus, Coalwood."

"You asked."

"Are you telling me you want a new partner?"

"Nah. You're gonna resign and get rich. We might as well see this through."

Riggs? God. "I haven't been in the Dells in years."

"There're two truck trails starting west of the first grass valley. One runs north."

"Okay, I remember that much."

"You've got AVL," he reminded her.

"Mine's old and crashed. Supposed to upload the new versions, but the tech keeps canceling on me. My old version's all froze up." AVL was the Automatic Vehicle Locator, a system via GPS that tied Lansing to all COs, and all COs to each other. When the system worked. "Anybody actually see the alleged deer hunters?"

"RAP line said only what I told you."

"When was the complaint called in?"

"Last night, sevenish."

She arched an eyebrow, said sarcastically. "God, that's almost like live and real time." More often they got reports days, weeks, or months after the fact, complaints with virtually no actionable information, which made them useless. "Exactly where in the Dells?"

"Swamps behind Snoopy's Camp."

Snoopy was Democratic state senator Elwine Hubbard Fishlock, who was a force as the state's most outspoken conservationist. As long as the rules applied to others. On his own land, Fishlock was king. Period. Elwine wasn't a regular violator but COs had had more than a few run-ins with him, which he seemed to assume turned him into some sort of authority of backwoods law enforcement.

"Elwine himself call it in?"

"Guy said something to make the dispatcher think he might be the caretaker, but he refused to give his name."

"Which dispatcher?"

"Mary Lou."

"She's damn good. But *leprechauns*?"

"That's what the report says. You ever seen one?" Coalwood asked.

"No."

"Way I see it, we have to entertain the possibility, to be fair."

"Riggs?" she said.

Her partner smiled. "Can't dance."

"Find Snoopy's caretaker?" she asked.

"Nah, mighta been, might not, who knows. Let's plow right in."

"The way Riggs does things?"

"Sort of. We don't have to go in shooting. I'm talking more figurative than literal Riggs."

"So what's your view on Ringo, matrimony and all such?" she asked.

"None of my business."

She switched topics. "What if somebody out here's hunting leprechauns?"

Coalwood looked over at her. "How do you *cook* the damn things?"

They both laughed.

"You think being the Missus would be this much fun?" Coalwood asked.

"Mind on business," Mary Vallier said.

• • •

The area of the dells was filled with forests of old gnarled oaks and a massive acorn drop, the mast crop the best in years.

They parked the truck about a mile from the river and hiked from there, looking for deer sign. Snoopy's Camp was south of them, a half-mile strip with river frontage. Most of the deer would not move down into the river bottoms until later in the fall. At that time of year they should have been up grazing on acorns.

"Fresh tracks and scat piles everywhere," Coalwood said quietly. "Plenty of bait here."

Soon they came across a line of scrapes and a couple of rubs on trees with diameters of eight or ten inches, suggesting some heavily antlered bucks in the area.

Coalwood said, "The leprechauns picked a helluva good spot to hunt. Split up? You go east here, I'll go south and then turn east and walk Snoopy's north property line. I should be about a half mile south of you."

"Meet back at the truck?" she asked.

"Can't dance," he said, smiled and marched away.

Coalwood: She loved the guy. Not in love with him, but loved him. Is this a fair distinction? She wasn't sure, but the realization, saying the words, even in her head, made her shiver like a sixteen-year-old. She neither loved nor was in love with Ringo Atola. I've got to do something about this, she lectured herself as she hiked, and the terrain began to rise. She had to pick her way through dense brush and when she found an opening saw a sort of saddle above her and aimed herself for that to cross the line of hills. The long climb made her legs tired. Coalwood could move through the heaviest woods like a ghost, or he could run like some sort of four-legged creature. His speed even with a full gear load was eye-catching and had surprised a lot of violators over the years.

She was trying to decide how to go over or around a large blow-down when she caught the faintest sound. She froze, closed her eyes, listened. Not just sound; it was . . . *music*? What the? Music in the dell in late morning during bowhunting season? Oh boy. Hunters taking a midday break? That might make some sense, which could mean a camp nearby. Ah, the leprechauns. The thought put a smile on her face she couldn't will away. Sometimes whimsy was good for the soul. She stopped now and then to fix the source of the sound and made a line directly to it.

Words rippled through the trees. Something about singing out of tune? What the? As soon as she questioned this she found herself singing, along with voices and the woods, the Beatles. The line about needing someone jarred her. Jesus, that song comes up in the woods after all that thinking about Ringo and Joe. Got to be a sign, not that I believe in such things, because I don't, at least not publicly. What I have is an open and inquiring mind. Getting closer she heard rhythmic clapping and a group of voices and as she hit the tree line and looked down into a clearing she saw twenty or more people in a ring, all of them in green outfits, singing about getting, no, not just friends, but *little* friends. Extra word in the lyric, what's *that* all about?

Vallier thought, hey, that lyric's not quite right, and she looked harder and saw the people were all tiny and as she walked into the open and they saw her they began to come up a small rise to meet her singing all the way and clapping their little hands together, and when they got to her, they enveloped her in a circle and hugged her, and each other, and kept singing, and she stood there with her brain in freeze mode and smiled and nodded and hummed, thinking, not leprechauns, Down syndrome folks.

"Good morning," she said.

"Lunch at noon," a man said. "No exceptions." He wore a green felt Robin Hood hat with a turkey feather.

"Noon-sharp," someone added.

She felt a tug on her trousers, "You hunting too?"

"I'm the game warden."

"We've got licenses," her initial greeter said. "Hunter safety too, hey everybody, show the game warden your license and hunter safety card." Seconds later all the people were waving cards at her. She felt wonderful and could not explain why, even to herself.

"You folks hear any gunshots over this way?"

"Arrows don't make gunshots," someone said. "I'm Alvin, like the chipmunk? But he isn't real and I am."

"You're *all* bowhunting?"

Alvin ordered, "Show her your bows." They all ran and picked up their weapons.

"You all sure follow the rules," she said.

"Rules are rules," Alvin said. "We do it right the first time."

"I'm sure you do," she said.

A woman came up to her. "Would you like to hunt with us? You've already got on the green."

"Thanks, I'd love to but I'm working."

"Work is work," someone said.

"When we get paid to do a job, the job comes first," the man called Alvin said. "Rules are rules."

They all said rules are rules and work is work.

Alvin said, "But tonight we're gonna sing and dance."

"And hug," a woman said. "We love to hug!"

And having declared this they all began to hug, openly, gloriously. 47 C-21s in their full human glory! Ringo Atola, you are such a gaping asshole! Do I, Mary Valliers, love to hug? Goddamn right I do! And Ringo doesn't.

She found herself hugging several people and Alvin broke up the love-fest yelling *lunch lunch lunch, noon noon noon*, grabbed her hand and dragged her downhill to an area where blankets were spread out, and a dozen picnic baskets serving as little tables. A woman took her hand and they sat down Indian legged on a blanket. "You wear green. We wear green. We all like green. It's Mother Nature's color."

Alvin yelled *manners manners manners*, and they all opened paper boxes and pulled out chicken parts and began to attack the meat.

Her hostess said, "Cold fried chicken. Not fast food, but real food, um um good." She held a drumstick out to Vallier who took a bite.

"Delicious."

"No rifles at all?"

"Robin Hood," Alvin said. "Not Dan'l Boone."

She took another bite of chicken. *Damn* good.

Alvin ripped into a breast and with a full mouth said, "Boone's down by the river." He was pointing in the direction of Snoopy's Camp and Vallier began to imagine some possibilities relating to the RAP report, but before she could formulate her plan, Joe Coalwood popped out of the tree line. He was carrying a rifle over his shoulder, and was accompanied by a young man who had not shaved in a while.

Alvin yelled, "Another *green man!*" Everyone cheered.

"That's Officer Coalwood," she yelled to the group. "He's my partner. His name is Joe and he *loves* hugs!"

"Hi Joe!" they yelled and ran to him and surrounded him and hugged him and patted him and the kid with him looked like he was going to lose his mind and Vallier thought she had never seen a funnier scene *ever.* Joe Coalwood was grinning and smiling and hugging back and the whole thing was like a damn fairytale.

The deer hunters in green tried to hug the young fella too, but he scowled and shoved and slapped them away, and Coalwood said with a menacing growl, "Mind your manners, asshole."

"Fucking little weirdo creeps!" the boy said.

Coalwood held up the man's rifle, pulled a silencer out of his coat pocket and showed Vallier. "Caught him over a fresh kill, his fourth."

"Related to Snoopy?"

"Camp caretakers's son, Fallon."

"Dude," Vallier said. "You guys work for the great state conservationist. Guess your dad won't be the conservationist's caretaker much longer."

"Fuck Fishlock," the boy said. "He cheats all the time."

"You shouldn't use language like that," Alvin said, piping up.

"Fuck off, shrimp boat," Fallon said and several men suddenly had cudgels in hand and whacked on Fallon's lower legs, forcing him to back up and put up his hands. "Maniacs!"

"Enough," Vallier said. "That's enough, Alvin. I think he's got the message."

"Come back tonight and dance and hug and eat," Alvin said, holding her hand, and she looked at Coalwood, and said, "Maybe . . . if we can."

Joe Coalwood gave his prisoner a hard push and the three of them began the hike back to the truck.

• • •

They took the truck to Snoopy's, confiscated the illegal deer carcasses, the man's weapon and silencer, wrote citations for him, and headed for Cadillac where Coalwood's truck was parked.

She was quiet almost all the way to town. "I'm done with Ringo Atola."

"Just like that," Coalwood said.

Vallier snorted. "Can't dance."

They both laughed and she said, "Ya know, Joe, *we* could dance."

"With the leprechauns?" he asked.

"Sure," she said. "Why the heck not?"

"Works for me," Coalwood said. "Pick you up?"

"Yah, six?"

"Okay."

"Know what? If I'd gotten pregnant and Ringo knew it would be a Down kid, he'd want me to abort. Asshole."

"Riggs," Coalwood said, looking straight ahead.

"Murtaugh," she replied. "Six sharp."

Reality

Maria Costangelo was called Bada Bing by other conservation officers. They would push their noses to the side and mumble "whasamattayou, Costangelo, you got it made, all your wise guy blood, some butt-wrench draws down on you and bang he's like disappeared."

"Yeah, yeah, whatever," Costangelo would say, knowing she had a secret. Guns scared the hell out of her, and though she shot and practiced incessantly and had for nine years, she was only marginally better now than when she had started out. She absolutely loathed the notion of being forced by circumstances, however remote, to fire a chunk of hot lead into another human being. If it happened, it would have to be forced. This she knew in her heart and admitted to nobody.

Nine years and she had pulled her automatic only one time, and never discharged it. Didn't have to. Thank God.

Newly married, she was eager to get home to husband Hughie. It had been a fourteen-hour work day, the opening day of the firearm deer season, a daylight to way-after-dark head-bumping with fools and the clueless, lifelong cheaters, and a few folks (very few) just making honest mistakes. All in all it had been a pretty lawful crowd for this part of Dickinson County, where lawlessness reigned some deer seasons. But this looked like a calmer, more doable stint and she felt relaxed, a foreign, totally unexpected feeling for opening day.

Hughie was making beer-butt chicken and she could hardly wait. She had not eaten all day and was famished. Okay, one measly cereal bar, but did that qualify as eating? This thought barely out of her mind, a white Honda Accord raced past her and began to weave from one side of the two-lane highway to the other, shoulder to shoulder. "Oh Shit!" she said out loud as she activated her flashing blue lights and tried to get the numbers off the plate as the vehicle slowed and pulled over and she called the county dispatcher. "Central, DNR One, One Thirty Six."

"Go, One, One Thirty Six."

"Traffic stop, run file, Wisconsin plate." She recited the plate numbers to the county dispatcher and waited, keeping her eye on the Honda.

"Thirty Six, Wisconsin plate comes back to a 2013 blue Honda Accord. No wants, no warrants. Want the owner's name?"

"Negative, Central. I'll be out of my vehicle."

"Central clear."

Costangelo approached the stopped vehicle along the driver's side, coming up so that the driver could not easily see her. She had an on-board camera recording everything, one of two in the state being tested. Most COs in the state made most of their contacts away from their trucks, not on roads in traffic stops, and in her own mind an on-board camera was just one more gizmo to screw with, one more thing to malfunction. But this was a classic traffic stop, the plate coming back to the vehicle, no big deal. As she got to the rear of the Honda she looked down at the trunk and bumper and saw what she thought was blood. Shit. This changed the whole deal. She was checking the blood smear again when the driver's door suddenly swung open.

"Stay in your vehicle!" she ordered the driver. "Repeat, do not get out of the vehicle and put your leg back inside!"

The leg did not withdraw. In fact, a second one appeared. Oh shit, I have done this exact fucking scenario in training, good God, not this, not this, please God, don't be a jerk! Please! I know how this shit turns out! "Get back in your vehicle!"

The man got out. Orange sock hat pulled down, sunglasses, camo hooded sweatshirt. "Hiya," he said.

"Sir, raise your hands and back up toward me. Do it *now*!"

"This is *fun*," the man said. "Is it fun for you?"

Goddamn. Instead of raising his hands, he leaned down and back into the front seat of the Honda, exactly the way it happened in the scenario training. "God, please not this."

Costangelo had already unholstered her Sig Sauer 40 semiautomatic, had it by her leg. "Sir, do not reach into the vehicle! Raise your hands! Sir! Listen to me, Sir!"

But the man pottered around in slow motion, his body making her think he was groping for something, and he was stretched out and bent over so severely he flashed his butt-crack and then his butt started backing out. She kept her focus on the front of him, trying to see his arms and when there was a flash of something dark she yelled "Sir, goddammit!" And he began to turn.

An instant later she was on the ground, punched in the stomach so hard it took her breath and forced her to desperately gasp for air, saw the man on the ground beside the Honda, on his knees, the acrid smell of something in the air, not gunpowder, the chemical stabilizers in the round. Stupid fact! Focus. How many shots? Had she shot? Had he? Headshot, sure I hit him in the head, but she watched in fascination and in horror as he picked up his pistol and started to get back into the Honda. Thinking fast, no damn angle from here, no angle, move, she told herself, instinctively rolling to her left one time, two times, stop. He was in the seat now, sitting up. Jesus, how could I have missed him? Pain in her guts burning like she had the sun inside her trying to get out. She exhaled, held her breath, sighted the weapon, squeezed twice and slumped face down on the asphalt, thinking no chicken tonight. Oh Hughie.

Trooper Chet Fong was first on the scene, lights flashing, sirens screaming like burning banshees in the night, Sleet starting to come in sheets.

So cold, hot. Cold. Hot. Oh God.

Someone beside me, voice calm, reassuring, gentle. "It's Chet, Maria. Chet."

"Did I get him?"

"Yeah, you *got* him. Be still, you're gonna be fine. I can hear the EMS three minutes, no more, hang on. You're gonna be okay, Maria, talk to me."

"Head shots, Chet. He got up again."

"It's okay, Maria."

"Head shots, right?"

"Yes, head shots, you stopped him."

"Did he kill me, Chet? Tell me, please?"

"No, he didn't kill you."

"Fuck it *hurts*," she said with a moan.

"I know," Fong said. "Pain is good right now."

"Did he shoot you too Chet?"

"I'm fine Maria, EMS is here. Do what they tell you."

"Don't let go of me," she said anxiously, and Trooper Fong didn't let go. "Call Hughie, Chet, tell him I'll be late for supper. Tell him I love his beer-butt chicken. Tell him, Chet. Promise me."

"I promise," the troop said as the EMS specialists knelt over her.

• • •

Ten days later in the hospital, Hughie, Chet Fong, her sergeant and lieutenant all gathered around her bed. She asked, "Am I dying? If so, don't bring my mother. She'll just make it worse."

Hughie said, "You can't make death worse."

"You don't know my mother that well."

They all laughed. "No more major surgery," Hughie said. "Couple of minor jobs is all that's left."

She felt like she was in a fog made of fine powder. "Head shots, right? All three?"

"All three," her sergeant said.

"How did he get up after the first one?"

"You sure you're ready for this discussion?" her lieutenant asked.

"I'm sure. I couldn't believe it when he crawled back into the damn car."

47

"You took out part of his brain and that caused him to jerk the trigger and the round ricocheted off the road and into your stomach below your armor and rained you with road fragments. Fifty or so small pieces."

"How?"

"We don't know," the lieutenant said. "Nobody knows. Your last two rounds opened his head like a melon."

"He have a name?" she asked.

"Caputo," her sergeant said. "One of your people."

"Not mine."

"Drove up from Milwaukee to kill his estranged wife. She was in the trunk.

"The blood," she said. "I thought it was a deer."

"Three months off on medical leave, then three months on light duty," the sergeant said.

She tried to grit her teeth, but could barely feel them. "No way," she said. "Back on duty as soon as possible."

"There's no rush," the lieutenant said.

"I don't get back quick, I won't be back at all," she said, and all the men nodded and patted her and she fell into a deep, drug-induced, and dreamless sleep.

FTO

"Oh good, they sent me a princess instead of a recruit. Call me Sang-Froid and I'll call you Perky. Word is you are perky, engaging, the sort of officer who believes in world peace and inclusiveness, whatever the hell that shit means."

It is the last Saturday of April, the traditional trout opener for what has seemed like forever to Dogtek, and this year is a real miracle, no snow, which is unheard of. It could mean a lot of potential business for us, thought Dogtek, so why am I standing here giving the hate-eye to my probie?

"My name's not Perky. It's Devin, Devin Cottin, and I'm supposed to report to CO Shelby Dogtrack."

"It's Dogtek, Perky, but you will call me Sang-Froid."

"You seem a little overanxious this morning, Officer Sang-Froid. Do you even know what that word means?"

Shelby Dogtek grinned outwardly and seethed inside. She had eaten male shit for years and these young chicks were prancy-dancing out of the academy, thinking everything was hunky-dory, no clue what getting to this point had cost the women who came before them. Most of the new ones she could melt down in less than a minute, but this Cottin chick hadn't even blinked. Worse, she was shooting back.

"Listen, Miss Perky, here's how this world operates. In this phase I do the heavy lifting and you watch and keep your yap shut. You got questions, ask *after* a contact, not during. You are to be seen and not heard unless I say otherwise. Got it? I don't see a notebook. Why don't I see a notebook? I wear a Praline Fifth generation recorder with a lapel camera. When I get home at night I dump everything into my laptop, which gives me permanent sound and video. Then I submit it to a program that listens, types a transcript, corrects it, and saves it."

"Miss High Tech."

"No Ma'am, this shit is low-tech toy class compared to the really good stuff out there. Some of the newest professional apps are major slick."

"This job isn't about slick."

Standing beside Dogtek's Silverado. Cottin says, "So far this job seems mostly about standing around trying to bust each other's chops. Are we going to work, or bullshit all day?"

Cottin got into the passenger seat and stared straight ahead.

Book on this kid says her appearance doesn't square with her attitude or her skills. She looked prissy and perfect and almost delicate and pampered, where in reality she's some kind of a hard case, and top of her class. Her greatly perplexed instructor Bill Quall, called a couple of days ago. "Ring her ass out, Shelby. Everyone here thinks she's the new you and I ain't buying that."

Dogtek found the recruit staring at her. "What?"

"Safety belt, Officer Sang-Froid."

Dogtek clicked her lap belt into place, started the engine, pulled out into the street. Her rookie looked straight ahead.

"Rule one," the field training officer said, "when you're in the truck or in uniform, keep your head and eyes on a swivel, and keep your mind on the task at hand, no exceptions."

"We're just leaving a hotel parking lot at the butt-crack of dawn," Cottin said, "the only vehicle moving at this hour. The streets are empty for Pete's sake. The game at hand seems to boil down to seeing who can dis the other one the most."

"Ah, you have how long on the job, four minutes?"

"I have common sense."

Mild weather, the morning disclosing blue skies, the two officers bumped their way north along rotten dirt roads that paralleled the

Escanaba River, which was murky and swollen with snowmelt. In deep summer the same stretch was a long shallow glide of water clear as vodka. Today it was ugly and agitated.

"Pack a lunch?" Dogtek asked her partner around noon. They had checked more than twenty licenses, but found no one actually fishing because of the high water. They had not exchanged fifty words since the opening salvo in the parking lot. Dogtek wanted to impress on the new officer that this job had been almost exclusively a male domain until twenty-nine years back. And it had not been easy. Still wasn't in some places, but she felt secure that the men she worked with gave her credit for the job she did and the good cases she had made, mostly alone because for a long time many officers refused to partner up simply because she was a woman.

"I adhere to a special high protein diet," the rookie said.

"Of course you do," Dogtek said. "High-end energy scams and vitamins in pretty packages. All crap."

"Whatever," Cottin said. "I need to use the ladies."

Dogtek laughed. "Yes, Miss Perky." She stopped the truck in the middle of the two-track.

Cottin started walking into the woods.

"Yo, Perk, you take front right tire, I take rear left. Always this way, never varies and gender of your partner doesn't matter."

"Like we've got secrets?"

"Like you will rarely be with another female partner and unless you want to get a rep for flashing Miss Puss, take the damn tire you're entitled to and try not to piss on your pants. I can't stand the smell of urine in my truck. The average mammal takes two seconds to micturate, but you can take longer and be accurate."

Task complete, the recent grad stood beside the truck and started to put on her service belt. "I can see this is somewhere between an art and acquired high skill," she said.

"You'll learn you can do it without taking off the belt."

"Seriously?"

"Yah I'm fucking with your head." Dogtek sniffed.

The rookie actually smiled.

They sat in the truck and ate in silence. It wasn't unusual for rookies to be hesitant and introverted by the sudden reality of being on the job, but this one chewed and stared straight ahead, saying nothing. No questions, no pass-the-time girlie inanities, nothing.

"What's your background, Perky?"

"Army brat, college, Army five years."

"Army what?"

"Engineers."

"Choo-choos?"

"Boom-booms."

"Ordinance?"

"Affirmative EOD specialist, B9D."

"Deployments?"

"One, Baghdad."

"You don't look old enough."

"Looks lie."

"College?" Dogtek asked.

"Northern. Go Wildcats."

"Hometown girl?"

"Alpena. You?"

Dogtek almost smiled. A question in a civil tone? Really?

"The Soo."

"Lake State?"

"Hard Knocks, no college for my lot in those days."

"Military?"

"Forest Service, Idaho. Hot Shot crew."

"Many fires?"

"One is too fucking many."

"I hear that," Cottin said. After a pause she offered, "Maybe we like got off on the wrong foot this morning?"

"Are you apologizing?" Dogtek said.

"Are you?" Cottin shot back.

Dogtek bowed her head, made a decision. "You want the straight shit?"

"What do you think?"

"I got a call from your top dog at the academy."

"Corporal Q?"

"Yes, Quall. He asked me to ring you out. Tops in your class but the instructors can't figure you out."

"Can anyone figure out another person?" Cottin asked.

Dogtek nodded. "Quall thinks you're another me."

"That good or bad?"

"Twenty-nine years on patrol, no promotions, I had enough points four years back to hang it up."

"Why didn't you?"

Dogtek shrugged. "Corny. I love this job, what we do, the whole damn idea of it."

"Not corny to me," Cottin said. "You're a legend."

"Some legend. There's a long line of haters."

"Your being among the first women, it's to be expected. Pioneers always pay the price."

"Hate doesn't evaporate like summer rain."

"More in your generation, I think. Mine isn't so hung up on gender."

"Even with all your hip-hop crap?"

"That's behind us, not ours. You married?"

"Troop," Dogtek said. "Takes a cop to live with a cop. You?"

"Nah, I need my space right now."

"Took me a long time," Dogtek said.

"I'm in no hurry."

"Don't be. Why are your instructors befuddled?"

"No clue. They tell me to do something, and I do it. They say I don't look like I'm trying, and I say, how's my score? That shuts them up."

"Similar experience," Dogtek said. "They don't just want you to perform, they want you to look like you're going all out in the effort, even if what you're doing is a breeze."

"How did you handle it?" Cottin asked.

"Didn't. Just kept on keeping on."

"Do it differently if you had to do it again?"

Dogtek nodded. "I'd act tired, grimace a lot, show some emotion."

"Even if you didn't feel it?"

"Even if."

Cottin said, "The Deli Scene, 'I'll have what she's having.' Meg Ryan. I screamed!"

"So did she," Dogtek said. "Sometimes fake is real."

"Why can't the world be straightforward?"

"Because half of us are men."

"Mars-Venus crap."

"There it is."

Cottin said, "Where to from here? Us, I mean."

The CO held out her hand. "Shelby Dogtek."

"Devin Cottin."

"We work together, do the job."

"I'm all over that, Sang-Froid."

The two women laughed.

"The distaff side," Dogtek said. "It's not for sissies."

Midsummer Day's Night

"Titania, that's an interesting name," the defense attorney said. "Thou art as wise as thou art beautiful."

The conservation officer in the witness chair sat passively, looking off into space, not responding, as she had been coached to do by the assistant prosecutor.

"Objection," the prosecutor said drolly.

"Objection to what?" the judge asked.

"Shakespearean quotes wrong-courtly, un-courtly language, ad infinitum and so forth."

"Overruled," the judge said, smiling. "Take another swig of coffee, Mr. Prosecutor. In a case about reptiles it's nice to hear something of a more pleasant nature, even if it's irrelevant. Mister Sabato, those're real nice words, but let's stick to the case, okey-dokey?"

"As you wish, Your Honor." Sabato turned back to the conservation officer in the witness chair. "Officer Titania, I assume you had reason to be in the home of the accused, would you please explain to the court how you came to violate the privacy of my client?"

"Objection," the prosecutor said. "Posing a charge in a question's clothing."

"Rephrasing," Sabato said, before the judge could jump in. "Please tell us your name and how you came to be at my client's home."

"My name is Titania Flato. Mrs. Lanie Nougat stopped me outside Walmart in the Soo one afternoon to ask me a number of questions about illegal hunting and penalties for violations. While we were talking her daughter Joanie held up a plastic gallon jug filled with copper belly snakes. There were air holes in the lid and the five-year-old held the jug up for me and said, 'Chink Stripes.' I explained that the proper name was garter snakes, but she said, 'No they're chink stripes 'cause they shit dollars!'"

Flato looked at the defendant. "I looked at Mrs. Nougat and said, 'Chink Stripes?' and she told me that it was just child gibberish, kid talk and I asked her what the deal was with the snakes, why did her daughter have a jar-full and she said she would have to talk to her husband and their lawyer before she could say more."

"Did you confiscate the snakes?" the defense attorney asked.

"I could have. It's illegal to make pets of any wild creatures, but I didn't want to disappoint the little girl."

"That's very considerate of you, Officer Flato. No big deal, right?"

"I didn't say that. I said I had a strong suspicion that something was just not right, and I looked at the little girl and asked her, 'You like snakes, honey?'"

"She told me, 'Not the bitey-bite ones–Bzzzzz!'"

I asked her, "Do you know what a bitey-bite snake looks like?"

Flato paused for effect. "The girl pointed at the van. 'They're right there in that door. Bzzzzz!'"

The defense asked, "What happened next?"

"I asked Mrs. Nougat what her daughter was talking about."

"Did she explain?"

"She told me it's kid talk and drove away. I wrote down her plate number, called it in, got an address, and went to that address."

"Had Mrs. Nougat done anything illegal?"

"There were wild snakes in captivity and she was acting suspiciously."

"In your opinion," the defense attorney said.

"My opinion based on training and experience."

"Oh, you have a lot of experience with reptiles?" the defense attorney asked.

"I wrote my senior research paper on Upper Peninsula reptiles," Flato said. "Does that count? And I have a lot of experience reading human behavior."

"Well and good, but it reduces to your *opinion*. In fact I might very well have more reptile experience than you."

"You're a lawyer, so that wouldn't surprise me," Flato said.

The courtroom erupted with laughter and the judge had to gavel them to silence. He pointed to Flato, said, "Good one, please continue."

"You might have more experience but it was my professional judgment."

Sabato said, "That's what this case comes down to, ladies and gentlemen of the jury, judgment or the lack of it." Sabato moved close to the CO. "You chased the defendant with no probable cause."

"The garter snakes were probable cause," Flato said.

"But you told the jury you were going to ignore those snakes."

"I was until the girl raised the issue of the bitey-buzz snakes."

The attorney puffed his cheeks. "What did you think the child was referring to?"

"Rattlesnakes."

Sabato said, "Bitey and buzz equal rattlesnake? That's a heckuva leap made pretty fast, officer. You jump over California king snakes, pacific gopher snakes, and long-neck snakes, all of whom rattle defensively and impressively by vibrating their tails in dry grass and leaves."

"Only rattlesnakes buzz in this state," Flato said.

"Not hognose snakes?"

"Only in fall in dry leaves. This was June. There were no dry leaves and the girl said the buzz was in the doors of the van."

"Suddenly you're a herpetologist?" Sabato proclaimed dramatically.

"I get paid to use my judgment."

"And it was your judgment to follow Mrs. Nougat and her six-year-old daughter home."

"They didn't go home."

"No?"

"No."

"Where *did* they go?"

"They crossed the bridge over to Soo, Ontario."

"Did you follow them?"

"No, I have video records of the time they went over and when they returned."

"Ah, do you pursue a lot of people with such zealousness?"

"The bridge records were subpoenaed later, after Mrs. Nougat failed to return home. I waited for some time, and then I called the prosecutor and explained, and he called the security and customs on the bridge and we drove over there and they showed me tapes and I got search warrants for the van and any other vehicles at Mrs. Nougat's house, the house itself, and their hunting camp out by Trout Lake."

"All over harmless snakes you were going to ignore?"

"Yes."

"So this escalates at light speed, from a situation where you were going to ignore garter snakes to a full-time full-court press using the garter snakes as your probable cause."

"Yessir, that's true."

"What happened when you got into the house?"

"The Nougats' lawyer—you—met me. You had obtained a show-cause to block the search writ."

"Did you search then?"

"No, the warrant was under the challenge you filed."

"Did you ever search?"

"Yes."

"When *was* this bogus search, Officer Flato?"

"Objection," the prosecutor said.

"Sustained," said the judge. "Stick with facts, Mr. Sabato, minus adjectives. They give me stomach acid, *agita* in the language of my kinfolk from the old country."

"Four weeks later."

Sabato looked at the jury. "Find any bitey buzzes, didjas?"

"No," Flato said.

"Garter snakes?"

"Yes, the same ones I'd seen at Walmart."

"And we're here now because of these same garter snakes, those you told the jury you were inclined to ignore?"

"Yes."

Sabato shook his head. "Which she was going to ignore, ladies and gentlemen of the jury. I'm finished with the witness, Your Honor."

The judge looked at the prosecutor. "State?"

"Yes, Your Honor." The prosecutor was Andrew "One-Lung" Bakalt, longtime county PA, a chain-smoker who had lost a lung to cancer and still smoked, though he'd cut back to a pack a day, most days. His voice was as deep as oil in the ground, and raspy.

"Officer Flato, when you returned four weeks later to the Nougats' house, vehicles, and property, what *did* you find?"

"As I testified earlier today, there were plastic holding boxes built into the minivan doors."

"For snakes?"

"Presumably."

"But no snakes in the containers?"

"No snakes anywhere in the van. It had been scrubbed clean, alcohol. Lysol, the whole extreme sterilization treatment."

"In your experience do people normally clean their vans in this way?"

"No sir, not in my experience."

"Did you expect to find snakes?"

"That long after the initial contact? Not really."

"But you searched nevertheless."

"Yes."

"Were you able to learn anything new?"

"There were framed photos of the Nougats' daughter. These were in her bedroom."

"What did the photos show?" the prosecutor asked with a cough.

"They showed a man holding garter snakes and a missassauga."

"Missauce, missags—that word always throws me. It's a kind of rattle-snake, correct?"

"It's the only rattlesnake indigenous to this state. Some people even call them Michigan rattlesnakes."

"You saw the photo. Then what?" One-Lung turned to the jury. "You've already seen the photo of the man holding the snakes. That was entered into evidence this morning." He turned back to Flato, "Okay, you saw the photo, and what then?"

"I asked Joanie who the man was and she said, 'Uncle Harp.'"

"Objection," Sabato said. "That's hearsay."

"Overruled," the judge said.

"Is your Uncle Harp a blood relative?" the prosecutor asked.

"Family friend."

"Mr. Nougat's friend?"

"Mrs. Nougat's."

"Not her hubby?"

"Apparently not. The wife and Uncle Harp had some sort of business arrangement."

"Explain."

"She was a snake mule. She illegally carried rattlesnakes to Canada."

"To Uncle Harp?"

"Well, Joanie was a little confused on the name. The man in the picture is known professionally as Uncle *Herp* over in the Canadian Soo."

"Is it an illegal business?"

"The reptile sales business appears to be legal by Canadian law, but smuggling and selling endangered, restricted or protected species is not legal on either side of the border."

"So these actions break their laws *and* ours?"

"That seems to be the case."

"But you had no evidence from any of this other than the photo."

"And the garter snakes. We had those."

"A circumstantial case," the prosecutor said. "You have no evidence of any snakes being moved from Mrs. Nougat to this . . . Uncle Herp."

"What we have is little Joanie telling us she gets new Chink-stripe snakes every couple of weeks, year-round. She said they get tired and have to go to heaven and she gets new ones from God."

"Objection," Sabato said. "More *hearsay.*"

"Overruled," the judge said. "Go on."

"I asked Joanie why she called the snakes Chink-stripes and she tugged the corner of her eyelid."

"You took that to mean what?"

"Chinese."

"Chink-stripes and Bitey-buzz?"

"Both species are sold on the black market as medicinals," Flato said. "High priced."

Sabato was immediately on his feet. "Thin circumstances, a mere child's words. Your Honor? *Please?*"

"Do you have children, Mr. Sabato?"

"Yes, Your Honor, three girls grown and married."

"Did you not listen to your girls when they were five?"

"That's irrelevant, Your Honor."

"No, it's not," the judge said. "I'd say it's crucial, even to the point I would not object if the child was called as a witness."

"*Objection!*" Sabato croaked. "It is improper and outrageous for a sitting judge to suggest legal tactics to one side. I demand a dismissal. You've gone off the reservation, Your Honor. This is not acceptable."

"No!" Mr. Nougat screamed from the gallery. "This is bullshit! Leave my kid alone!"

"Order in the court," Judge Jack Tar said. "Control yourself, Mr. Nougat or I will find you in contempt. I assure you that you will *not* like that development. You're not the defendant here, your wife is."

"I'm sorry Your Honor. I know that, but my kid ain't guilty of nothing. She's a sweet, good little girl."

"And she is accused of nothing, Mr. Nougat. We just think the jury ought to hear from her."

"Grounds for appeal and reversal," Sabato raged. "*Mistrial,* this is a classic mistrial scenario. I move for a mistrial, and for you to recuse yourself. A judge is supposed to be impartial."

"I'm very partial to the truth, Mr. Sabato. Does that offend defense attorneys?"

"Your Honor . . ."

"My chambers after lunch," the judge said, standing up, his face florid.

• • •

Flato thought they could have been done quickly but Judge Tar apparently needed his midday repast at a set time. Judges were among the rare professionals who got to absolutely fix their hours and those of everyone around them.

Titania Flato and One-Lung were joined outside the courthouse by Flato's DNR sergeant, Dirk Bernhardt. Flato ate a hot dog from a cart and One-Lung had coffee and a cigarette and coughed.

"I don't know about this kid thing," Bernhardt said.

"You sure don't," One-Lung said. "Please keep your legal naivete to yourself." He turned to Flato. "Good job in there, one word answers, good use of silence and delay in response as a shield and sword."

She chewed, he smoked, and the sergeant drank Coke from a paper cup. One-Lung looked at her. "You having qualms?"

"About the kid? Of course."

"The Feds are pressuring me to drop this case," One-Lung said.

"*What* Feds?"

"Fish and Wildlife."

"Why? They never talked to me."

"No explanation. Just drop the charges and apologize for the CO's zealotry."

"They want me to apologize?"

The prosecutor nodded once and lit another smoke. "I mean, really, it's just some garter snakes, right?"

"It's a pipeline to who knows what," Flato said.

"All we can prove is that it stretches across the river."

"It's a classic Lacey Act case, you *know* that."

One-Lung exhaled smoke. "Calm down, we're here, aren't we? I just thought you ought to know what's going on down in the public prostate."

"What's Fish and Wildlife's motivation?"

"My guess? They have something going and we're crossing their lines or short-circuiting something. The media's already the laughing stock of law enforcement, Big bad cops snatch little girl's pet 'gardener' snakes."

"That can't be helped," her sergeant interjected.

Flato said, "I agree, but it could get worse." She turned to One-Lung. "Why wouldn't the Feds not come to us in the first place? Isn't this the time of peace and cooperation between all law enforcement agencies at all levels in this great country of Homeland Security transparency?"

"Spin wins," One-Lung said. "Not reality."

Flato looked at her sergeant. "Is this my call, yours, or Lansing's?"

One-Lung said, "This is the state's call, which is to say it's my call and it's a go."

"If it's winnable," Bernhardt offered.

"We'll win," One-Lung said. "The question is at what price?"

• • •

"Are you comfie, Miss Joanie?" One-Leg asked the now six-year-old.

"I want to talk to *her*," the girl said, stabbing her little finger at Titania Flato.

"Not me?"

"I smell cigarettes," the girl said, making a face. "She smells good, like my snakes."

One-Lung invited Flato to ask the questions, whispered, "Just let her talk."

"Hi Joanie. Did you have some lunch?"

"Mum brought it from home."

"I object to this, Your Honor," Sabato said.

Said Judge Tar, "So noted. Let's hear what this young lady has to say."

"Do you know why you're here?" Flato asked the girl.

"Nope," the girl said. "It's boring."

"How're your Chink Stripes?"

The girl pouted. "God took all of 'em and I'm never getting no more."

"I'm sorry to hear that," Flato said.

"It's okay, they're up in Chink heaven."

Flato used her finger to pull an eyelid. "Chink, like that?"

The girl did the same. "Chink. They're funny looking."

"Objection," Sabato said, "leading the witness, irrelevant."

"Overruled."

"The stripes don't have eyes like that, do they?"

The little girl pondered this and opened her eyes wide, said "No their eyes look like this!"

"So why are they called Chink?"

"Cause Mum and Uncle Harp call 'em Chinks."

"Did they tell you to call them that?"

"I don't know," Joanie said, looking up and over at the judge. "Is he the boss of us?"

"He sure is," Flato said. "He's a real nice boss."

The girl said, "Okay."

"Joanie, can you tell us about the Bitey-buzz?"

The girl animated with a buzzing sound so realistic and eerie the jurors and almost everyone in the court looked down at their feet, Sabato included.

"Thank you for that, Joanie. It sounds so real! Do you play with them?"

The girl flashed a big smile. Then she mimicked vomiting so realistically even Flato backed up. "Can't play with them things. They bite you and make you real sick and make you *puke.*"

"Have they made you sick, Joanie?"

"Nope, just Uncle Harp, but it don't matter."

"Why not?"

"Uncle's got real strong blood."

"But you don't?"

"Mum neither."

"What about daddy?"

"Daddy works all the time. Chinks is Mum's."

"For what?"

"Uncle Harp. He has lots."

"Do you know where Uncle Harp lives?"

The girl furrowed her brow, "Crosst the river. He's a Can-tuck."

"Canuck?"

"Yah, Oh . . . Can-a-da," the girl began to sing with perfect pitch.

• • •

"Officer Flato, you have further evidence?"

"Yes we subpoenaed Mrs. Nougat's personal savings account. She has a balance of . . . ," Flato held a note in front of her, "$72,733.57."

"And the date of the most recent deposit?"

"One day after our Walmart encounter."

"Check?"

"Cash, Canadian converted to US greenbacks."

Mr. Nougat shouted, "You bitch, I'm working three fucking jobs and you've got seventy fucking grand stashed?!"

"Bailiff," Judge Tar said calmly. "Please take Mr. Nougat outside and let him breathe in some fresh air."

• • •

Two days later the jury found the defendant guilty on all counts and the judge condemned the money account, which allowed the state to confiscate the illegal cash.

Titania Flato was almost to her truck when a red-haired man in a camo jacket caught up to her. "Nice outcome," he said.

"Thanks."

"Course, you just shit on two years that the RCMP had a man inside. Uncle Herp's operation was an international hub: China, Taiwan, Korea, Japan, unreal. He has ten thousand reptiles at a time, sales in the multi hundred millions and now it's all right down the shithole. Uncle Herp disappeared yesterday."

"Who're *you*?"

"Templeton, Fish and Wildlife. You traded less than a hundred grand for a few fucking copper bellies? It's ridiculous."

"You should have talked to us."

"You fucked that doggie, girl, not us. Uncle Herp left one message to pass on to you. It says, 'tell the game warden over there with the fancy name she's dead meat.'"

Flato watched as the man strode away and felt her knees go rubbery and then she laughed out loud. Dead meat over harmless reptiles? This can't be real. Can it? This is what, your fifth death threat in fifteen years?

"How comes these things to pass?" her namesake had asked in Shakespeare's play, which she had read dozens of times throughout her life, knew it almost by heart.

Five death threats? I must be doing something right.

The Real Twelve Mike

Tamarie Bullywick did not expect a gunshot and reacted instinctively, bouncing off the roof of the Silverado, jamming her neck. "Shit," she muttered out loud: All the windows were down to help her hear better. As soon as she recovered from hearing the shot, she put the truck in gear and started forward with her truck completely blacked out. She soon saw a small beam of light blink on and off and by the time she was closer to it, she saw a silhouette dump what looked like a large animal into the pickup bed.

She turned on her blue emergency lights and spotlights and accelerated forward, but the other truck took off fishtailing and she got up a hundred yards behind it on the icy two-track and picked up her microphone. "Central, Two One One One is in pursuit." She gave her location. The two-track dead-ended at a massive cedar swamp so the guy was not going any farther than that. It had snowed two days in a row, heavy wet, October snow, thick and gumbo-like, quick to melt in the sun, but just as quick to turn slippery when the temp dropped, and fast turning to ice, as it was doing tonight.

Lakes and ponds had been iced over for a week now, most nights down to almost ten degrees, winter stutter-stepping its way into place.

Bullywick drove as fast as she dared. The guy was black now too and she focused hard in case he tried to flip on her. She knew that two vehicles running black at night on these roads was a potential disaster. But she had been trained to do this and had been doing it for the better part of nine years. She guessed a crash lay ahead and seconds later she caught a glint of the truck ahead sliding sideways to the left, hitting something and rolling and flipping, end over end, like a toy.

Oh boy. She stopped, jumped out and ran to the wreck, which rested on its roof. She shone her flashlight into the cockpit. Empty. Boot tracks beside the driver's door. Some spots of blood, then a good pool of it. *Fool.* Quick look at bed of the truck, no deer beneath. Blood and hair, but no corpus. She found the carcass fifty feet back from where the truck had hit a stump which caused the vehicle to flip.

"Central, Two One One One is out of the vehicle. My guy rolled his truck and is running. I have some blood and boot prints and will be on the dog."

"Backup headed your way," the multiple county dispatcher said. "Fifteen minutes minimum."

"Two, One One One on foot, will check in with positions. Run a file?"

"Central ready." The CO passed along the truck plate as she went to her truck, pulled her Remington .308 out of its scabbard and started tracking. The blood wasn't heavy but it was steady. She guessed he'd wrapped it with something. Good. The bleeding would slow him down eventually, probably pretty quickly. *Does he have a rifle? Should have checked the cab of the truck. Shit. Assume he does. First rule of the chase, know what you're following.*

"Two, Triple One, Central. Plate comes back to a ninety nine Ford Taurus, owner's name is Tivoli, Carolyn R., out of Mancelona."

"Can you call the owner and ask who has her car? The plate is now on a ten-year-old Dodge Ram pickup."

"Central clear."

Bullywick's lungs were burning, heaving. Her legs were rock solid. Cold air always got your lungs until you got acclimated. No way a normal civilian could last twelve minutes in this cold and shitty footing. Catch-up was a matter of time. She kept running. *Rifle's heavy, bulky, pain in the ass. The division needs to downsize just for deals like this. The .308 will drop an elephant at a mile, but elephants were few in the Yoop and a one-mile shot unheard of in a region that was 75 percent swamp and heavy bush. Wrong weapon for the job, this crap is not .308-friendly.*

He had started running south from his truck but was gradually veer-ing westward. He's lost, running without a plan? Blood sign was spotty, intermittent, no change. No destination in his flight, his only goal is to get away from me. No way he can last.

Breathing more evenly now, steadied, low sweat starting to bead. Suddenly his tracks cut sharply west and she followed them to the lip of a seven or eight foot drop down onto a pond. She shone her light, saw his boot prints. He'd run right across the middle. *Light snow on black ice, watch your footing, girl. Be snotty-slippery footing.* She moved across the pond at a steady clip and saw the other bank and was looking for a place to make landfall when she heard a sickening crack and kept running and then she was through the ice waist-deep. The cold sucked all the air out of her and she used the rifle to pull herself back onto the ice shelf and once up, slid to the shore and dropped to her knees in the snow. She looked at his tracks and followed him up and found where he had stopped and milled around. *Why? Watching me? Sonuvabitch, did he see me go through the ice? Did he watch me struggling? If so, he was leaving me to freeze. Sonuvabitch!*

"Asshole!" She yelled out loud. "I'm coming for you, asshole!"

She heard her radio and stopped. "Two One Eleven, Central. Carolyn Tivoli says her brother, Thomas Hall Arnheim got out of prison last week. His former brother-in-law, Larry Arena owns a 1990 Dodge Ram, black, but it has no plates and was parked in a field near Valuetown. She never loaned her brother her vehicle. He must've stolen the plate, she claims."

"Thanks, Central. Have you got a physical description for me?"

"Six-three, 180, heavily tatted, shaved head, nose posts, multiple ear-rings, age twenty-five."

"Got it Central. What was he in for?"

"Aggravated assault at age eighteen. The trial results were recently tossed and they let him walk."

Fucking great. Thomas Hall Arnheim. Why do these pukes always have so damn many names? His tracks were staying due west through a series of drumlins. She kept her eyes between down and ahead and kept running forward to the side of the tracks, *right after left, right after left, right after left, of all the careers I might've chosen, right after left, and I picked English? Gawd, girl. Look where that took you, right-left, right-left. I love Shakespeare, love him, that whole bloody prejudiced and screwed up time in human history, right-left-right-left, Elizabeth, the virgin queen, antipathy of a virgin, nobody dared remark on, unlike now when characterization was art made by graffiti specialists in public johns. What did the Old Shepherd say in the Winter's Tale, left-right-left-right, click light on, okay, still got tracks, why ain't he bleeding more, right-left-right, yeah the Shepherd, c'mon girl, execute, pound that ground, pound that ground, Shepherd, yeah, okay, "I would there were no age between sixteen and three and-twenty, for there is nothing in between but getting wenches with child, wronging the ancestry, stealing, fighting, left-right-left right, don't think tired. Don't think, run, pursue, catch, punish, get control, Hark you now! Would any hit these boiled brains of nineteen and two and twenty hunt this weather? God yes, Dear Will, if you only knew the facts of now, you might even have written just for this night for what am I but a shepherdess in green, left-right-left-right, breathe, breathe, breaths, how . . . long . . . can . . . this . . . asshole run?*

Wait, slow, trail curling again, almost due north now. Is he trying to circle back? Stupid, dude, stupid.

"Central, Two Triple One, I haven't heard backup."

"They're at your vehicle, Triple One."

Left-right-left-right, up-down, pound, pound, pound that ground. "We may be circling back toward the vehicles, Central. Tell backup to hold there."

"Central clear."

Left-right-left-right, free of drumlins now, flattening terrain, open country, a field? Odd and far off, lights. What lights? What the hell? She checked the blood trail and boots, bee-lining for the lights, whatever they were.

Closer now. Small cabin. Damn. His tracks went to the front door, which was standing open. Rifle at ready, slow your breathing, slow your heart, slow your heart, think peaceful thoughts, think midnight mass and after an orgasm. No, too long since either. Slow your breathing anyway, this is the real deal, not some training exercise.

She stepped inside, rifle pointed, moving deliberately, found a man and woman of fifty in the living room, a younger woman in her twenties, all of them naked and blue from the cold. They all pointed at the back door.

The older woman said, "He told us he'd kill all of us if we told the cops where he went."

"Not to worry, nobody told me anything."

"Are you all right?" the man asked, "you're soaked and you look awful."

She passed out of the house without comment, needed back in the cold before her system tried to shut down, outside, found his path, now due north, arrow straight, no veering. She went back to the house. "What's due north of your place?"

"Jacobsen's Farms. Pigs."

"How far?"

"Three miles," the man said.

Back on the follow, keep your nose down, left-right, left-right, boots pounding the icy ground, left-right, getitgetitgetit, I feel no pain, I recognize no pain. I am fresh, I am fresh, left-right, left-right, steady breathing, get it right. Don't fail me, Willie boy, Honor in one eye and death in the other and I will look on both indignantly. For let the gods so spare as I love the more of honor than I fear death. Yah, good shit, the best, left-right, left-right.

"Central, we're now headed for Jacobsen's farm."

"Your status, Triple One?"

She heard deep concern in the dispatcher's voice. Palpable worry. "I'm just peachy," she said over the 800 mhz. Liar, liar. "Triple One clear."

"How far?"

"Three miles." There was a black layer of huffing gray clouds not ten feet ahead and she saw his rifle coming up and laughed, yelled, "I'm inside your reaction circle, ass-jacket."

Bullywick struck the man like a linebacker with a grudge, driving him back and down onto ice which cracked and turned immediately to a nasty smelling sludge, swallowed both of them. *I am in hell, but I have him cuffed.* She yanks him to his feet and she slaps him from frustration, lights him up with her SureFire, sees that his head and neck are bloody, a bloody shirt stuffed in his shirt neck and people had her by her shoulders, pulling her away and she is yelling breathlessly, "There stands a wretched creature, bruised and burdened with adversity."

• • •

Later, stretched out in an EMT truck, IV in a vein in the top of her hand, a bearded guy looking down at her and she says, "Shakespeare or God?"

"Quite the gap there," the man says.

"Not so much. God gives life and the Bard sustains it."

"Good point. How do you feel?"

"I stink," she said

"A shower will solve that problem. Is there no quit in you?"

"What?"

"Dispatcher says it was two hours from your first call until the deps pulled you off the fucked up tat dude."

"Left-right," she said. "Times a million or two."

"We think you should spend the night in the hospital."

"Because of that douchebag? That is not happening," Tamarie Bullywick said quietly, suddenly feeling unusually relaxed. "Did you assholes drug me?"

"For your own good," bearded guy said.

Bullywick said, "It is a tale told by an idiot, full of sound and fury, signifying nothing, our little life rounded with sleep and now cracks a noble heart. Good-night, sweet prince."

All through the academy cadets had been made to run as far as they could in twelve minutes, at first just in workout clothes and later loaded for bear. It was the most brutal exercise they did and it hurt every time. Instructors recorded how far you ran in the allotted time.

Two hours, let them beat that. It was her last thought for a while.

Basket Case

Sergeant Cashellen Verlaag could not understand why she seemed to attract eccentrics and nut-bags looking to her for their salvation, but here it was, oh four hundred and it had happened again. Verlaag, nearing retirement as a conservation officer, rolled out of bed and into uniform, and went into the kitchen to start coffee with an ancient machine that sounded a lot like a dog eating dry food from a tin bowl.

"*Mom*," a voice said. Fifteen-year-old Maryssa Verlaag, high school senior, dead ringer for her mother. "*Another* fruitcake?"

"Could be," Cash said. "I got a message from Vipsania Apfel. She claims she's captured six New World Order soldiers in spacesuits."

"You should, like write a book," her daughter said.

"Who would believe it?"

"I would."

"You don't count, hon. You're my daughter."

Next into the kitchen shuffled bed-hair hubby Sig, whom she called Nazrat, Tarzan backwards. Sig was the opposite of Tarzan: small, physically unimposing, shy, frightened of almost everything, yet the finest man she had ever met and newly retired as an IRS special agent. "What *this* time?"

"Vipsania Apfel."

"She's *still* around here?"

"Apparently."

"That poor woman."

Apfel had been a prison guard in Iraq and had blown the whistle on Abu Ghraib, for which she had been beaten and shunned by the US military. Two weeks before shipping home she had been in Baghdad when a suicide bomber ignited her death-belt, killing forty people and wounding Apfel, who lost all the fingers on her left hand.

The strange woman had shown up in Iron County in 2006 and Verlaag had run across her in a makeshift illegal camp up on the remote East Branch of the Net River, drying two hundred trout, pike, perch, and walleyes.

"You do know there's a limit, ma'am?"

The woman said, "My appetite exceeds all possession limits. The river and woods are my grocery store and like a smart shopper when you find a lot of something in supply you ought to buy as much as you can afford, or in this case as much as you can dry and preserve for later."

Verlaag saw the deformed left hand right away, along with significant facial scarring. Apfel wore a sort of buzz cut, which hid nothing, her skin dark from living rough and in the elements. "How long's this camp been here?"

"For as long as I have needed it."

"You know you need to have a permit and the limit to camping in a spot is two weeks?"

"There are too many rules in the world for people to follow and some people don't follow any rules at all, ever."

"Rules have a purpose."

"To remind us that we are peons."

Verlaag laughed. "Can't disagree with that. How long are you *here?*"

"It is not allowed?" the woman asked.

"It is, I'm just wondering how long you're here."

"Not long here, I have my own places in the hills far away from the winds and the storms."

"You live outside year-round?"

"Yes, of course, in preparation."

"For?"

"The New World Order, One World Government, black helicopters, they are coming for us. *All* of us."

Conspiracy nut. "You think they won't find you out here?"

The woman smiled and showed a sly twinkle in her eye. "You didn't."

"Until now," Verlaag pointed out, which put the woman into a heavy sulk.

Verlaag could sense the woman was hurting deeply and in some ways not even close to being in touch with reality. "You need to cut back on fish numbers and move your campsite every two weeks. Please?"

"You will arrest and incarcerate me, take off my clothes and piss in my face and make me pose for pictures for your friends to laugh at."

Verlaag was taken aback. "*What*?"

"God intends to punish me."

"For *what*?"

"*Cum paganis satanas*, the devil is with the pagans," the woman said, looking off into the distance. "Abu Ghraib."

"You were *there*?"

"I blew the whistle."

"God should reward you."

"I could have and should have made it public much sooner."

"But you did it, that's what matters."

"I brought dishonor to my brother and sister soldiers."

"Hey," Verlaag said, "they brought that on themselves."

"They will come to get me one day, but they won't find me," Vipsania Apfel whispered. "Nobody will find me."

It had been a strange encounter, one of many over Verlaag's career, and she had never seen the woman again, though she heard occasional reports of a hermit woman all across the north county hill country.

"What's she want?" Sig asked. "And do you want your brekkie?"

"Peach pancakes in the microwave. I'll take them and a thermos of coffee on the fly."

"Is this an emergency, then?" her husband asked.

"I haven't talked to this woman in six years and she calls me out of the blue. I'd say yah, it's an emergency."

"Where is she?"

"She gave me GPS coordinates."

"That's all?"

"It should be enough," Verlaag said.

"You want company, Mom?"

"*You* have school," she told her daughter.

"Don't be a grouch. I just thought my mumsy might like company."

"Thank you. I don't."

"What exactly does the woman want?" Sig asked.

"She wants me to take custody of six Nazis who are soldiers in the New World Order. In spacesuits. All women."

"Mom, that's like crazy," her daughter remarked.

"Not to her, it's not," Cash said.

"How did she call from the woods?" Sig asked.

"Superpowers," their daughter interjected. "Maybe she's a superhero hiding from the forces of evil."

"Apparently Apfel is not the only person around here who is out of touch with reality."

"Mom, that hurts my feelings."

Verlaag kissed her husband and whispered hungrily, "Nazrat."

Sig grunted, "Bundolo! Kreegah!"

"Attaboy, don't lose that thought."

"You two are totally bogue," their daughter said disgustedly.

"Bogue's still in vogue?" Cash asked.

"GOMB, YOLO, Mommy-O."

"This from my daughter who struggles with French?"

"What it is, *Mater mein.*"

Verlaag loaded her four-wheeler into the bed of her Silverado, stopped in Crystal Falls to fill her fuel tank, set GPS coordinates into her Automatic Vehicle Locator system, and her dashboard Garmin GPS, and headed north. "Central, DNR One One Fifty is in service."

• • •

Working her way north she set her 800 mhz radio to a Lansing DNR frequency. "Station Twenty, One, One Fifty is in service. Anything shaking?"

"Negative, One One Fifty, Twenty clear."

"DNR One One Fifty, Central."

"One, One Fifty."

"We've just had a report from the Feds of a lost balloon, something to
do with an around-the-world race, the balloon in question last seen over
Minnesota."

"And?" Verlaag said.

"Feds say it could be down somewhere in the northwest county. They
have some sort of GPS tracking unit aloft, and this is where they think
they lost the signal."

"Coordinates?"

"BOLO only at this point."

"What's this balloon look like?"

"Three hundred feet of Mylar holding up an insulated, pressurized
gondola, crew of six."

"Pressurized. Does that mean regular clothing or special?"

"Spacesuits the alert says. With helmets."

Verlaag laughed. Six women in spacesuits. "Would this be an around-
the-world race for women balloonists?"

"It would. How did you know, One, One Fifty?"

"Central, I think I'm on my way to fetch them as we talk. I'll update
her status later. Want my destination start coordinates? I'll have to leave
the truck and take the four-wheeler."

"Ready to copy coordinates, One, One Fifty?"

Verlaag passed the numbers and said, "One, One Fifty clear."

"Good hunting, One, One Fifty. Central clear."

Around the world for women only? I love this planet a world where
even women can partake in totally meaningless whimsical activities.

Central dispatch was on the horn again thirty minutes later. "One, One Fifty, Central. Homeland Security is dispatching choppers and personnel to the target coordinates."

Homeland Security? *Shit.* "Negative Central, negative. Tell them to standby and wait until I verify this thing. Right now it's all tentative, copy?"

"We'll tell them, Central clear."

Homeland Security helicopters? This will send Vipsania right off the deep end.

After snaking her way across the north county's two-tracks into the northwest wilderness, Verlaag pulled over and perused maps. The coordinates were right on the line with south Houghton County, about three miles south of a landmark called Finnlander Ridge, and right on the Ontonagon-Iron County line, an area COs called the tricounty corner, which was nasty, mostly vertical country. Her best bet looked like an old tote road snaking off Forest Highway 4500. Is this where Apfel's been all these years? It was an area far from anything that might even be loosely construed as civilization.

"Station Twenty, One One Fifty will be out on my four-wheeler and away from my vehicle."

"One, One Fifty, be advised Homeland Security is alerting us to a possible border violation with suspects in northwest Iron County."

Border violation? Good God! "Negative, negative, is your El-Tee in?"

"Affirmative."

A calm male voice came across the radio, "One One Fifty, Twenty One Hundred." The RAP room supervisor had been a topnotch field CO, and was also a military combat vet.

"Twenty, One Hundred, can you get Homeland to stand down? I had a call from someone in that area claiming she has contact with a crew of six Germans and a balloon. I'm headed there now. The informant is hinky—a conspiracy nut. Choppers will spook her at best and God knows what at worst."

"I'm on it, One, One Fifty. Be careful. Station Twenty clear."

If Homeland Security could be headed off, Lt. Barry Sample would be the one to make it happen. Verlaag unloaded her four-wheeler, and verified she had a full fuel tank. She always kept it full, but always checked it and had looked at it in Crystal Falls and now looked again, just to be certain. She did not want to run out of gas up here. It looked like six miles to the coordinates Vipsania had given her. Thank God she had the low-slung Polaris RAZR 1000. With this she could snake over, around and through virtually any obstacle. And she could also run like a rocket if she needed to.

$$\bullet \bullet \bullet$$

"Stop or I shoot!" a voice commanded. Verlaag had stopped to stare at an endless carpet of shiny silver fabric stretching up into a rare grove of first-growth white pines. This area apparently had been too remote even for old-timey loggers who pretty much used winter to go where they liked. Usually the crews swarmed like ants and disappeared leaving a hole in the forest. Harvesting, loggers called it, but it was the same thing. Pay a low contract to the state, chop a bunch of trees, and sell high. In most places the strategy left nothing behind but greater nothing.

"It's me, Vipsania."

"I can see that for myself, but there are black helicopters in the area. I seen 'em!"

Homeland Security, officious bastards. Assholes. "They are here to help," Verlaag said, not buying her own line and sorry she'd said anything.

"They're the enemy. Here to help? Do you think I'm stupid?"

"Of course not." Certifiably left field, maybe, but not stupid. Switch directions. "Where are your prisoners?"

"They are secure."

"Are they all right?"

"They are secure."

"Where?"

"Exactly where I secured them. I can feel the choppers in my bones."

"There's no One World Government, Vipsania, no New World Order."

"I have captured Nazis as proof."

"They're balloon racers, not soldiers."

Long silence. "Explicate."

"An all-woman balloon race around the world. This team is one from Germany."

"War everywhere and people are racing balloons?" Apfel asked, her voice cracking with nerves. She sounded irritated, befuddled.

"Better than making war, eh?"

"Yes, of course," Apfel said.

"Are your detainees healthy enough to travel?"

"Yes, of course. But they are vapid, empty creatures. There is no threat to America if this is the kind of soldier the One World Government sends."

"They are civilian balloon racers, not soldiers. Can we talk face to face, woman to woman?"

"Yes, of course."

Verlaag was startled. Apfel popped up not six feet from her, her camouflage making her blend perfectly with her background. "Geez, you are good," Verlaag exclaimed.

"I will starve if I am just average."

"Good point. Where are the women? Can I talk to them?"

"You are not alone, but I told you to come alone. You have violated our agreement."

"I *am* alone."

"There are helicopters."

"Where?"

Apfel looked upward.

"Gone right now."

"I made them pull back."

"So you admit to be with them. You just lied to me." The woman's rifle barrel came up.

"I *didn't* lie. You know how higher levels of command involve themselves in stuff that's none of their business. A balloon went missing along the border and Homeland Security leaped in to save the day. Don't point that weapon at me. Homeland Security is part of your country, our country, not the New World Order. They are us and we are them and so forth. They are trying to help. You have six people detained. I can't put them all in my RAZR. Do you expect me to walk them out of here? These people are not like you and me. They are balloonists, pilots. They fly in the air, not walk on the ground."

"You may have them," Apfel said. "They eat excessively," she muttered.

With this said, Vipsania disappeared. There, then gone, leaving Verlaag blinking. *Fruitcake!*

Verlaag left the RAZR and walked ahead to the tree line against a hill, saw a rectangular trapper's cabin built into a hillside and pushed the door in. She found six women in black and red jumpsuits, silver spacesuits piled in the corner with helmets and oxygen masks. All the women had short blonde hair, blue eyes, high Aryan jawbones, lantern jaws. "Good morning ladies."

"*Gut morgen*, We are crew of Germany Reunited, *Deutschland Wiedervereinigt*. I am Kapitan Asta Bormann."

Another blonde piped up. "You shall not usurp our collective authority. We are all kapitans: Asta, Krista, Dagmar, and I am Elke. Take us to your leader."

Verlaag had to fight laughing. Take us to your leader? Good grief!

The first speaker said, "*Osten verloren in ihrer vergangen hut.* This means East—she is lost in her past." The woman rolled her eyes.

"Are all of you all right?" Verlaag asked.

"*Ja Wohl*," Kapitan Elke said, "but of course we luuse zis race becuzzzz one of us makes za wronk kal-ka-leyshunulation of zawinz. *Dumbkoff*."

The six women all began shouting and pushing each other and Verlaag backed outside and activated her radio. "Twenty, One, One Fifty. I have our missing fliers. They are all well and accounted for. Homeland has a chopper somewhere near here. Tell them to look for green smoke and I'll talk them in. Put them on DNR One."

"Doing it now," the dispatcher in Lansing said. "One One Fifty, did they back off?"

"Just in time, thanks."

"We'll send them back in."

"Tell them no weapons, all is calm and copacetic here. One, One Fifty clear."

The girls put on their spacesuits and carried their helmets. They lined up behind Verlaag and she led them to a clearing near her four-wheeler and popped smoke, shaking the can to get the plumey coils rising upward.

"Our kondola iss on za hill behind za shack," Kapitan Asta said.

"It will be sent to you," Verlaag said, hoping she was right.

She felt the chopper before it flew into view and hovered over them. It landed in the clearing, whipping debris everywhere and the chopper's crew came out in black uniforms, brandishing weapons.

"All clear, all clear!" she yelled, waving her arms to get them to sling their weapons.

One of the crewmen came forward. "These the aliens?"

"They are a German balloon crew."

"We will take custody from here," the sergeant said.

Verlaag shook hands with each woman and watched them file into the belly of the helicopter, which lifted off with its turbines screaming as it flew away over the trees. *Wait until conspiracy nuts get hold of this deal,* Verlaag thought.

"You have honor," Vipsania Apfel said, popping out of nowhere again.

"Don't *do* that. Please!"

"Our business is concluded," the hermit said and fired her rifle in the air, making Verlaag drop to the ground. When she got up, the woman was gone. *Good God.*

• • •

"So, Mommy-O, space aliens?" her daughter greeted her.

"Balloonists," Cash said.

"Like the creepy guys that make scary animals at kiddie parties?"

"No, all women, Germans, racing around the world."

"How stupid," her daughter said dismissively.

• • •

In bed that night with Nazrat. "Rub my back, hon. Between that truck and the RAZR I'll be lucky if I can still walk when I retire. Ooh, those hands."

"Kreegah? Bundolo?"

"Do my back first, okay hon?"

Fishing for Glory

The conservation officer casted and retrieved with metronomic regularity, working the water, every inch, expecting every cast to be the one, yet hoping it would not.

The lake was small, not ten acres, surrounded by maples denuded of leaves, a rim of sphagnum around the circumference. It had been a nasty job to get the aluminum pram through the tag alders and loon shit into real water, but if you wanted a big fish, there had to be a struggle. Granpa had preached that. You want big fish, you gotta work for 'em. God don't give no big fish to nobody don't deserve it. The struggle was minor, really, not more than a quarter-mile boat drag and once she was on the water and in the envelope of peace the lake created, the struggle was immediately forgotten, reality reduced to cast and retrieve, thinking through her wrist, varying speed, waiting for that tap to tell her to set the hook.

Granpa Dusinberre had taken her out to Harsen's Island nearly every day all summer and they filled coolers with walleyes. Granpa even kept carp he called nigger food. They always dropped the carp with an old man with rheumy yellow eyes. Granpa called him Willie Fish, but she never knew the man's real name. Granpa liked Willie, that was clear to her, but he was always the nigger. On days she couldn't fish, Granpa took Willie along. Later in life she recognized it as racism, but racism tempered by something else she couldn't identify.

Call a man a nigger, like he wouldn't mind, and take fish to him *and* his place was not even close to convenient or on their way, it was in fact *way* out of the way. Her grandfather had been a hard man to figure and she never did solve him, but he was kind and attentive and full of information and advice, which turned out to be equal parts bullshit and real. She knew he always cared about her and rooted for her. His death, while she was in training, had hit hard, forced her to suck it up and reach deeper inside herself.

How many fish had they killed over the years? Certainly enough to populate this small lake, but the old man refused to bow to any rules. "What the hell do them bone-ass desk jockeys in Lansing know that I don't know for myself?"

She interrupted memories to reposition the boat, anchoring deep over the loon shit.

No hits yet, work the shoreline carefully. There was an unexpected drop-off there, a black hole in a black hole under a sky the color of dirty motor oil and spitting ice-pellet snow, the contrast making the snow look like cornflakes. Her hands were cold, but steady casts kept her warm enough. So nice to not be in the truck.

How would I explain a chore like this to the clueless, those folks locked in factories and office mazes? Well, maybe not factories, not like when you were a girl and the entire neighborhood was populated by shop rats and motor-heads. God, how they railed and squawked when I went off to college, and it got louder and nasty, especially when I declared criminal justice as a major. That decision had very nearly sent neighbors in their saltbox houses off the deep end. "It's not a proper job for a woman. No odds in it. Too damn dangerous. You'll never be as good as a man, never get married, never have kids, never satisfy God's plan for all women." They wigged out when I told them how I felt.

That switched the focus and pressure from her to mom and dad. "You don't want grandchildren?" they had asked her parents. It's that old man's fault, neighbors said, raising that girl-child like she was a boy. Just not proper for a young lady. Now look at her".

Cast, retrieve. Cast to the target, let the line sink until there was slack, retrieve.

How did my one family, same as all the rest when you really got down to it, how did my family command so damn much neighborhood attention? It was like all noses were pointed at 59122 Dover Avenue. Until the day you came home with a sixty-six-inch muskie. No talk after that, only praise and jealousy. She be a female Ted Williams, neighbors proclaimed to mom and dad. Fools, idiots. Sixty-six inches brought nothing but praise, and soon I'm that weird kid who doesn't know her damn place in the scheme of things.

You have to learn that if you listened too closely to people, they'd put you off balance and keep you there. They spit up whatever they think-feel but without real thought, just on impulse. Like the time you had two tequila shooters on top of three beers and Sean Hospital had touched you and caught you on fire and the next thing you knew you were buck-naked on top of him in the back seat of his father's yellow Olds 98, screaming like you're a banshee. Afterwards you felt really mellow and asked him about camping and fishing and hunting, and he had made a gagging sound.

"That stuff is so pleb," he had said.

Pleb? She had no idea what the hell it even meant, but guessed by tone it had been a put-down. Too bad. That night still stood out in her mind in terms of pure electricity, while most others were barely remembered. *His loss, not mine.*

This isn't a job, it's a way of life, one envied by a lot of folks and understood by few. Cast left, retrieve slowly, slower, slowest, pause, yes, like that, yaaah. People think game wardens hunt and fished twenty-four seven, which is true if you understand people are your quarry, not fish and game. People are so clueless and a day like today is a gift if you care to see it so. I love this!

She repositioned the boat again, picked up the thermos, and filled her cup with coffee.

A pile of mergansers flooded down onto the lake north of her. A raft of thirty. They were such odd creatures and fish-killers extraordinaire. "Go away," she told them. "I don't want competition today."

Fisheries class, her first one, a professor by the name of Ann Frank had begun class, "No, not *that* Ann-with-an e Frank, but yes I'm a Jew like her. My family owns an aquaculture venture off the coast of Scotland. Fishing in my blood, you might say, and I would not object. Hook and line too." The professor proclaimed, "I love the surprises that fishing brings, the explosion of action, your heart racing."

On a weekend fish with Ann and her husband Bolton, Ann said, "Fish are like men. They want to be on top or bottom, never between." They all laughed at the not so-subtle double entendre and Ann then announced in her professorial voice, "You will always find the most pleasure in a small hole in a small water body."

Dusinberre pondered that, put down her rod, rubbed her hands, and looked at her hydro-chart. She saw that the deepest hole was quite close to the shore, not out along the ledge drop-off.

She rowed over to the hole, anchoring with two anchors to keep the craft positioned in one place, stationary. She took out her little Bugs Bunny lunch pail and got out a peanut butter and grape jelly on raisin bread sammy. Granpa had told her, "Even God eats PB&J." He was so full of shit, and so MUCH fun.

She felt a chill of anticipation, a ferret zipping up the inside of her spinal column. "One hit," she said out loud. She had never in her life lost a fish she hooked, not once, not ever, a gift from Granpa Dusinberre.

First cast and retrieve across the bottom of the hole she thought she felt a tentative bump, no more than a brief, soft shudder. She cast back into the same spot and let it sink a while longer. *Down, wait, wait, wait. Okay, long enough. Now creep it, creep it, s-l-o-w-l-y, feel the bottom, feel it tap. Pause. Lift the pole tip slightly. Tap. Resistance? Yep that's a tap. Set!* She jerked the rod tip up with all her strength, felt the hook bury deep and set as the rod bent into a U, and she kept the line taut and began the long haul and fight, pulse and crank, pulse and crank, pulse and crank until it came grudgingly to the side of the boat and she got a hand on it and held tight as she put down the rod and touched her radio transmitter on her coat. "Central, One One Eighteen. I have Glory."

Glory Livermore, thirty-six, fell out of a canoe last night, probably intoxicated. A downstate woman with four little kids up in deer camp with three of her pals, drunk and dead, one road leading to the other.

"One, One Eighteen, great job," her partner chirped over the radio. He was in his own boat at the other end of the lake. "You never lose 'em!"

Good to be known for something useful, she told herself, and to get a whole day on the water and not in the faces of idiot deer hunters.

Gulf of Goths

They had named their daughter Eudora after the writer and until she was fourteen she was a studious girl, polite, thoughtful, sensitive to others, outgoing, happy tomboy, jockey, never still.

And overnight beloved Eudora became another person, wanting only to wear black and colorless clothes and compressed her vocabulary to no more than a few words and phrases. *If you say so. Whatever. I have no interest, whatsoever.*

Golden Child turned Miss Morose almost in a twenty-four-hour cycle of the clock and CO Alexandra Gamerov and husband Melville King were at a loss. School counselors shrugged, kid shrinks shrugged, the family doctor and her nurse shrugged, their priest shrugged, as did her teachers and her friends.

Only Grandmother Baba Gamerov didn't shrug. "Miss All American Girl becomes Miss All-Black listening to that stuff, Rivethead, Nine-Inch Nails and she wants me to call her Doomcake? I refuse. I will not accept this. She needs a good kick in the pants. Doomcake, for God's sake. It's an abomination!"

"This is God's punishment," Baba insisted. "She turned me prematurely white and made my breasts sag like *due otri piatte*! All that hunting and fishing and camping in the woods and sleeping on the cold, damp ground, eating all that junk food, I'm telling you it's all unnatural and now look what it makes! Civilization has taken the last five hundred years to decide a woman's proper role and it is not in the *bois*. The child is lost forever, for eternity, and you have only yourselves to blame."

Classic mother-speak. Alex pushed the heel of her hand hard into her eye socket. Her mother was consistent, if not humane, considerate, supportive, empathetic, or interested in anything in life, save one: Herself. So it went.

Baba would be no help, and Mel wanted terribly to help but he was a nurse for a cardiac surgeon and could barely handle the workload and demands of his job, much less the vacillations of a teenage daughter. He tried, but this was a time when employers were strict constructionists in easing burdens on employees' work lives. There were too many people in line for any opening, and willing to take huge cuts from their previous incomes. You had to toe the line. It was my-way-or-the-highway time and a lot of states were gnawing away at unions, putting even more pressure on people.

She had Mel's support, but Eudora was mainly her problem and while she didn't have the flexibility of a stay-at-home mom, her job gave her flex time and split shifts and this helped. The plan? There was no plan. How did you counter a 180 in someone's personality? Somebody you adored?

Sitting at the kitchen table, cradling yet another cup of coffee, she got a cell phone call from Emil Grayle, the village constable. "Gamerov, you hearing anything about Goths?"

"The barbarians or kids who dress weird?"

"Very funny. Kids."

"Not a thing, Emil. Why would I?"

"Street word."

"Street word in Vokal? We have seventy year-round residents, Emil. We're not even a town. Legally we're a hamlet. There are no traffic lights and there's no street talk. What the hell is going on?" Vokal's kids were in the Saint Lac consolidated school district; there were no schools within the boundaries of the hamlet.

"Neveryoumind, word is the tree goths, grass goths and crows are gonna have a rumble at the boneyard Friday night."

"There's a football game in St. Lac Friday night."

"Not for the goth crowd, there ain't."

"We've got how many goth kids in Saint Lac, four, five? And you're telling me they're splintered into three factions?"

"There's four at the high school, more in the middle school, a couple in the elementaries, and your daughter is said to be the ringleader of the whole caboodle."

Gamerov closed her eyes. "What exactly does that mean, Emil, the ringleader?"

"Ask your kid. There's firearms involved. Don't say you ain't been told."

"Thanks, I guess. What is it you expect me to do?"

"Ain't it obvious?"

"Not really."

The constable hung up without further comment. His call pissed her off, and worried her. Now what? The ball was clearly in her court.

• • •

That night, dinner. "New with you?" Gamerov asked her daughter, whose hair was dyed black, her face white and sallow.

"Same old," Eudora said unenthusiastically.

"Really, same old?" Mom asked.

The girl looked up from her chicken breast. "Are you like in badge mode or Mom-mode?"

"I'm not sure. Which do you think would be more appropriate?"

"I have no interest whatsoever," the girl said.

"Tell me about tree goths, grass goths and crows."

Eudora looked warily at her mother. "It's not *stupid*," she said.

"Did I say it was stupid?"

"Whatever."

"Do not use that tone with me, Eudora."

"Get over it," the girl mumbled.

"You want to be treated like an adult? Okay, here's how that works. Emil Grayle called me tonight to inform me that my daughter is and I quote here, "Ringleader," end quote, of some sort of Goth confrontation planned for Friday night. Is that direct enough for you? No? Then add this to the calculation. Emil told me firearms are involved. Now, Ms. Goth ringleader, or who or whatever you are today, when you take high school students and throw in the word gun, you are headed for a high alarm for all cops."

The girl looked aghast at her mother. "*Guns? Guns!*"

"Guns."

The girl flashed momentary panic, but steadied herself. "Do you believe everything you hear?"

"You know very well that I don't, which is why we're talking, to which I would add now that I seem to have your attention, we've not done much of since you went Goth this past summer."

"This is *not* the time," Eudora said.

"When *is* the time?" her mother asked.

"*Guns?*" the girl said in an extremely anguished tone, got up, and ran to her room, slamming the door behind her.

Alex Gamerov poured more coffee for herself, waited a few minutes, went to her daughter's bedroom door and knocked respectfully. "Can I come in?"

She and Mel had always respected their daughter's privacy and Alex did not want to step over that line now. "Honey?"

"I have homework," her daughter said through the door.

Mom pushed open the door. The girl was sitting on the end of her bed scowling. "I have no *rights*, is that it?"

"This is not *about* your rights, Eudora. There are serious allegations of the kind neither the constable nor I can ignore. We can't."

"*God*, Mom, it's me, Eudora. Do you really think I would have anything to do with guns in school?"

"You've been taught to handle firearms, you hunt, you're skilled."

"I'm also not crazy! Mom, this is what happens when a few people are different and others don't like the difference."

Alex Gamerov took a deep breath. "Newtown."

Eudora rolled her eyes, but did not withdraw or retreat. "You think I'm that fucking lunatic Adam Lanza?"

"You know I don't."

"But you've already assumed the gun rumor is true or you wouldn't be in here interrogating me. Adam Lanza was a sick fuck, Mom. Crazy." The girl made a sour face.

"I never mentioned a name."

"You don't have to. The media have pounded names into TV-heads, but Mom, most shooters in schools aren't Goths. They're sick kids. If you even put on a trench coat now, you're automatically Goth. Back in the early sixties all college kids wore trench coats. It was in."

"Not any more," Alex said.

"No, not with the Baah-group. It's in with some kids. Black is beautiful, or didn't you get that memo? I mean, *come on*."

"Black is beautiful is about race."

"Not always and not now. The whole point of Goth is to look at yuck stuff and try to find beauty."

"Blood, vampires, death?"

"Yes, Mom. All of that. We're human beings. We're all going to die. Whole religions try to teach their people to respect but not fear death, but if Goths do it, it's wrong."

It struck Alex Gamerov that her withdrawn, often moody fourteen-year-old had been doing a lot of thinking. She was being entirely rational now, and convincing. "So, you started acting Goth to come to grips with dying?"

"Mom, *listen to me*. One doesn't become Goth. You are or you aren't, and one day you realize it and you start to dress the way you think, the same way the Baahs dress to reflect what they think."

The conservation officer felt wired. "Stay with me, please. You are or are not Goth?"

"Right. You think like most other people, or you don't. You're inside the box of the big group, or you're outside that box. Like you, Mom. You're a CO and you have to live and think outside boxes others build. You're trained to not think like others."

Gamerov stared at her daughter.

"Goths hate guns, mom. And all violence. Think about it. Americans love guns and violence. Look at movies, comics, TV, whatever. Goths are the opposite."

"You're telling me there's no guns involved this coming Friday?"

"The constable's son Trent started that rumor. He's on the football team, heard some kids had plans and would not be at the game and it pissed him off. He decided to undercut us, using his old man."

"By alleging a *gun*?"

Eudora nodded. "Nowadays you don't need a gun to make your point. All you have to do is mention that word and that's it. He said gun to his dad and after Newtown and all the crap afterwards, here we are talking about it, aren't we? Trent's no dummy. He played his old man like a banjo. The word 'gun' is the new way to get attention."

"What *is* Friday about?"

"There's a dude on the Internet with a blog called Goths in Trees and he puts up really cool, really different photos of people trying to capture the Goth look. He criticizes their look in a constructive way and he asks people to send in photos."

"At night in a graveyard?"

"Not in a cemetery. That's bogus, like the gun. It's at Elle McGhehey's house. Her dad's got floodlights and they have colossal oaks in their back forty."

"Crow goths?"

"Brandon Lee, Edgar Allan Poe, Nevermore, they like to dress up like crows."

"Tree Goths?"

"What we're trying to become."

"Grass Goths?"

"Us now, before Tree Gothdom."

"This is like some kind of upgrade, a change in status?"

"Mom, are you *thick*? It's a lark, it's Goths making fun of Goths who show off their Gothnicity, you know Smithy Posers?"

The conservation officer's head hurt. "You and your friends want to make fun of other Goths?"

"Right on, you are so mundane."

"I am?"

"It means normal, Mom."

"And you?"

"I'm Goth mundane, at least for now. Next year, who knows?"

"I buy it," Alex Gamerov said. "Not sure I understand any of this, but I think I buy it."

"Of course you do, Mom. You're Goth."

•••

Friday night at the McGhehey house, Constable Emil Grayle crashed the photo shoot at 10:30 p.m., Maglite in hand, pistol in the other. "Nobody move," he yelled.

"Put the gun away," Alex Gamerov told the man.

"Gamerov, you're here and you ain't got down on this?"

"She realized she's one of us," Eudora Gamerov told the constable. She stood by her mother, both of them dressed in severe black, including knee-high patent leather boots with multiple silver buckles and platform soles and heels.

"No guns here, Emil," the conservation officer said.

"Yah, well I maybe better take a look-see for myself. This is a big deal."

Gamerov said, "If it's such a big deal, why did you wait until Trent's game was over before you came out here? Football takes priority over a gun threat?"

The constable walked out without further comment. Eudora's friends all cheered and clapped and whistled at the game warden, who said, "You guys are so mundane."

They got home before Mel, who looked at his wife and whispered, "Grrrr, that outfit turns me on."

"You're too tired," she said.

"How do you know?" he shot back.

"That's all you ever tell us."

"Yah, well step into my horizontal office and let's discuss this," he said, taking her hand.

"*Whatever,*" she said.

Heads, Tails, and Other Vague Body Parts

"Good grief, there's a plate of head in here," Norval Churr bellowed as he slammed the fridge door.

Norv, as other kids knew him, was the fifteen-year-old current attachment of Geriomo Smoon's alluring and astonishing physically developed fifteen-year-old daughter Vachel Lindsay Smoon, second smartest child in the Creston-Vale school district, senior class valedictorian by rank, most of her peers two years behind her in school.

Vachel went to the fridge, looked inside and made a growly snarly sound and said, "Mom, Stench is doing it again!"

"Honey, I worked shiners until six this morning. Can I please sleep?"

"It's so . . . gross, and we like have a *guest*?"

CO Smoon stumbled into the kitchen in her pink onesy. "I'm Geri," she told the strange-looking boy with huge ears.

"That's Norval Churr, Ma. He likes me. Actually I think he likes some parts better than others but he doesn't talk much so I have to pretty much guess."

"It's good to be liked," the mother said. "Doesn't the future of the Earth depend on it?" *Not that you would know. When was your last date? Two years? Gawd.*

"That's so gross, Ma. Norv's a boy, a sophomore, a pet. *Look* at him. He doesn't know about birds or bees and all that euphemistic mumbo-jumbo cover-story lingo."

"I know there's a plate of heads in the fridge," Norv said. "Does that count?"

She yelled up the stairs. "Yonder, get your darn butt down here and take care of your specimens."

The boy Yonder, aka Stench, thirteen, a freshman, already six-two with ranges of white-capped zits all over his face, wild hair, and with darty, dark eyes, the unmistakable countenance of a lab rat. Yonder came downstairs silently and looked at Norval like a bobcat might look at a fawn.

"Norv, meet Yonder, my kid brother. We call him Stench."

Yonder sniffed. "No room in the freezer here or downstairs."

Geriomo joined her son, who towered above her. She opened the fridge. "*Kittens* and *rabbits*?"

The boy sighed and shuffled his big feet. "Somebody dumped the kittens in the creek and I claimed salvage rights." The boy made another sniffing sound. "See, not even a little ripe. The rabbits got run over when I was doing the lawn on the rider-mower. I didn't see them until it was too late."

Geri eyed her son. "Too late? Likely story. Not paying attention, off in one of your fogs," she said.

"No biggie, Mom. All great scientists have collected specimens. It's no different than the commercial food chain. People like pigs but do they know how pork gets into the Piggly Wiggly? I think not, and they don't *want* to know. Scientists, however, we want to know, we *must* know, we have to know."

"You're no scientist," Vachel told her brother, "and if you're moving that plate of heads downstairs, please go outside and around, not through the house. We don't want to walk through a ribbon of fumes of the recently departed tickling our nostrils."

"Ever the bromidrosiphobic," Stench said.

"You are a very sick and deeply disturbed child," Vachel told her brother.

"No more child than your companion," Yonder said, adding an exaggerated head nod.

"Wait," Geriomo said. "I have two fawns in the stand-up fridge, so there's no room in there." Smart tossed a key on a green lanyard to her son. "Blue evidence locker in my office."

"That's full of steelhead and salmon," Vachel told her mother.

"No, I moved those fish to the district office yesterday afternoon. There should be lots of space on top the other stuff."

"Other *stuff*?" Norval interjected.

"Cadavers for necropsy. Bodies, if you will. Want to see?"

"I guess," the boy said.

"Vachel, do not tease that nice boy," Geriomo said.

"He wants to see, Ma. Donchu Norv? You want to show me your manly man side, look death in the eye, all that good stuff, right?"

"I guess," the boy said.

"Vachel, leave that young man alone. *Ti-pi.*"

"I *know*, mother, but it's like *frozen*?"

"*Nak-ka*," Geriomo said sharply.

"*Eh-eh-eh*," the girl keened. "*Miki-luk.*"

"*Na-ka. King-oo-vi?*"

"I'm just having some fun with him."

"Mean is not fun, it's bullying."

"Is that like Canadian you guys are speaking?" Norval asked.

Geriomo looked hard at her daughter who said, "Okay?"

"No." The boy was clearly a driver in the slow lane, a poor reason to be picking on him. Geriomo tried to teach her children to talk in Inuit when they wanted to keep conversations private. She had grown up in Alaska, her folks both anthropologists. The family had lived with their subjects until Geriomo went outside to attend Michigan State and while she was gone, her parents had drowned in a hunting accident. Geriomo decided to remain in Michigan, got her degree in wildlife management, worked for the DNR as a biologist for a while, but found it boring and moved over into law enforcement. Thank God for her health. She had always made it a point to stay in shape. The physical tests of the DNR academy had been a nightmare, but she had made it through and had been a CO now for eight years, five of which she had been on her own in the county.

Hubbard Kenty, her partner and former trooper, was known for his lead foot, which led him to a head-on with a massive bull moose, killing both of them more or less instantly. At least she liked to think so. Hub had been a good guy with a happy-go-lucky, off-the-wall view of life. As a trooper he'd given out popcorn balls on Halloween, and GET OUT OF JAIL FREE cards during traffic stops on the Fourth of July. Geriomo missed him and so did her kids who called him "Uncle Hub."

"Go outside," Vachel told Norv, who dutifully shuffled out onto the upper deck.

"You cannot audition boyfriends," her mother said.

The girl made a face. "You don't *know* that's what I'm doing."

"Vachel, I raised you. I know what you think before you think it."

"Like one of your violets?"

Violets, her word for violators. She wished at times that she could think like them, if thinking was the right word to describe what went on in such mixed-up heads, but most of the time she decided, she would rather stay ignorant of their innermost thinking.

"That boy is not a game, Vachel. He's human."

"Ma, he's a sophomore. They're *never* human!"

"OK, why is he here?"

"An experiment."

"You're *using* him?"

"I won't hurt him. He's like a dildo, hey?"

"Vachel."

"Yes, I know what you keep in your dresser!"

Geriomo sat in the nearest chair and laughed out loud, sighed, and looked at her daughter. "*Aiie!*" send that boy home now. You and I need to talk."

"A real talk about actual body parts by name, or more metaphoric bullshit?"

"Actuals."

"Okay!"

Vachel went outside and was quickly back. "He never would have worked out," the girl declared.

Her mother gave her daughter a questioning look.

"Stench dropped two catheads on the deck. "There's a puke-pile beside them and Norv's nowhere in sight. Never breed with a quick puker," Vachel concluded.

"A new philosophy?"

"Inescapable, but more along the lines of unpleasing aesthetics, and like nobody cleans up their own puke, right Ma?"

I will laugh at this ten years hence, Geriomo Smoon told herself.

"Is it difficult, Ma?"

"Is what difficult?

"Having the kind of talk we're going to have."

"Depends on if I can remember how it works, or if I have to make it up as I go."

"*Ma*."

Dancing Hula in Felony Forest

Her last day, twenty-seven years in a green uniform, nine thousand, one hundred, and twenty-four days spent in every imaginable weather condition (including a water spout in Lake Gogebic), over every kind of terrain, and yet, and against all odds and sheer chance, she had made not one major case of a lifetime, the sort of thing that left a story behind when you were gone.

Not one case, not even close. She'd made cases, lots of them solid cases for all sorts of violations but a big, mass felony case, not a one and not so much. It was well, like humiliating.

Not to mention inexplicable. It wasn't one of those things others talked about to her face, but she was sure there was talk behind her back; she could even feel the pricks of derision at district meetings when everyone gathered. She imagined their words: always average, never a go-getter, your plain-old brown wrapper of an officer, a blivet and a face with no name and gliding to an end of the lackluster skein.

It irked. It hurt. It made her steely eyed and determined. None in more than a quarter century, but today was today, not yesterday, a fresh, unmarked slate and this could be that big day for the case. For the one.

It has to be. Because this is the last day forever.

Why am I like this? It's what happens to any officer who follows a legend into a county. Her predecessor had made so many major collars they called him Big Case. But me, in the shadow of such glory, nothing, not even a chance to sit in my own name. Oh yeah, what happened to Big Case? Yah, I know your partner, how's he doing? God, your partner was a thing to behold. All this sucked big time. But she was too proud and too stubborn to transfer. She was determined to prove herself here, no reason why not, just a matter of recognizing a big case when it rolled up on her. A matter of time and patience.

But a major case had never come my way, and now I'm down to the proverbial and final last patrol, my last set of downs with the ball in a long career, yet, and here is also a gift, a totally free day, with no directive forcing me into a boat, or to anything or anywhere specific. On my last patrol day I can go and do what I choose to do. Not that they want or expect this. The higher-ups no doubt expect me to go quietly through the day and slide into the obscurity of retirement and the long slide after that led to whatever the hell comes next, which has many names, even more theories, and scant evidence qualifying it as anything more substantive than air castles.

Not that I want to trust to blind faith. Done that for a quarter century, and see where it had led me. No, not fate and no blind acceptance. For once I'll listen to Dylan Thomas, "Do not go gentle into that good night, Old age should burn and rave at close of day; Rage, rage against the dying of the light." Okay so what do I actually do? What do I focus on, driving serendipitously whereby I can cover a lot of blank miles, hoping to collide with a fate that had always and effectively avoided me, and hope to end an eight-hour shift no differently than the past many thousands spent the same way? No, not that.

Deer, bears, wolves, fish, what? Think it through. It's September for cripe's silly sake, Labor Day, the last gasp of tourists and . . . get out your notebooks and look back at this same date for many years. Huh, drug bust last fall by the interagency drug team out near Tula, and, of course, this past summer they had been spent countless hours by multiple agencies patrolling the snot out of the same area, which makes and made no damn sense. Why do cops think the other side is dumb? Uneducated, probably, but not dumb. They can be as wily as foxes. If I wanted to grow drugs . . . I'd . . . she got out a plat book. If I wanted to grow drugs, I need water, cover, and geographic anonymity. There are farms south of Imp Lake, which have always rubbed me wrong, though I've never been able to say precisely why. Saw corn silage there, year after year. Now I'm wondering, she wondered, who does the farmer sell to? There're no animals on that farm, not that I've ever observed or heard. So it's not silage for his critters. And it's a far fling from Tula, and close to Wisconsin for fairly wasy transport north and south. A long shot's better than no shot. Imp Lake it shall be, my final roll of the dice.

It's sort of laughable, this last-day fixation, but never having made a major case has always made me feel somehow like I had shirked duty, which I never had, not even for an hour. Just couldn't. It's just bad luck, that's all.

Remember when the city cop saw a naked young woman jump off a footbridge in the city park in July? He jumped in immediately and hauled her to shore and been hailed a hero, given the gubernatorial medal for saving a life. Nobody pointed out that the water there was three feet deep over a pea-gravel bottom. Years before I had witnessed the same thing, walked out on the bridge and told the woman, "Stand up, you're making a fool of yourself." Unlike the city cop I know every fact and nuance of every square foot of the county, had made it a point to learn it all, so that when something happened, such data was already in my head and could help me quickly sort things out.

Did that preparation pay off? Chump change only, no significant cases or results. Same situation, different solutions, identical outcomes, why was one glorified and decorated and the other one unremarked? Strange darn world.

Now I get to roll the bones one last time and Imp Lake wins. No regrets, no looking back, go and do, this can be the one. I hope.

All right, consider tactics. Just drive on up and say howdy? No that would never works and I have not even a shadow of probable cause, never mind any compelling evidence of anything, much less a crime, even a minor one. You can't blast onto private property on conjecture, just can't, and right now your ability to take a next step is contingent on a smart first step. Stop stalling and go do it.

As a drop-back partner she had Carmen in her backpack, Carmen, her personal drone, which had cost her close to two hundred bucks and had yet to earn a nickel of return. The drone's real name was EYE-SKY 1 but she called hers Carmen after the silly damn game she and her sisters had played all those years, "Where in the world is Carmen Somthingeeavo?"

She liked flying the drone, liked it a lot. It had a 16 megapixel photo resolution, and 300x magnification. She'd bought the camera separately, rigged the mount all on her own, Leica digital, another eight hundred smackers and never mind the lack of payoff. The logic was simple enough. DNR budgets were stagnant at best and they had no money to spare for a plane to fly night shooters and over-baiters. She accepted the reality and created her own aerial capability.

She had, of course, dutifully passed the drone idea to her sergeant, even showed him the set-up and gave him a demonstration of what it could do. His reaction had been immediate: "Waste of time and money, there ain't no budget."

Six months later there were two state drones being flown by COs, she was not one of them, and her name had never been mentioned in concert with helicopter drone craft. She shrugged it off.

Maybe there will be something in plain sight at the farm and all I'll have to do is pull into the farmyard.

Don't fool yourself. You ain't one to get the gimmes. Stand off, let Carmen do the looking, see what she can find for you.

She took a circuitous route to her destination. She knew an abandoned road nearby, one now mostly grown over with popple and birch land scrub brush. Nature was reclaiming it, but some good hard surfaces remained. The old stretch of macadem was north of the farm and a good place to hide the truck.

She parked and hiked to the old hardtop where she assembled Carmen, ran though the pre-flight checklist, got a wet-finger read on wind direction, and told the bird to fly. "Get 'em Carmen."

It was quite amazing technology for a thousand bucks: But what if Carmen goes down, what can I do legally to recover her? If she was down on government property, no problem. But down on private property? If she was government-owned property I'm pretty sure I could notify the landowner and go fetch. If it was an actual aircraft and not so toy-like, there would be no question of going for it, public or private.

She's not real in size, but her capability is real enough.

Stop worrying. She's never failed you before and she won't fail you today, not this day—of all days. She put her mind to flying instead of crashing and worrying, pulled her cloth hood over her head and watched the laptop monitor she put on a stump. She used her plat book and a quadrangle map to guide Carmen over standing corn. *Never thought about this before, but with a hard freeze possible any day now, why is the corn still standing? Random fact: Corn won't germinate in soil that's fifty degrees or colder. When does dirt this far north ever warm up?*

She guided the drone down a long row, activating the Leica's still-photo function on a regular basis. She had programmed for an automatic dump into a mission file on her computer, a file she had labeled "Last Chance."

There's something odd about the corn rows, but you need to stay focused on flying and do analysis after Carmen is safely home.

Mental Note Number One bumps Mental Note Number Two. You've thought this was odd for years, something not right, but not enough to pull you in for an up-close look. Dry corn was dry corn, what's the difference? Carmen flew up a row and she turned her right 90, and left 270 to run south along another swatch. Flying was mesmerizing and she understood how pilots could get addicted. The activity was methodical, somewhat instinctive, and could be very creative in some circumstances, especially if you let your mind lag behind the craft.

What the hell was that? A flash? What the fuck?

Check controls, all good, what the heck? Yellow red-white, I know I saw something. Bright, a burst. Circle, descend, take another look. OK, up, 90, 270, steady, Carmen flying with no more than whispery nudges from her forefinger against a small plastic extrusion. OK the map and plat book say the farmer has two forties, the second one across an unnamed creek, she's a long way off now, maybe near the outer control limit. Hope this wasn't the day I out fly my drone's radio leash and prang the poor girl. Be still, stomach.

Eyes on, concentrate, creek down to a trickle, let's look at the second forty, big jack pine stand with hint of some sort of yellow, a hut maybe, set back deep, more yellow and red flashes now, all along the corn rows. It's green corn in September, that's not right. Wrong color, wrong time of year. Green is for mid-summer, yellow is for fall. That's out of place, something seriously wrong, the old non-sequitur in the woodpile, OK, lower look time, descend watch for obstacles, careful now.

She hovered the little craft ten or twelve feet off the ground and ripped off a long line of still photos, turning the craft ninety degrees after each shoot. That done, climbed Carmen back upstairs above the trees. *What next? The building in the red pines? Why not, you're here, she's there and operatin fine. Do it all, girl, leave no stone unturned, this is your last damn chance.*

Again, down lower, lower, low hovering, swinging the nose, it made her think of square dancing. Got the structure into focus and what else . . . what the hell is that? Next to the structure, a small quonset of Korean War vintage, covered by a camo net, the kind you saw in newsreels of World War Two, stretched over artillery and tanks hiding from aerial recon. Green stuff under the camo tarp, she could see that, took Carmen closer, fired away with stills and saw it was military-type netting for sure. There was one displayed outside General Jim's surplus in Clare.

Flash! No color this time. Light, bright light, blinding! Muzzle flashes? Jesus! Pull Carmen up, climb, climb, no more side trips, bring the girl back safe to her home in your backpack.

The small chopper landed twenty feet away and toppled on its side. She fetched the craft, removed the photo card, popped it into her computer. Hood over her head again, she unloaded the take. *The corn? Reaction immediate. It doesn't look real. Look closer later. Skip to the end, skip to the flash, what the hell had that been? Clear photo of an asshole in a Cabela's ghilly suit playing sniper. She lit a cigarette, her first one in six months, inhaled deeply, studied the photos. Sniper for sure, guard over a dope grow. A big-ass dope grow, a monster dope-grow.*

What corn farmer has snipers guarding his fields? Stupid non-question. None. Can feel my heart rate elevate, okay, calm down, regulate your breathing. Be calm. You are in charge, stop hyperventilation before it takes the controls. Next, the tarp. Definitely a tarp, camo, loose mesh, the green underneath too blurred to see with any distinction. Back to the yellow structure and along the corn rows, blinking red and yellow like some sort of psychedelic mirage and her mind thought curtain and Casbah and she laughed out loud. You're outta your mind, woman. Wait, no value judgments yet. Use your brain, not your feelings. Black posts in the corn rows, she could see those, had two good stills and all that blinking yellow and red and finally, gloriously an amazing close-up of a . . . hula dancer? She rubbed her eyes. Hula dancers hung from wires strung between the black poles in the corn rows. And among the hula girls little black pine trees. What the hell?

All right, tie it up. Shots at the drone. Probable cause? Was the shot at the drone, or at another target, something she couldn't see from where she operated Carmen? A coincidence? No matter, the damn barrel was pointed almost straight up and that's reckless discharge of a firearm in my book. What about the stuff under the tarp? No way to tell, no positive idea, just weirdness at this point. Hanging hula girls and black pine trees? Those were real for sure, out of place to be sure. Call U.P.S.E.T., the UP Substance Enforcement Team? No, they'll take the information into processing and I'll never see it again. Probably nobody will. What could this mess be but a dope grow? Real! A legal one? Nope, it was way outside those idiotic rules. HIPAA hamstrings cops. The Health Insurance Portability Act of 1996 makes scaling the confidentiality wall an insurmountable hurdle, forcing agencies to spend resources, get warrants, and serve then. And only then will the Feds tell you if the grow was righteous or not. How the hell could agencies even pretend to be on the same team? Idiocy.

Got to think clearly here and now. She disassembled Carmen, pushed her into her ruck, put the laptop in its case, and started for her truck when she heard dogs closing on her position. Moving fast. *No bear-hound practice is allowed now and bear hunting has not yet started. What the heck? Not hounds, something else. Shit, girl. Run!* She ran full-out to the truck, and threw her gear inside. She had slowed twice along the way to brush her ball cap on the ground.

Whatever the hell is coming, I want it to come right to the truck so I an see and if needed, photograph it. Even a nose-dead dog could follow the trail I left for it, or them.

She radioed the county, let dispatch know she was back in her vehicle, said nothing beyond that. Her engine start would activate her Automatic Vehicle Locator system and let Lansing know she was in the truck, motor running, no need for radio contact.

She kept her eyes on the trail she'd come out on, felt her heart thump. *Tree huge pit bulls came flying at the truck with three more behind the first wave.* She put the truck in gear and pulled away as animal bodies thumped against her doors. *What . . . the . . . hell?*

Conclusion One: This is something.

Conclusion Two: You can't handle this alone. She set her 800 mhz to the district frequency.

"One, One Four Zero, One, One Twenty Seven."

"One Four Zero."

"Where are you?"

"Highway Thirty Two Ten, just north of Smoky Lake."

Good. Less than ten miles. "You want to grab lunch? Say Nimrod hilltop, ASAP?"

"Say again, One Twenty Seven."

"Nimrod. Hilltop. Think."

"Gotcha," One Four Zero said. "One Thirty Six is with me. We just joined up."

"One vehicle?"

"Two."

"Four-wheelers on board?"

"Affirmative."

"See you soon. One Twenty Seven clear."

• • •

One officer had become three and One Four Zero was famous across the state for his electronic and computer acumen. Not to mention he had the work ethic of a logger on boar-foot pay.

She turned her truck into Nordine's Food Plaza, gassed up with the state credit card, wrote down her mileages, and went inside to buy rubber sandwiches, pickles and roast beef, and American cheese. She stood at the counter, in line, waiting to be served and did a double take. Hula girls, red tops, yellow grass bottoms, colors so bright they burned your eyes, each dancer holding a ukulele, Bahama & Copy Air Fresheners. *And Look . . . look . . . black ice deodorants for vehicles.* "How much?" she asked the cashier, who had a gold ring in her right eyebrow.

"I ain't rung you up yet. I only got me one hand."

Wordledge saw two hands. God. "Those deodorants, how much?"

"Black Ice, three bucks."

"And her?" Pointing at a grass skirt dancer.

"She'd be four bucks. You like girls or something, not that I mind, dude. I'm cool with it, sayin'?"

"Give me five Black Ice, five hula girls and the sandwiches." She peeled three twenties out of her pocket.

The girl said, "Like you gave me too much, ma'am."

"It's a tip," Wordledge said. "Keep the change."

"I'm like totally down with that," the cashier said. her head wobbling from side to side like a bobblehead doll's.

The other officers were already at the Ottawa National Forest HQ parking lot. Nimrod was a legendary hunter, name of the local high school's mascot, Officers used it as a crude code for the village. The hill meant the ONF lot, the only hill for miles.

She dropped her tailgate, put down the deodorants, and sandwiches. "Bad day in the truck?" One Four Zero asked with a smirk.

"Eat, jerkoff."

One Thirty Six guffawed. "In that specific order?"

One Forty chirped, "Asshole."

Wordledge said, "I need your focus, men. All of it and right now."

One Thirty Six said, "Men? You usually call us boys."

"Serious shit?" One Forty asked.

As she laid out her morning, their jaws dropped lower and wonder in their eyes switched to predatory smiles and nods as anticipation of action grew.

She let them see the photos and One Forty said, "How the heck did you get these?"

"Drone."

"But you're not one of the test fliers."

"My own drone."

One Thirty Six. "How long you had it?"

"Over a year."

"Let me guess," One Forty said. "You showed it to the sarge."

"Even flew it for him. He told me it was too expensive, a waste of money, nothing but a damn toy."

"And now the department's testing them," One Thirty Six said, "And your name's nowhere to be seen or heard."

"There it is," Wordledge said. "Focus, men. Forget all that crap and pay attention to what we have to do here. She spread out the deodorants. "Who uses Black Ice?" she asked, and watched their lightbulbs pop on.

"Felony Forest," Thirty Six said. "I heard about this stuff from an UPSET dude. Shit doesn't work," he said. "On smokes neither."

It was commonly believed that Black Ice would mask dope smoke from cops.

Wordledge said, "What if it's not weed they want to mask? It doesn't have much odor unless you're right on top of it. What else has a smell needing to be blocked?"

"Meth," One Forty said.

"Meth," One Thirty Six agreed. "She-it. Must be a damn lab back there."

"Got to be thousands of deodorants strung in the corn rows," Wordledge said. "At three and four bucks a pop."

"Big investment for a small op," One Forty said. "Pit bulls?"

"I counted six."

"I hate all dogs," One Thirty Six said. "*Especially* pit bulls."

"Animal control," One Forty said.

"No outsiders," Wordledge said. "Just us."

"We may not be enough," One Forty said.

She told them, "I saw only the one jerk with a rifle and the dogs."

"With a rifle is the key observation in that fact," One Thirty Six.

"UPSET is made for this," One Forty pointed out.

"UPSET's a bureaucracy. Their clock is a glacier. By the time they get done dicking around this opportunity will be long gone."

The men nodded, both said, "Okay."

She told them, "We have to assume the shooter saw my drone. The clock is ticking. He fired at the drone, didn't hit it and sent the dogs. Want to hear what I'm thinking?"

Both men nodded.

She drew the farm on her notebook pad. "The stream separates A from B. Main farm is on A, the shit on B. The main concentration seems to be here." She drew a small x. "Which makes this spot a pinch-point." She tapped her pen.

"Ergo the sniper in the pinch-point where he can see the most," One Forty observed.

"There it is," she said. "The dogs came out to my truck here." She drew another x. "I'm thinking he's holed up in the narrow area, pinch-point but will cheat his position toward where my truck was while he waits for his cavalry."

The three studied the little map with a topographical literacy civilians would be baffled by. With little discussion, they all saw the same picture, understood what the others understood. "One Thirty Six along the center line toward the pinch, which is about forty feet high. He'll be up there somewhere, watching. You get the high ground. One Forty comes up the creek from this direction." She drew a small arrow. "I'll come down the creek from the opposite direction and we'll all meet in the middle."

"Rules of engagement?" One Forty asked.

Wordledge said, "Order, 'Drop your weapon.' One time. Then put him on the ground."

"We don't *know* that he shot at you," Thirty Six said.

"Give two warnings and you'll be out of surprises," she told him. "But it's your call. We'll use the sun," she told them.

● ● ●

Five o'clock all three moving in, radios squelched, ear buds in.

"Got one soul," One Forty whispered over the 800 mhz. "Thirty yards, his back to me."

"Alone?" Wordledge asked.

The radio clicked once. Yes.

"Your call, One Forty."

She kept moving up the creek toward the rendezvous.

"One Twenty Seven, One Forty is secure with one in custody."

"Thirty Six moving up."

Wordledge came out of her crouch and raced up the creek bed until she saw One Forty and his prisoner, the man's face a mess of cuts and blood. "He only thinks he can fight," One Forty quipped.

Thirty minutes later they confirmed a huge meth lab. Weed too. She called the Gogebic County Sheriff's Office, got the undersheriff on the phone, explained the deal. He told her backup was rolling.

They found the six pit bulls, freshly shot. Wherever the lone shooter was going, the dogs weren't welcome.

Wordledge looked down at the prisoner, Hispanic male, sixteen maybe. Who can tell? Just a kid. "You got help coming?" she asked him.

"*Puta*," the boy said, and spit blood. Wordledge hoped there was a tooth in the mix.

No more bad guys showed.

But Gogebic County came in force. The U.P.S.E.T., followed by G.I.A.N.T., the Gogebic Iron County Narcotics Team, a cross-border hybrid. State troops were the last law enforcement to arrive, but there were three cars. Then reporters trooped cautiously in at the end.

The very last in, the tailend Charlie, was their beloved and anal sergeant, who cornered her. "You retired two hours ago."

"Don't worry," she said. "I won't file for overtime."

The three officers split and headed their separate ways. One Forty stayed with the other cops. He would sign the report she would write for him.

Wordledge's family was waiting at her house in Ramsay, three grown kids, two grandsons. There was cake, champagne.

• • •

She watched the late news. It was all about U.P.S.E.T.'s major bust. The next morning she found an AP story, which also told how the U.P.S.E.T team had monitored the lab for a long time and calculated the raid for when cooking was not under way. The last sentence in the last report said, "DNR officers assisted."

Trailer Fly

Michigan State Police lieutenant Patrick Kneff had his charm dialed up to full-on, but it had not worked its customary result and eventually he sighed, forced to come clean with the truth. "Charity, we are desperate here."

Conservation Officer Charity Riordan had known Kneff for years. Patrick's wife was one of her closest friends. He was one of those types who breathed "Trooper" and marched around with a ramrod back, but he was a good guy and a hopeless prude in all things related to women. Sex only in the dark, his wife Ruby had told Riordan. "Light and naked bodies seem to embarrass him."

"Not *we*, Patrick. You mean *you* are desperate and that forced you to come to me."

"Straight talk now," Kneff said. "Man to man."

Riordan rolled her eyes and saw him gasp, let him simmer in his own juice.

"Uh we've ah uh used uh ah our only female troopers, uh. We can't use them ah again. They'll see us coming, uh a mile uhway."

"You might want to reconsider your word choice, El-Tee."

Kneff paused and pinked like a redfish in a frying pan. Riordan added, "I am not an enthusiastic booster of poontang pinch parties, even when I'm not in the lineup. These are victimless crimes, Patrick."

"There's sexual slavery," the lieutenant managed.

"Agree, so go after that, not some slob johns."

"In or out?" an exasperated Kneff said.

"Word choice again," Riordan said, turning him redder. "If I say no will you guys have to scrub the detail?"

"Yes," Kneff said.

"If I don't go, you don't go, like that?"

"There it is."

She could see him weighing words, but too uptight to let them loose. "What's my motivation here?" she asked.

"You pretend to be a prostitute," the lieutenant said in a whisper.

"No you moron. I know what a hooker wants and that's to make money. Duh. I mean me, Charity Riordan, your female colleague from the DNR, your wife's best pal. What do I get?"

"Eternal gratitude," Kneff mumbled, staring down at his gleaming patent leather oxfords.

"If it can't be spent, poured in a glass, put in a bank, or eaten, it's neither eternal, nor gratitude."

"You dicker like a hooker," Kneff said.

Riordan let the words hang. This was kinda fun. "Words, Patrick, words, and how would you, *of all people* know how hookers dicker . . . a word I employ only because you got it up first."

"A letter of commendation to your chief for your file," the lieutenant offered.

"You do know that thunder surrounds the capital, Patrick. Just what I need is my big boss envisioning me in a hooker's gear and fuck-me-heels. She heard the state trooper gasp. "Here's the deal, I do this for the boys in blue, and you get me the latest version of an infrared scope."

"You have to get that equipment through your own purchasing channels and budgets."

"Normally, but this isn't a normal deal, is it? You need me to say yes and I just stated the price, which given what you're asking seems like perfectly acceptable terms."

The man's shoulders slumped. "Deal."

"*Before* I go out on the detail, not at the same time or at a date to be named later."

He nodded. "OK, before is fine."

"New not used, fully functional, not some jerk's broken cast-off."

"All of that," Patrick Kneff said.

"Good," she said. "See how easy that was?"

"You can be a pain," the lieutenant said.

"I know," Riordan said. "It's an art. Does this little op of ours have a name?"

The state police loved to name operations and details. "Operation Trailer Fly," the lieutenant said.

"Who came up with that?"

"Regional command."

That meant Marquette. "Do you even know what that means?" She knew his idea of outdoor activity was an acre-square lawn or riding a golf cart. Fly fishing would be like Mayan to him.

"It's a fishing term, Patrick. You put on a large fly to attract the trout's attention and you tie a second fly behind the attractor fly. The attractor fly gets the trout's attention and usually it takes the second offering, the trailer. So if I'm the trailer, who's the attractor?"

Kneff looked to be in great pain. "There's just you and the take-down team."

"I thought we wanted the john to take me down."

"We do."

"You'd better talk to Marquette. I think the op's missing something, the flashy attractor. I think this detail, by its name alone requires two females, not one."

"We don't *have* two."

"Technically you don't have any, Patrick, by your own admission. I'm not one of yours. I'm a loaner, a volunteer and there's just one of me. You *need* two."

"Where from?" he asked through clenched teeth.

"County deps, Park Service, it has to be another woman."

"Region wants this done, it's part of a big push statewide."

"Well, you'll just have to talk to them."

"I don't want to talk to Marquette. I hate talking to Marquette."

"And I don't want to be the damn trailer. I'd rather be the attractor, first team, not second team."

The lieutenant shook his head. "Never mind, I'll figure something out."

"You could dress drag," she offered, scoring a scowl. "When is this thing supposed to happen? My sarge needs to know for our chain of command."

"It's not," Kneff said.

"What about the infrared?"

"There won't be one."

"That's not fair. You promised and I agreed to help you. Do you know what sort of emotional adjustments a woman has to make just to agree do this sort of slimy patrol?"

He nodded, said, "Yes, I don't know."

"And the infrared?"

"Yes, I mean no," he said, his frustration growing fast. "No detail, no reward."

"I didn't scrub the detail, *you* did."

He said nothing. Riordan said, "I didn't scrub the mission, did I?"

He nodded, said, "No."

"Right, you did. I kept my end but you didn't keep yours. I earned the infrared with my attitude alone, my willingness to demean myself as a woman and law enforcement officer."

Kneff was chewing his lower lip so hard there was some blood. It looked to her like he would swallow his tongue before he'd utter another word. "I'm deeply disappointed, Lieutenant Kneff."

"Sorry," he mumbled.

"Because you disappointed me or because you're gonna piss off Marquette."

"Yes," he said. Then, "Should never even think you can help. You COs don't think like normal people."

She smiled and watched him march away stiff legged. He stopped when he got to the door, turned and looked at her. "*You.*"

"Sir?"

He went through the door and did not look back.

Three Hours in the Chair of Wisdom

This was not on the schedule, in fact the whole notion of it was so dainty-girlie it made her grumpy, but here she was at the hairdresser, summoned like some commoner by hair-care royalty, the summons issued with some compelling rationale there had been no way to refuse.

Ergo here she sat in the chair as still as a cadaver on a morgue slab, frog on a biology lab table waiting for some geeky student to hack away, guinea pig in a psych lab, helpless as a lab animal, the clear and unforgiving spotlight steadily on her. It was not a happy moment. It almost never was, not once in her life.

"Ohmygod Ruthie . . . honey . . . your hair looks like mice been nesting in there and mind you how many times I got to tell youse youse got to be in the chair mont'ly or at least six wicks an' I know that sounds 'spensive and tell me true girl you would trade a few sheckels to avoid that look you come in with, matted rat dog. I do swear this is the worst it's ever been, a look I might add here would put a man's feet to flight at first sight. Youse stay on this schedule, youse'll never find a man, hon. You want a regular fella, youse got to pave the way, dear. It's in your hands, not God's, though a great part is in my hands too, if youse'll just come in when youse're 'posed to."

"M. C.," Mildred Pythia Culvert, had been married five times, all to men named Frederick, which she ranked by their performance in bed, not in order of matrimony. Chronological Frederick Four was Performance Fred Number One, and they'd still be married, she insisted, if but a few weeks into their sexual bliss and legal union his heart hadn't blown out its arteries and killed him instantly while he was installed atop of her.

"You want the usual rush job, Ruthie honey, the rush job on your mouse nest? Or can we relax for once and do this thing right with artistic flair in the full three hours that top results require?"

"The whole three, please," Ruth Brennan said with a forced smile. She was sitting stiff-backed like she was installed in steerage class on the latest soak all passengers, no-frills airline flight from Lansing to Tampa. Most women could not tolerate Pythia Culvert for anything close to three hours. If a wagging tongue could be translated into iron-pushing terms, M. C. was the world clean-and-jerk champion, by a wide margin.

The woman's jaw started ratcheting when you came through the door and did not stop until you were a half mile away in your car on the way home. She'd start with a verbal clean, and go on all day till well past dark when her mouth and eyes closed simultaneously to complete the long delayed jerk.

Three hours was more than enough to crush even the average extrovert's tolerance for drivel.

Contrary to appearances, Ruth Brennan was neither an extrovert, nor average. What she was, was a sponge, with a gift for full and accurate memory of every word she heard and everything she saw, and even better she could retain such drivel indefinitely and pull it up like it was a book on a shelf right next to her. Psychologists did not yet have a term to describe her unique ability.

No mere and petty gossip, Pythia Culvert was the self-declared font of all knowledge and dirt, real or imagined in Luce County, a twenty-first century Delphi Oracle of Colossal Proportions. At five-nine and three hundred admitted pounds (another hundred or so went unclaimed), she moved with the grace of Alice B. Toklas and focused like a magnifying glass set out in the sun by a kid to fry ants on a sidewalk.

"I was named Pythia, from the Greek word *pytheuls*, which means to eat. It's not pejorative hon, really it ain't. What's a compost pile if not rot and from that rot cometh new life, am I right? See in one of my former lives—we've all had a bunch, donchu know—I was the Oracle of Delphi, the one over to Greece? Not the one makes car parts down to Lansing, and people and minor gods too, they come to me, though there ain't been a rush of minor gods recently, but in the past they come, all right, everybody comes to me for answers to life's problems and pinchy quandaries. What I am in modern verbology is an aficionado of public souls."

Ruthie knew the woman had an inflated opinion of herself, but it wasn't selfish. She truly believed she was on the Earth to help folks, and she tried. Though in Ruth's mind, Pythia Culvert was mainly a world-class gossip and when she was on the beam, she tended to draw more gossip right out of folks who seemed hardly aware of what they were revealing.

"Now I know when a girl like me modestly propounds to have answers, there is likely to be lingering doubt among the pawpaws filled with doubting Thomases, but you listen close and then tell me later I ain't hit the nail on the head more'n I missed."

In this preposterous claim Pythia was absolutely right, which is why Ruth Brennan was putting herself through the entire three-hour ordeal, because it was an ordeal, physically and emotionally and pick any dictionary you want for the word and definition that makes you most comfortable.

The salon was called Hair Oracle and Pythia's chair was in the center of a circle of six hairdressers, whom Pythia pointed out, she "commanded the way that Bernstein guy does all that snappy John Phillip Sousa stuff and why we don't got more red-blooded American marches these days makes no damn sense to me, our kids being at war all over the damn world. I mean my nephew Harry's been deployed ten damn times now and not one new march coming out of them music-making big shots out east."

The arrangement of chairs struck Brennan as downright odd, like a center circus ring at the big top, but nobody seemed to mind. Regal Pythia with straw-colored hair as dense as a lion's mane had an estrogenic voice spewing torrents of words in waves, floods, tsunamis, oceans of words and thoughts drowning all they sloshed over.

Mostly you just sat and watched and listened as the master of revelry went on and on, and when time came for other actors to say their lines, she'd let them know, but this show, make no mistake was about Pythia and all others were supporting cast.

Court assembled, chairs occupied, Pythia began, "Sweetest Sue, youngest and new, what have you for we who are here today?"

"It's Molly," Sweetest Sue said saccharinely.

"Miss Molly youse may speak your mind here in the Hair Oracle, Honey. Like Vegas, what gets said in here stays right here, so what shall it be, dear?"

The speaker was fiftyish, short gray hair—double crow's feet around her eyes like crackled glass and the windy whistling cadence of a troubled carp. "My grandmother-in-law, God bless her, is ninety-four, a South Bend gal with Golden Dome blood thick in Catholic cells, once removed from a ship, out of Cork or thereabouts and here so long she forgets who's speaking when she hears her own brogue."

Pythia smiled benignly, her eyes sparkling. "Ma, we call her, which is Gaelic for boss. Some years back her youngest daughter married a fella of the Jewish persuasion in New Rochelle, New York, and since has converted to Jeweydeism, whole hog so to speak, and old Ma's never said a word, nor been quite the same. See, she expects religious conversions to flow the other direction, Jeweydeyitics to Catholics, as it was in the time of Jesus, who she insists was the first Catholic, Catholicism being the only Christianity back in the start."

"Never a word about the conversion?" Pythia asked.

"Nary and a Silence of the Lambs quietetude," Molly said, "except every year she expects, no—she *commands*—all her blood kin to draw Christmas names and give gifts of a minimum of one hundred American dollars, minus shipping and the wayward and objectors are compelled to participate even though she and her spouse and kosher flock do not celebrate the birth of baby Jesus. This is an insult to my aunt and her kin and a financial burden on younger folks. Why would she keep to this nonsense, and what do we do about it? What *can* we do?"

Prounounced Pythia, "It's clear the boss is clinging hopelessly to hope, like a dingleberry clings in stubborn wooly desperation that her child has not gone over to the dark side. I would suggest the family pool resources, fly Ma out to this New Rochelle place and put photos of her daughter in her First Communion dress in the front of the room, have them tear their clothes and recite, *Baruch dayan emet*, which means Blessed is the one true judge. This done everyone should express regrets to Ma for the loss of her daughter and at the same time rejoice at the gain of a fine new son."

"She'll die," Molly said.

Pythia pursed her lips. "So there's your backup plan. Shall we have a snort in the fort?" One of the hairdressers produced a bottle of Captain Morgan spiced rum and a portion was poured in a dozen small paper cups and distributed and Pythia said, "With solidarity with the ewe in pain, *l'chayim.*"

Brennan expected hosts for communion, but it was down the hatch neat and back to the show and business at hand, Pythia scanning the circle, steadying her gaze on a hairdresser named Mazie and her client, a redhead named Charlemagne but known locally as Charlie.

"Last we heard," Pythia said to Charlie, "your sister Louisa was caught up in a downward cycle if I may be so insensitive to express her troubles so indelicately."

"I can be a lot more direct," Charlie said. "Sis was born with a charcoal furnace betwixt her legs, which was made by God, like all the other parts, to render wood to ash. Claims she's had hundreds of rutting partners, with no plans for a cutback. We're all worried."

Pythia snorted. "If the sex is good, what's the worry? One of my Fredericks didn't know a clitoris from a pig's knuckle. Your sister has her a gift, why not celebrate it?"

"It's immoral," Charlie said. "And unhygienic."

"There ain't no morality in fucking," Pythia said, "only in who you tell about it. If sis can't keep her knees together and her mind on Jesus, tell her to keep her pie-hole closed. Drinks around!" Pythia declared and out came the rum again, chugged down, cups tossed, everyone sitting back with greatly relaxed eyes.

The oracle tapped Ruth's shoulder. "Ruthie hon, what're you bringing to the multitude this morning?"

Brennan had not expected this, not after what this was costing her. She whispered through clenched teeth, "This isn't part of the deal."

Pythia patted her shoulder. "Relax and trust your oracle, honey."

Brennan took a deep breath. "This is embarrassing."

"Keep going," Pythia said.

"Well I have to look stuff up in the *World Book*. And it makes me feel dumb that I don't know more than I do. It makes me feel, like flawed, you know?"

"Nonsense," Pythia said. "Looking in the *World Book* don't mean you don't know stuff, even if you got to look it up again and again. The point is you know where to look, which is the same as knowing the answer by heart and at the same time gives you a lot more clear space in your brain. What the heck do you think that whole Google thing is about 'cept a *World Book* on people's computers. Spice the mainbrace! Drinks around!"

"You done good," Pythia whispered as they waited for their rum portions.

The fourth client declined, but the fifth hairdresser introduced Mrs. Bob Harrie Senior who said, "I'm Mrs. Bob and I am seventy years old and my husband Mr. Bob and I are members of Christians Without Borders, Mentors and Walls. Our twenty-one-year-old grandson York is a spirited young fellow still at loose ends and without direction in his young life. Mr. Bob and I have prayed and prayed and one glorious morning we awoke, Mr. Bob said, 'Wheeke has a gift.' What Mr. Bob meant was that York has loved to hunt and fish since he was a wee lad, hunt and fish, and start fires. York's nickname is Wheeke which comes from the sound a young pig makes when you stick a big knife in it. Wheeke! Wheeke!," Mrs. Bob shrieked, freezing the whole room in abject horror. "Well, Mr. Bob and I set Wheeke up in the animal disposal profession and if a neighbor or area farmer has a wolf or bear problem, they call Wheeke and he eliminates their problem. Praise God, his services are in high demand and over the last year alone he's got three bears and seven wolves, four coyotes and a bobcat or two. He has found his true vocation in life," Mrs. Bob concluded. "But now we'd love to find our Yorkie a bride. Now Wheeke don't much take to girls, so I am here for suggestions."

Not a single response. All the women stared at the woman like she had just stepped out of a starship and through the silence Mrs. Bob smiled benignly and insipidly as if she was being baked in amazing grace.

Hair done, Pythia walked Ruth Brennan to the door. "Get what you hoped for?"

"Even more, thanks for calling."

"There's a reward for this, right?"

"I'm submitting your name but I can't promise it will come through. I don't make the decision for such matters, but this is a solid lead and we'll see where it takes us."

Brennan followed the woman at a distance to a farm near Engadine, broke off and headed home. She called her lieutenant. "You at the D office?"

"Ruthie?"

"Yah, you are not going to believe what I've got," the veteran conservation officer said. "Be there in twenty minutes."

One and One Is a Future Crowd

Mary Thomisine Kyd knew she was unusual, had known it since she was five and already twice as tall as her kindergarten classmates, a difference teachers, doctors, and social workers insisted would even out over time.

It didn't.

Mary Kyd, distant kin of the famous English author Thomas Kyd, Shakespeare's contemporary and possible colleague and collaborator, was six-foot-six and two hundred pounds of muscle. Division Two volleyball All-American, she had opted to become a cop, not just any kind of cop, but a conservation officer, called a game warden in her old kin's sixteenth century.

In college at Ferris State Mary Kyd had majored in English literature and criminal justice and had done everything she could to learn all she could about her ancestor, the writer. Failing to secure a place in law enforcement, she would end up a reporter for the *East Yoop Gazette*, her dad's weekly rag with circulation that went all over the world. Papa Kyd looked forward to the day his daughter would take over the editor-publisher's chair. It had nearly broken his heart when she announced choosing a badge and gun over a notebook, not that paper notebooks really existed anymore, except as artifacts of old-time reporters from a far different era when millions of trees died to bring news to the public. Pa Kyd was a veteran of the AP in Korea and Vietnam, and longtime outdoor editor of the *Saginaw News* before moving the family to St. Ignace in the southeastern Upper Peninsula.

There was in Mary's mind some poetic thread reaching from her to playwright Thomas, whose specialty was eye-popping violence, a difficult effect to create in an audience with a ruling queen with a penchant for lopping the heads off legitimate criminals. Some folks in Thomas's time merely ran afoul of her majesty's erratic moods and ended up with their heads chopped off and spiked, body parts dropped in various parts of London as grisly reminders of the penalty for crossing her majesty, discarded like so much fertilizer to give root to fear among the hoi polloi. Thomas Kyd wrote of crime and passion, violence and madness, the same things Mary Kyd dealt with every day in her job.

Never mind that Kyd died penniless and broken at thirty-six, her very age now, and died a snitch to boot, having accused playwright Kit Marlowe of heresy, said accusations made only after weeks of brutal torture of Kyd after Marlowe accused him of the same offense, the sort of professional back-biting and a falling out that quick-stepped from sad to tragic. Released from prison, Kyd was persona non grata among all player companies and condemned to obscurity. Marlowe, meanwhile, stayed out on bail and was murdered in a barroom brawl. Kyd's fault, some insisted.

She had been tempted to write, but the politics among such creatures was more base than among the basest criminal class, which described the fish and game poachers and violators who were her daily clients.

Happy in my job? Sure. You bet. Completely. But who among us is entirely happy?

Then Pop died and left full ownership of his piss-poor flagship business to her, not the weekly, which was a hobby at most, but his damn junkyard-scrapyard, Kyd's Lots Of Treasure, a play on Stevenson's work. More theft than play, but that argument had fallen on deaf ears when she tried to explain it to her dad.

It wasn't enough to be a full-time game warden, but full-time nursemaid to a junkyard in a time when massive unemployment was sending everyone scrambling to find stuff to steal and sell, not just to peddle *to* her, but to steal from her as well.

She had tried electronics and dogs, all to no avail, and one day her CO colleague Tommy Butch called her to regale her with a tale of a raid on a dope house in Flint, where the raid team confronted an animal perfect for her security needs, and after hearing Tommy's pitch, she agreed to take possession after all legal requirements had been satisfied, all legal hurdles cleared, and evidence no longer needed.

That had been three years back, and since the day she'd brought Susie home, problems with local marauders had ended. Her sign Beware of Killer Dog, did not, however, deter out-of-town ganking crews. As with strangers across all time and all places, they had to learn the hard way. So it had been, so it is, and so it shall be.

The system was simple. She had a steel fence ten feet high, which all but the most uncoordinated fools could easily scale. No electric current in the metal fence. No walls topped with broken glass or punji sticks, just a big wall painted electric red, and inside the fence, one very large sign, think billboard size, a sign declaring, You Are Now in Deep Shit.

Now, any fool would know a red fence was not likely to stop a determined thief, but if someone touched the fence, their touch triggered sensors that hooted in Susie's ear and sent her loping across the grounds to investigate. See, Miss Susie, as Mary liked to refer to her, took the sensors as a call for food. Usually Kyd found perps confronted by the five-hundred-pound lion, with Susie growling and urine pooling on the shoes of the whimpering intruders.

Tonight when she heard the alarm, she wondered what entertainment there would be, because that's all Susie amounted to was entertainment. In truth she was as tame and nonviolent as the meekest house cat, but she could play the man-eater and Kyd, in thinking about this, decided this was yet another thread tying her back to her ancestor and legendary playhouses. In fact, she used a line from Shakespeare from time to time to greet all of Miss Susie's stops.

Kyd, on a study abroad one summer in Oxford, had discovered in the Bodleian Library, the *Scot's Discoverie of Witchcraft* from 1584. She had loved the old university town northwest of London. Contrary to its title, the venerable old tome was a how-to on staging tricks, a handbook with the specialty of bodyless heads resembling that of the the actor Leon

Rippy. Kyd wondered often how many makeup artists and press people in Hollywood knew about the resource and how much it affected certain things today.

Scot's taught her to fashion astonishingly realistic (and grotesque) heads, human and animal, male and female, which she placed on eight-inch-diameter poles all around the junkyard. In daylight you couldn't see them, but once the night lights came on, the heads lit up—if you were inside the fence. Many of the heads were set by Susie's usual stopping spot, to assist the old girl in getting the full attention of the miscreants, the heads set five feet off the ground, at eye level and not visible until Susie roared, the sound triggering sensors that illuminated spotlights on all the heads, replicas of Mr. Rippy. With Susie growling, Kyd would say over a loudspeaker, "Here we have a company of course and evil fellows, Susie. Shall we dispatch them anon, or are you of a mind to play? You have seen a kitty play with prey I pray, lads? Plucking off a toe or an ear. You've seen that, right?"

The reaction was unanimous and immediate. Tears, shaking, rapid chin nods, pissed-in pants. She'd call the local constabulary to come fetch the trespassers and she always filed charges.

Tonight's alarm presaged more sport. She considered the invasions a form of stage performance, and smiled for her ancestor, hoping he was looking upon the offering, *She looked skyward. Gone but not forgotten, Tommy boy.*

Alarm sounded, Mary Kyd picked up her shotgun and went to find Miss Susie.

Who was nowhere to be seen. Immediate stoppage of her heart and dry mouth. What if some of the assholes had hurt Susie, killed her? It would be your fault. No more floodlights, no more performances, no more pissed on two-hundred-dollar sneakers, just darkness, still and cloudless and heavy as wet wool. Shit.

Kyd retreated stealthily to her home and sat at the second-story window looking out on the junkyard below. A growly groan awoke her and as her eyes adjusted she looked down to find Miss Susie and a mountain lion, cougar, panther, nittany lion, whatever, no longer indigenous to Michigan. Susie batted the cat and pounced heavily and the two rolled around in the dust and Kyd thought, great, I have to watch my damn cat getting her ashes hauled. Eventually Susie got tired of it and made a show of wanting to be fed. Kyd fetched raw meat from the cooler and feeling more than a tad nervous stepped out on the porch and set the meat where she usually put it, and the animals leaped on it and began tearing at it.

She had to think what to do. You could legally keep big cats if you filed and met guidelines and qualifications, as she had done with Susie, who was tame when she arrived. But this animal, though action was tame and lovey at the moment, was neither tame, nor domestic in nature, and ten minutes from now, might turn to killing. Big cats were unpredictable and used swagger to intimidate. Worse, what will happen the next time an intruder comes over the red fence? Goddammit goddammit all. Or Susie got preggers? I can sort of manage one cat, but two? Don't even know if a cougar and a lion can make kittens. I never should have listened to Butch and taken the lion. Knew then it was poor judgment, my damn ego overriding common sense. I'm both betrayer and betrayed, like Thomas Kyd and Kit Marlowe. If I report this, the visiting animal is probably as good as dead. As too is Susie. If my cat was a magnet for this one big cat, there would be another one eventually. Not could, would. Even if the next one doesn't vault the fence it might wander the perimeter and drive Susie to distraction. Or get after area pets or kids. How could I have been so damn stupid and thoughtless?

Choice brings consequences. Always has, even when your choice is forced by torture. I tell people about their choices every day. Now this? She couldn't even look at Miss Susie as she got more meat and the shotgun, took it outside for the cats who immediately came to her.

"I am so sorry," she whispered, raising the barrel.

Mile-High Humble Pie

This is how the assignment came down to CO Alice Daynight: DeMint James, Western U.P. manager for Montrose-Foret Timber Company, called the Marquette District office and growled at the El-Tee. "We've got squatters on property along the Net River in Iron County. I went out there to tell them to move on and they pulled weapons on me. Now you goddamn DNR people can earn your goddamn pay."

El-Tee immediately called the sarge, who said, "Send *her*." Her being Alice, fourteen years a conservation officer, fourteen hard nose-to-nose years with violators and her own command.

The El-Tee loathed her, once declaring at a district meeting in front of all of her colleagues, "You are outrageous and unprofessional."

She had shot back, "Which of those two assertions bothers you most?"

Of course she knew: For fourteen years she had fought, never surrendering, never pausing, never taking even one step back, and carping like a banshee at other officers she felt couldn't meet her standards, males or females, of any rank.

Her old man had been a marine in Vietnam, two tours, taught her to suck it up and press on, charge or die, which gave rise to his nickname, "One Word," that word being "Charge." Daddy One Word had set the bar high and she had been forced to stretch almost every day to reach it, the El-Tee not making it any easier with his snark-and-bark attitude.

Dissing her with a personal objective pronoun: her? Like a woman was so much dog shit on a man's boot? It disgusted her, it angered her, it hurt her, and the worst of all: She agreed with him. Women did make lousy cops, too damn needy. Not her, but other women. She was the exception that proved the rule because she did not need help from a goddamned living soul, at her job or for anything else.

El-Tee was a sneaky creepy, trying to wear her down over time with his subtle but pointed put-downs. He was old-school, boys were put here by God to do this and women were here to do that, end of discussion, no crossovers. In his mind, women lacked resolve, commitment, and worst of all there was that biological clock thing ticking like a time bomb in every uniformed uterus, and once a baby was in the picture the woman became mom first and cop second, jeopardizing her own safety, the safety of others, and above all the mission. El-Tee didn't lecture or proselytize, but she knew what he was thinking, because it was the same thing she thought. Women folded under stress, needed extra support. She was the exception, could handle anything and everything. Had done it all these years. Alone, goddammit, the way One Word wanted, the way he *demanded*.

Which led her out to the Montrose-Foret Timber Company property one late October night with early season wet snow falling, five inches down and more coming and forecast to last another twenty-four hours, up to a foot of snow. It would cripple the area for a couple of days. But Daynight didn't mind the snow. Snow helped her see better at night, gave her an edge.

She'd called DeMint James to get directions to the squatters and asked him why he hadn't called her directly instead of calling Marquette. "We top dogs like to sniff the butts of other top dogs," he told her with a dismissive laugh. Such a gaping asshole.

Once into the area, she hid her truck three miles away and hiked onto the property on foot, preferring to face whatever it was head-on, not to scare them into running from her truck. The plan was to confront these jaybirds and get the problem solved now, not to drag out the damn situation, which was how it often went with squatters and off-the-grid types.

The plan worked perfectly until she got ambushed by a half dozen bearded men who lit her up with flashlights, swarmed her, and began to beat on her before she could react. Very quickly and unhappily she found herself face down in the snow, but kept struggling and somehow got to her pepper spray and swished the air, but caught herself a nasty dose, which blinded her as the attackers continued to kick and punch her and began pulling off her clothes. Sometime during this, they got her boots off and she had gotten one arm free and jammed the heel of her hand upward until it hit something that audibly cracked, which immediately reduced the pressure on her. Next thing she knew she had rolled free of the tangle and was on her feet and running and it struck her as she ran with flashlights dancing behind her that she was headed toward the river, just like a gut-shot deer, a situation that rarely ended well.

She ran for minutes or hours, had no idea how long or how far, only that the pursuit fell back. It didn't relent exactly, it just gradually fell back, a fact she attributed to her own adrenaline overwhelming her attackers. She'd lost her watch in the wrestling, and her duty belt with flashlight, baton, and Sig Sauer 40. The pursuers had fallen back but continued to buck forward in silence, not screaming, just following relentlessly, and she made her way along the river, her feet hurting, and next thing she knew, she felt nothing below the knees, and realized she could go no farther. At least she still had socks, but they weren't going to be enough.

No choice, she stopped, found a piece of dead wood with some serious heft for a club, and burrowed wildly into a pile of brush and timber debris to let them get close so that she could launch a counterattack ambush before they could react. Once into the woodpile, she tried to think logically and calmly, took off her top layer, wrapped her feet in the sweater, dug through the snow into leaves and pushed her feet into the leaves, hoping for some insulation, curled her legs, and soon felt sleep nipping at her like a feisty dog. Life, like the night, went black, like she had tumbled into a chasm. She wondered how long it would take to hit bottom, or if she would fall to eternity and that this was the portal to death and whatever came next.

• • •

Alice Daynight awoke to see dim light outside. She couldn't feel her feet or tell if it was still snowing. No radio, no weapon, no boots. *You are fucked,* she told herself and began trying to get up, only there were no more leaves and her feet were sockless and no longer wrapped. She was under some kind of a blanket or tarp, and when she tried to sit up, hands roughly shoved her back down. "Stay down Mister her-him, her-him's feets is all frozed up. This lil piggy gone him's market, freeze foot counter, I speck."

The hands that held Alice Daynight were strong and she smelled cloying breath redolent of whiskey and cigarettes.

"Let me up," she pleaded weakly.

"Lachu up, her-him gone fall kersmack! on her-him's ass-bomb and all dere is to'at." The voice made a sound like a sandbag dropped on cement.

"I can't feel my feet," Daynight said.

"Her-him's tellin us her-hims don't feel them's feets, I guess when we seen 'em skins gone go eeky inky black, her-him's little pigglies ugly as polly woggles swimming dem springtime puddle." A piercing cackle shattered the silence. But Daynight was too exhausted to react, lay back docilely and whispered a weak and derisive, "Baah." Aimed at herself, her inability to keep going. *You are a weak sheep, a loser. Her-him is an odd construction, intended to identify me as a her playing him, a him with her qualities, or some kind of queer blend?*

From her back she saw a specter close to her face, a high wide flat forehead, a Neanderthalic ridge above the eyes, heavy cheekbones with knots the size of mature walnuts, eyelids thick and puffy, a narrow nose set too high, thin at the top and red and bulbous at the bottom, a mouth stretching all the way across the face with no east-west terminus, a pointed cleft chin under thin lips at the apex of acutely slanted jaws, a cluster of cream-colored warts to one side of the chin, greasy black mop hair strands hanging down like a rasta gone wild with the consistency of worn-out whiskbroom bristles, and that *smell*!

"Where am I?" she asked.

"Seen worse is truth I t'ink. Come down his way from Newfieland with my Mum-mama was way back in thet then and when. Up there was livin' in him village with Mum-mama's man, whiskey face got lots them dogs, all bark-bark, shittin', oh them dogs do shit-shit-shit for sure, him-them's up there call him Happy Valley."

A laugh shattered the air.

"You Ass Flyneboys had himselfs up there, flyne dem Uncle Sam jets down like Canada goose-goose, landin' I seen 'em plenty times, watch 'em close, watch 'em close." The voice made a whistling sound so real Daynight thought a jet was trying to land on top of them and she flinched, her head jerking around, looking for the source of the sound.

"Was dere night-nights, calls him's Max Hermenal, them Uncle Sam You-Ass flyneboys hims buyin' hamboogers, okay ketchumup, okay pickle-dillies, okay mayo, okay onions raw, hold moose turd, Chief," the voice said softly with the detached tone of a gospel reader at a Catholic mass. The voice moved closer and lowered, "Him moose-turd yella-yella like him puppy shits," she confided, and whined like a new-baby pup thirsting for an open pap. "Cheese I sometimes eatem all, eatem all, goddammit! Maggie slow down b'fore you th'oat-choke, frites too, with ketchumpup You-Ass style, not no vinnygar like from him Angleterre, where that Queem him's at, they say. Him majesty Queem galavant Kanada-Country they say but never her-him come no Happy Valley, Newfieland. Never saw him queem up dere I don't t'ink, but mebbe so, mebbe so, long time ago, and never know."

The woman hummed a few bars of "God Save the Queem." "Mama told me her name Margaret, but you-Ass flyneboys up blue yonder call him-me Maggie, Ski-Mow Maggie, bought him hamboogers and I aten 'em, aten 'em oh yes, hold the mooseturds, Chief." The woman put her lips to Daynight's ear and whispered, "You know Ski-mow pipples?"

This voice named Maggie was asking for a response, but Daynight was having a hard time following any of her rambling.

"Down here in You-Ass just fucking Indin, hey? Same like Ski-mo, same same."

The woman leaned even closer. "You heard him all her-him. Now you, Sisser."

Did she say Sister? Is she insane? Or is she even real? "My feet," the conservation officer said.

"Frozed up I tole her-hims can't hear, Sisshater. Her-him we seen gallomphing through them snow barefeets and bareleckted all bluebiddy-blue-blue-blue like him springs ices. Me and Sizzy pull her-him out dem woods pile into truck, fetch her, let's go, let's go, let's go! alla time her-him making crazy chatter-chat how them-hims jumps her bones mean have him's way, hump-hump squirt squirt, but her-him get loose and run like big-eye deer."

This cannot be real. I am Alice in the rabbit hole, Dorothy flung like a Frisbee in a shithouse across Kansas.

The woman paused to take a deep breath. "Damright, her-him's frozed foots can kill Sister. Got to get her-him warmbled up. Gone take some days, some things don't fix up fast as break?"

Daynight thought by the tone of the woman's voice and her soft touch that she meant no harm, but what she intended was far from clear, as was her sanity and connection to reality.

"Her-him slurp some soups, warm her-him up inside first first. Her-him stay right dere, still as fawn in grass move, Okay. Her-him got piss we put Sister over pot and let her-him pssssh." The sound was a perfect mimic of a stream of urine slashing the cold air. "Like dat, her-him hear? Don't Sisshater her-him worry none 'bout them-hims, *non-non-non-non. Nous avons le dos de notre sœur, oui-oui-oui-oui-oui.* We don't tell hims nothing."

"People are asking about me?"

The woman grinned her snaggletooth grin. "No You-Ass flyneboy. Just him wit' dem black trucks." She mimicked a quiet truck motor. "Hair cut real short like You-Ass Flyneboys, but Maggie know what she see, Sister."

She pushed her face against Daynight's. "Hims shows pitchers, I say ain't seem her-him. I say make him good deal two hambooger, hold the mooseturd."

"Him say, no good, 'You see her-him, call talk-him number.' Give me pepper, see?"

She pushed it so close to Daynight's face that she couldn't read it.

"I can't read it," the conservation officer said. "Me no reader neither," Maggie admitted.

"Get Sizzy bynbye, she read mebbe turd grade, mebbe four? Her's words is good."

Daynight flashed back to a summer in the forest service, fighting fires, smoke filling her eyes, unable to orient herself, like now. Back then in Hell's Canyon, dropped onto rocky saddleback, the pilot a rookie in crown-fire thermals, the art of hovering not his forte, she had crawled down onto one of the skids and dropped the last eight feet to the slanted ground, rolling and feeling the wash of the Bell bubbletop as it took off to fetch two more bodies into the fight, first woman in her crew, she had earned her place, side by side with men, comrades in fire, now two women, comrades in cold?

She had grabbed a shovel and assaulted the fire with flaming madness, her crew boss standing nearby grinning and saying, "Pace it, girl." She had lasted five minutes, turned, vomited, and fell to the ground where she lay for a quarter hour or more as other fighters came in, this her first summer of adventure and derring-do. Smoke had stayed in her clothes and nostrils the rest of the summer, which turned to terror, as everything in her life seemed to, the two being the inner and outer skins of the still-forming creature she called herself. They built fire lines in the mornings, before the freakish noon winds acted like a bellows and sent the fire creature racing and crowning up draws and over razorbacks, sending them in pure flight ahead of the flames, cursing and praying and crying, all of them covered with soot and sweat and stinking like galley slaves, skid-marks in their drawers, eating T-bones and ice cream every night, all supplies dropped in by parachute, even stoves, small iron creatures that, when chutes didn't open, as they sometimes were wont to do, burrowed into the earth like unexploded bombs. A crisp muffled sound, boomph, followed by a wisp of gray-brown dust.

A smoke jumper impaled on a pine stub, legs apart, yellow football helmet still on, blood coagulating below on tawny pine duff, a half-dozen vultures overhead, a serendipitous pig-in-a-blanket gift for scavengers. The nametag stenciled over the breast of the white nylon jump suit said he was Van Donkert, a dead Dutchman, crucified by pine driven up his ass and through his heart. They left him hanging, called in the location by radio. Ought to have worn a helmet on his ass, she told herself, adventure and terror highly sensitive to details. Later, caught under a burning tree, someone pulling and tugging, beating on her. No, there was no tree, just the beating and then under a brush pile, and what? This is so confusing.

"Root," the voice called Maggie said. "Some eat good, some him not so good, this good, root soup, eatem up, Sister." Maggie spat for emphasis and patted Daynight's head with a damp cloth.

Days spun on, she imagined, or were they really? Impossible to tell, she was trapped on her litter, unable to move, her feet healing but burning, like they were being cooked back to health.

Maggie's dwelling was a shed-like affair longer than wide, with an exposed tarpaper and canvas interior and leafless slash piled against the outside, kraal-like to break the wind and snow and make the place blend into the landscape. It was situated in a grove of scrub oak and jack pine on the southeast edge of a rocky knob, away from the prevailing winds coming down from Alberta.

There were two main rooms with dirt floors and several tattered hooked rugs scattered to serve as wafer-thin stepping stones across the cold surface. Heat came from a woodstove, a squat black antique with cast iron lion paws, made by the Kalamazoo Stove Company.

The two women cooked on that stove, and the constant opening and closing of the belly's door kept a pall of blue smoke hanging in the room.

Maggie had no last name, this somehow having been obliterated over the course of several purported marriages. By profession, Maggie was a prostitute, untidy in her hygienic practices, a foul-talking slattern who bantered loudly and near-continuously, almost always in a gibberish that made it difficult to understand precisely what she meant, if anything. Gauging by her domestic situation, Alice guessed that Maggie was not among her profession's elite, but the spartan surroundings also bore testament, Alice supposed, to a possible degree of integrity, that being she wouldn't do *anything* for money. Just some things. Could apply to me too, Alice decided.

Reeking of smoke and normally covered with a layer or two of old dirt, Maggie was far from physically attractive. Her head seemed at least two sizes too large for her neck to support and no doubt this might contribute to her perceived difficulties in the flesh trade. She was short-tempered and demanding, yet sensitive to the CO's comfort and welfare, downright brutal with Sizzy and inexplicably gentle and solicitous with the many cats that wandered in and out of the place, even those that squatted along the tarpaper walls, and left the place stinking like an amphetamine cookery.

It seemed to Daynight that by now, certainly by now, the search would be on for her and her truck and with the Automatic Vehicle Locator on board, finding the truck should be a piece of cake. It was only a matter of time and as time went on, she found herself repeating this little earwig.

"My truck?" she asked Maggie one day.

"Uh-huh, her-him's truck done went take swim-swim, sploonk." Here she used a sound that reminded Maggie of a massive weight dropped into a deep pond.

"You know where it is, this swim-swim?"

"I know, I know," she said.

Sizzy seemed a pleasant enough girl and was equally considerate of cats, evidence of fine breeding in some circles, and religious fervor in pharaonic Egypt before the greatest sandstorm in history buried everything, god-cats included. Maggie's shack cats prowled the premises keeping the place free of mice, screwing and fighting with equal enthusiasm, especially at night, their cries and shrieks echoing inside and bringing odd smiles to Sizzy's rotund face. The girl told Daynight she was twenty or two-times-ten, and she'd gone to school too, finishing grade two-times-three. Sizzy had fawn-colored cheeks, acne scars, and licorice stick lips.

Her hair was black and tied in a tight-hair yarmulke. She favored a natural-colored deer hide dress that hung well above her thick, hairless legs. There were approximately one hundred rubber bands around her left ankle, mostly in natural neutral colors, with a few red and green ones and two huge blue ones. The conservation officer noticed that when Sizzy got nervous, she plucked at the rubber bands with her thumb, snapping them against her flesh like out-of-tune banjo strings.

Every day Sizzy toured a trapline but the girl, unlike mom, professed no vocation. Daynight assumed she was Mama's dogsbody.

One morning the two women came in arguing, jabbering sharply, and set several net bags on the floor, filled with hubcaps. "I seen 'em dere," Maggie thundered at Sizzy. "I'm say okay T'underburr, okay. Cat-ill-acks, okay. Lin-cones, okay-okay, but what her Sizzy gets?"

"Two-times-two," Sizzy said weakly. "Two-times-two." She tried to hold up two fingers on each hand but her fingers lacked flexibility and she signed three.

Four Dodge hubcaps were on the floor in two sets of two.

"Shit her two-times-two," Maggie said with a snarl and turned to Daynight for moral support. "I say him pay first, pay first, then fuck, okay? Sizzy get him plates, T'underburr, okay, Cat-ill-ack, okay. Lin-cones, okay, but not no damn Dodge. Dodge is shit!"

Here, thought Daynight, was Chrysler's corporate image problem in a nutshell.

"No diff!" Sizzy said, louder and more forcefully than normal. "All same, Sizzy like Dodge, all damn same, two-times two, her pig 'em up, pig 'em up.'"

"*Not* same," Maggie hissed. "Dodge, him *shit.*"

Maggie looked at the CO again. "T'underburr, Cat-ill-lack, Lin-cone, Dodge, Her-him say now."

Damn, this was forcing her off the fence she had so carefully tried to maintain between the women, both of whom she was grateful to. We had here two women, mother and daughter, four Dodge hubcaps, and a raging cumulonimbus of emotional rage. Daynight opted only to shrug.

"Her-him, *her* side," Maggie roared angrily. "No fuck for Dodge. I fuck, Sizzy get plates, no damn Dodge!"

"Look," the conservation officer said, "before we write off one side against the other, let's decide exactly what it is that each side is for." In the mediation business, backing up was the best tactical approach.

"Not *for*," Maggie squawked at Sizzy. "Nor for, *right?*"

Sizzy nodded assent. "Not for, only two-times-two."

Maggie amplified. "We have. Hims had. Now we have. All there is. Not for, to have what is, *lui faire comprendre?*"

The hubcaps in the tarpaper shack, Alice Daynight concluded, were decorative items, treasured gewgaws, semiliquible assets, perhaps even some sort of cargo cult specie.

Every now and then more hubcaps appeared, but no more fights ensued and as Daynight grew stronger and her feet healed her hosts gave her muckluks to keep out the cold.

"Those men who chased me, I want to find them," she told them. "And I need to let my people know I'm all right."

"Hims no more look-look," Maggie said in a flat voice.

"Which hims? Bad hims or good hims?"

"Any them hims, him-radio tellum her-him gone, tsk-tsk, no more leads."

"Shit," Daynight thought, *They think I'm dead.* "Where is my truck?" she asked them for the umpteenth time, "and don't give me that swim-swim singsong shit."

"Fish water. Truck, him go down fish water," Sizzy said.

"Can you show me where?"

"Her-him no go outside, hims will get her, do bad t'ings."

"I'm better. I need to let people know I'm safe and I need to get those people who attacked me. You can either help me, or get out of my way."

"Her-him no go out," Maggie said. "Bad him not far, not far."

"Show me *just* how not far," Alice tried.

Both women crossed their arms, set their jaws, and shook their heads.

Here then was an object lesson in self-reliance. Once you accepted help, you were a hostage to that and the values that came with it and your freedom of choice was gone. "Sorry, ladies. Confronting badass is what I do. Now, I *need* clothes." They had kept her unclad all the while they were nursing her back to health.

Sizzy fetched buckskin pants and a tunic, both dyed white, various old sweaters smelling of mothballs, but warm. Wool socks.

"I need a gun," Daynight said.

Blank looks. Silence in the room.

"You can't live out here full time the way you do without a gun," she told the women. "Don't worry, I'll return it. I just want to borrow a gun." Then it struck her, something was amiss with the law.

"I don't care where you get your weapons or if you carry concealed without permits," she said. "Not my business. I just want to borrow one to help me do what I have to do."

"Them hims make her-him worm food," Maggie said. "How you bring back bang-bang when you worm-food?"

"How far away are these bad guys?" Daynight asked.

Maggie made a dramatic sniffing sound. "Smell hims, uh huh."

"From here?"

The two women nodded.

"How far?"

"Mebbe mile bird-fly," Maggie said, pointing.

• • •

Fully dressed for the first time since that night, Daynight stepped outside, found that the shack was located in a tight grove of scrub oak and jack-pine, on the side of a knob of boulders, and sitting so that prevailing winds sweeping down from the Canadian prairies would have the least effect. The sky was dark and gnarly, like something was brewing. Daynight's feet still hurt, but they were at least warm and working.

"Go night better," Maggie offered as they stood outside. "Bad-hims gets drunks, slips. Then her-him be safer."

Daynight studied her savior. "Gun?"

Sizzy pulled a Colt .45 from her coat and pushed the handle at the CO, along with two clips.

The weapon was old, but well cared for. Daynight checked the action and inserted a clip. She smelled the weapon, not recently fired and not a virgin, which almost made her laugh, the description pretty well describing her love life. *Why do you think of such a thing at a time like this? The human mind was a very odd thing.*

The snow from the storm that night was gone. Leaves were off the hardwoods leaving a yellow and russet carpet in the forest. The sky was ominous, but sun was peeking through swirling clouds. "I go tonight," she told them.

"No," Maggie said. "*We* go. Her-him, Sizzy, Maggie, three hers better than one her."

Sizzy went inside the shelter and came back with two AR-15 rifles, handing one to Maggie.

"No I have to do this alone," Daynight insisted.

"Her-him do alone last time, how that work?" Sizzy asked.

"That was then, this is now."

"Same bad hims, same same last time, uh huh," Maggie said. "We go, all for one."

All for one, one for all, what was that from? She looked off into the distance. *These women are a problem. I cannot take them into a situation that could go bad, not armed. Not at all. But their point is well taken. The* last time had been a disaster and the women seemed to know the quarry. No surprises this time. "Okay, we three, but only me with a weapon," she told mother and daughter.

The women shook their heads. "Three hers, three guns," Maggie said. "Now we eat and rest," and she went back inside, followed by Sizzy. Daynight took a deep breath, exhaled, and followed them. *Sometimes choices in life boiled down to no choices at all.*

• • •

Past midnight, the air spitting snow, they were not a hundred yards from the camp, one small log building built into the side of a hill and almost invisible until you were almost on top of them. Smoke came from chimneys, but no human activity since eleven, the three women had sat the whole time quietly, each wrapped in a blanket, patient. They had counted five men, which might or might not have been the number of assailants who jumped her that night.

It had taken some convincing but she wanted the women to wait outside as backup, and stay outside until she called them. They had brought her to the place, but now she wanted them to lay back and not get involved. Safer for everyone that way. "All right," Daynight said. "The time has come."

• • •

The stench inside was almost beyond belief, but Daynight eased open the door and slid inside into the darkness, broken only by a small light somewhere beyond her, and all around her the worst snoring imaginable. *Were there lights in here?* No way to know, and now that she was inside she had a flash. There was too much dark. If she initiated anything in this, she could come under fire and never see it coming. This realization chilling her, she slid back outside, eased the door closed.

"Too dark. We need to wait for daylight," she told her companions.

"Burn it," Sizzy said.

Daynight knew that was an invite to disaster, would prompt panic and shooting. "No, we wait for first light, take them as they come out, one at a time or in a group."

It was a great plan until the first contact came from a man who jogged in from the woods, not from out of the cabin and he shouted and raised his rifle and Sizzy shot him in the leg, dropping him, and ran over and jumped on him and bashed his head like a melon until he was still.

By then people were stumbling out of the cabin, half-asleep, some with weapons, some not, and Daynight got the drop on them and guided them to one side to Maggie as she waited for the last one to come out, which he did meekly, demanding, "What's the meaning of this?"

Absolutely nothing, which was the sick part of the whole deal, from the initial group assault to this.

• • •

County jail in Iron County, all the perps logged in and out of her hands and her sarge showed up. "Jesus, Alice, we thought you were dead."

She thought of Mark Twain's words. "The reports of my death have been greatly exaggerated."

Sarge stared at her like she was a ghost. "Who shot that one?"

"I did."

"With what?"

"Colt .45."

Sarge sneered. "That don't quite fit what I heard from the EET guys."

"Well, it is what it is, Sergeant."

"There are reports," he said.

"What day is this?"

He told her. It had been ten days since that night.

"I know there will be reports. Can I at least get some sleep?"

"First tell me the story and then you can go and we'll start back at it tomorrow at the Crystal Office. The El-Tee wants to be there."

She told him a very abbreviated story and told him she had been forced to flee from her savior-captors. Pure luck that she stumbled on the bad guys and even found a gun to use.

Daynight knew he wasn't buying it, and decided to lay it out in detail, which she did.

"So you did not shoot one of them?"

"No, but I will say I did. I owe those people. They were just trying to protect me."

"This ain't like you," her sergeant said.

• • •

The next day, almost all of it spent in the Crystal Falls DNR office in a vacant cubicle they had gone over it and over it, the El-Tee staring and not saying much, letting Sarge do most of the talking and work.

There would be a shooting investigation, and she was on temporary suspension until that was done. "Take the time and recover," Sarge told her.

El-Tee walked her out to her personal truck. The work truck was being recovered from the river, but was likely totaled. She had gotten her other stuff back from the cabin that night.

The lieutenant looked at six cool bags in the bed of the truck. "Been shopping?"

"Yah."

"Not for you, is it?"

She shook her head.

El-Tee chewed his bottom lip. "You remain, by all standards, an outrageous woman," he said, "and a damn fine conservation officer. Those women who helped you? Right thing to help them and protect them. I'll keep the spotlight off them. They are transient good Samaritans for public consumption. I'm glad you're back safely, Alice. You are a unique piece of work," he concluded. "You needed help and you accepted it. Good for you. Right decision. I'd have made the same one."

Piece of work. Is that good or is that bad, what's he trying to say? Wait, slough off your defenses, Alice, he just called you by name and praised you. Said he's glad you're back.

He's going to help protect Maggie and Sizzy. Stop reading so damn much into everything. You can't do everything by yourself. Your old man got that wrong.

Facing Perfection

"We never make time for *us*," Monty whined. "See what I'm sayin'?"

Bailey Cross grimaced. "Jesus, Monty, you can't *see* what someone's saying. You *hear* it, or you *understand* it. Lose your stupid clichés."

"So," he said and she cut him off.

"Is this starting a sentence with *so* some kind of damn virus? I hear every idiot under the age of thirty-five doing this all day every damn day."

"No sex in a month and all you can talk about is how I *express* myself? God, Bailey. The baby takes precedence over everything except your job."

"We've talked about this," she said.

"You've talked, I've listened, that's how it is with you, issuing orders, expecting them to be followed, and never questioned. Life isn't like that."

"It would be easier for everyone if it was. You get too emotional, over-react, pout like a child."

"I'm not pouting now," Monty said. "I'm trying to get you to talk to me, not at me."

"I see no point," she said in her aloof voice. "I like the status quo." Which was a lie. She faced conflict all day, every day in her job as a con-servation officer, and wished for, and prayed for perfection and calm when she was off duty. Why can't Monty understand how important it is for us to work together for perfection? It's a shield, a way to protect us, a way to put some predictability into our lives. She picked up her coat. "I am not going to engage in juvenilia."

"Where do you think you're *going*?" her husband wanted to know.

"Out."

"What about the baby?"

"What about her? She's fine, you know what to do."

He glared at her, his eyes pressed tight. "Typical, you walking away, avoiding reality."

"Whatever," she said, closing the door to their Spruce Street home. She got into her personal truck and motored up the county road toward Big Bay to her friend Jalani Dalani's fishing camp on the Heaven River. Indian-born Jalani taught biology at Northern Michigan University, had been her friend since her first year in Marquette County, thirteen years back.

Before marrying Monty her entire life out of her DNR uniform had involved trout fishing with flies. In those days she had fished every opportunity, however brief.

Monty lacked such inspiration in anything, was not eager to connect to anything, even a child, his own. The latest brouhaha was just another round in the we're-not-us-because-there's-a-kid ongoing fight. She didn't buy it. Monty worked eight to five at the bank, an *eight-to-five* job; How hard could that be? She flexed and split shifts to have time with the baby so that one of them was always there. Her job was hard, physical, scary at times. His was none of those things. The thought of eight hours in an office made her shudder.

Their life worked fine, was almost perfection. Couldn't he see that? "God."

The off-duty game warden stopped at Lefty's gas near the campus and got a couple of sandwiches from the cooler, and some chips. Lefty knew who she was but was the kind of person who left her alone when she was in civvies. She liked that, appreciated not having to hear the refrain, "Got a question for you." Said questioning almost always stupid, or a masked complaint about rules or another imperfect human.

She had grown up in Grayling, fishing the Au Sable and Manistee, Big Creek, any water with a trout population. Her whole family fished, as did most everyone in town. Everyone fished for trout, and tourists added to the wader-clad horde, stomping around in hats proclaiming "Grayling: A Drinking Town with a Small Fishing Problem."

In those days her best friend was Bucky, who had incredible instincts for fish, ones she lacked and had to train into herself. They fished together every day, were always hanging out together, and even spent a couple of days rolling around naked on the riverbank in a clumsy experiment that brought more embarrassment than satisfaction, but she had been as equal and eager a participant as her pal.

One day the fishing partners were staring down at the Coffee Creek, watching some small fish finning in sun-drenched shallows. "Stupid trout," Bucky proclaimed, after which he launched into an explanation of how smart fish, meaning the large ones, lived their lives in near-total darkness and did as they pleased, safe from predators. Bucky's grandfather called these hell trout, the only ones worthy of a trout-man's time and pure interest. The notion of a trout-woman was beyond his ability to disbelieve.

Bucky was smart, but too undisciplined for college and after high school had enlisted in the Army and ended up in the Seventh Cavalry, Third Squadron, the so-called "Eyes and Ears" of the Third Armored Division that led Operation Iraqi Freedom. Bucky was among the first soldiers killed by an IED in the Al Rashid District of Baghdad. He was awarded the Purple Heart and a Silver Star posthumously and she had stood by the flag-draped coffin with his grandfather, listening to the high school band play "Garryowen," ripping the hearts out of all present and all the old man could say was "Fucking waste of a good trout man." That was 2004, her second year in the county. It seemed impossible to believe. There had been a moment at the funeral when she'd wished they had gotten married.

Bailey parked her Chevy truck at her friend's camp, got into her waders, slid on her vest and pack, and got into the water, not bothering to string up or select a fly until she could find feeding fish. Once she found them the catching was steady if not spectacular, which was to be expected in June. Evening was the better time to fish in this part of summer, and with a bright sun and blue sky, slow was to be expected, though she had to admit to some disappointment, because Jalani confided she called this stretch Heaven's Sweetwater. Bluebird sky, June, the fish would come later.

Late in the afternoon she stopped at a glissade beneath a dark brown pool at the bottom of a long riffle. She sat and listened to the current harrumphing and clearing its throat and somewhere in the cascade of sound thought she heard a distinctly sturdy splook—not a fish rising, but a substantial fish feeding without fear, a hell-trout gorging during the dead hours in the light, which happened so rarely it might be considered miraculous in some circles. It was almost like the fish had a character flaw, a genetic defect that made for dumb behavior.

If it rose again. Big fish had the irritating habit of feeding one time on the surface and not again, at least in earshot of the angler.

"*Drat*," a voice yipped, its owner beyond view. Cross heard a reel clicking urgently, and a fish splashing in resistance.

The CO made her way around the next bend and saw an old man netting a brook trout of dimensions that defied imagination—well over twenty inches, a good two feet in length, its back black and cold, its belly alive with the colors of wildfire. The man released the fish quickly, and plopped down mid-river on a flat rock. He took off his hat, pulled out a purple bandanna, and wiped his forehead.

"Heavenly," Bailey Cross said, announcing her presence.

The man didn't even glance at her. "Hellish is more to the point," he carped quietly, staring out at the river.

She looked up into the sky, saw nothing. "What did it take?" she asked. "There's no hatch."

The man pointed across the river with his little bamboo rod. "See that naked stick out there, just bouncing in the water?"

"The curved one?"

He grunted and stood up. "Just watch."

Within seconds there was a tiny, almost imperceptible rise below the stick. The man peeled off line and pitched a reach cast across the river, his fly lighting without a sound two feet above the stick and passing dragless within an inch of it.

Splook! The water exploded, and the bamboo rod bent as the man set the hook. The fish ran, but the little rod was stout and the man was soon releasing the trout at his leg. It was another large brookie, almost two feet long and thick-bodied, glistening like an emerald trapezius muscle.

"Hellish," the man said, as the released fish scurryied to a hole across the river. The old man sat down on the rock again. "A big fish can rise small, but a little fish can't rise big," he said.

She had learned this from Bucky when she was a kid. "Heavenly," she said again.

"See for yourself," the man said, making his way across a slippery stone bottom to the shallows and the bank.

"I've never seen a brook trout that size," Bailey Cross said. "Much less caught one."

"You will," the man said. "This spot's yours until you surrender it to the next angler."

She looked around. "There's nobody on the river but us."

"All possessed trouters find this place sooner or later. You'll have company, but the spot's yours until you give it up. I expect you'll even get offered a few bribes or threats to move on," he added with an amused chuckle.

"Was that the same fish?" she asked the man, trying to see what fly was on his line, but it was too small to see.

"Can't say," the man said. "Everyone comes here thinking this is heaven, but it seems to me the purest of hells," he concluded with palpable disgust.

Cross was too amped to engage in further conversation and edged her way upstream to the sitting rock. She locked her eyes on the bouncing stick and saw from this angle it was shaped like a French curve. It was her experience that it was rare to find a large fish feeding on the surface except during major hatches, and virtually never in sunlight unless there was a good breeze and hoppers in the bank grasses, but as she stood and watched she saw another small sip and her heart began to race. She stood quietly, watching, and saw another sip. Having matched wits with an occasional large fish, she knew it would stay in its feeding lane if the fly wasn't directly overhead. One inch off might be as bad as a galactic mile. She thought about the rise and tied on a yellow sally, a yellow stonefly.

She waited for the fish to rise again, then cast two feet in front of the stick, mended out the drag and told herself to let it ride past the fish's likely station and only then lift it quietly and gently and cast again. With a sally you usually wanted to disturb the water, like the bug was trying to lift off, but this first time she wanted it just to flow quietly over the target. Given that she was mentally into the second cast she was unprepared for the crushing attack on the fly, but she set the hook and quickly got the fish onto the reel, as it surged upstream against the current, leaving her mouth agape, the surging fish cutting the water like a red-hot scalpel through butter.

The head-pounding below the surface was violent and consistent. She'd handled big fish, but this was something different in terms of pure strength and she was sloppy in netting it, the fly coming loose and snagging the netting, bending the hook, making the fly unusable. She looked for another yellow sally, but discovered that was her last one. She picked out a green caddis and tied it on. She'd seen no splashy rises to caddis and none flutter-hopping in flight, but it often worked, and green was her lucky color, even when there was no identifiable hatch. Deep down she guessed she was seeing tiny, microcaddis, #22s or smaller, but the sally had worked just fine.

A fish smacked her next cast like a starving hermit finding a venison roast over an unattended campfire. She set the hook, brought the fish to net, and released it.

By the time she got into her fifth fish in less than an hour she was beginning to wonder if hell-trout had bred a super dumb-ass sub-strain, or if she had stumbled upon a pod of stupid big brookies. She began to use scissors to nip a groove in the creatures' dorsal fins before releasing them to dart away.

There were six more fish in the next hour, in all eleven brook trout, all around twenty-four inches in length and four or five pounds in weight, production line fish, all in one place. It was insane and spooky. As far as she knew she did not catch the same fish twice and she wracked her brain trying to fathom why large brookies would be schooled in accessible water in daylight, not just schooled but apparently all packed beneath the dancing stick, which she was coming to imagine as a magic wand. Trout school in lakes, okay, but not in rivers, especially not in runty rivers like this one.

After fish fourteen, Cross sat on the flat rock and noticed the surface had been polished and she wondered if this had been going on for decades or centuries, which was a stupid thought, but she was crawling around desperate. She thought, I mean, each fish is the trophy of a lifetime, every fish almost identical in length and weight. What were the odds on *this*? This was infinitely more rare than the odds on winning the state lottery.

After the eighth fish she'd begun switching flies after every catch, but the results remained the same, the length of time, and savagery of the fights almost identical. It didn't matter what she threw, or how well or how poorly. Catching giant brook trout here was a lock.

By catch twelve she began to experiment with casts to see how far the trout would come to the fly. Number fourteen came six feet from its hide and took the fly with savage greed. Six feet! It was all very confusing, totally unlike any fishing experience she had ever experienced, or even imagined.

"You about done?" a stentorian voice boomed from behind her. She turned to find a short man wearing a bright red Stormy Kromer hat. He had the physiognomy of a rodent.

"You been at it for a while," the man said. "I've heard it said some fish here so long their hearts give out."

Cross grunted and stood up.

The stranger added, "Some just mighta been saved if they'd had the good sense to get out earlier and seek help."

Cross didn't answer him. He was trying to wedge her out of the spot and she was not about to leave, not with his attitude and pushing. She had always enjoyed the solitude of trout fishing, and generally other anglers shared the same values, and if you came to a river and found yourself near someone, you'd get out and go around, usually several hundred yards to give them plenty of breathing and fishing room. Nobody had ever given her a list of river rules; she had found them out of respect and courtesy of others, and the golden rule. Not every trout-chaser followed them, but most did and trout rivers tended to be serene, orderly places where you could fish hard or daydream and not worry about interruptions.

"A gentleman would step aside," her kibitzer said.

Cross said, "A gentleman wouldn't be downstream of me running his pie hole."

"No call for that tone of voice," he said.

"And no call for you to be back there," she repeated, made a false cast back at him and put a fly within a hair of his ear as a warning to give her some space.

Clearly, his presence and her reaction flummoxed her and her next cast was a gross, amateur fat loop that splatted the fly on the water not five feet from her leg and thirty or more feet from the bouncing stick, and as she reached down to pick up the fly a brookie charged all the way down-stream and ate it, almost out of her hand!

"Guess that cast will put them down," her visitor said, obviously not seeing her take the line and the fish not six inches from her knee and let it go.

The next cast went under the stick. A trout struck, she made the set, and as soon as she had it set she kept the rod down and straight-lined the fish under the water.

"Too bad," Jerkwad said with a laugh. "This ain't a woman's game."

But he plodded around her, went up around seventy-five yards and sat there as she caught fish after fish and eventually he moved up into the woods. She was releasing fish number twenty-four when Mr. Obnoxious cursed her venomously and departed for good. It was getting dark and she considered making camp for the night, but if she left this spot would that constitute surrendering it? Could she even leave the sitting rock? Questions without answers. She sat on the flat rock, ate a sandwich and a Mounds bar for energy, and after awhile, stood up to cast again. This had to end, sooner or later. Had to.

But it went on all night, no stars, no moon, no light, just cast, set, net, release while mosquitoes pocked her exposed skin and left welts that itched devilishly, and at some point during the night, she stopped counting and indeed lost count of the number of giant trout she had caught and released.

As the sun rose she looked into a mirror of skinny flat water and saw her face was swollen and red.

She told herself that in totally unexpected situations it could be difficult to extract oneself, but in the morning sun and rising temperature she knew she had experienced more than her fill and with no other people in sight, she shouldered her pack and gear and walked upstream until she saw a path upward and used it to climb out, carefully carrying her rod tip behind to keep from breaking it.

There was light on top and the old man who had given her the hole the day before. She smelled fresh coffee before seeing him. His camp consisted of a pup tent and not much else. His waders hung from a tree by their suspenders and she saw that the waders were as much patches as original rubber material. His rod was leaning against a bush. He poured coffee into a mug, held it out to her, and smiled.

"You lasted a long while," he said.

"I don't understand it," she said.

"What's to understand, and why would one want to? It just is. That's what matters, the moment, right?"

"All the fish were identical," Cross said. "Every one of them, and each a different fish. I think fish biologists would say it isn't possible to have so many big fish clumped together, except in a hatchery."

"Gets boring," her host said. "Everything the same, no variety, no chance for failure, its perfection beyond imagination and skill and you can't do anything wrong. That's the hell of it."

Bailey Cross sat down cross-legged with the man. The coffee was strong and hot and she tried to think about what he said, but she was soon asleep and awoke to find herself alone.

"It was boring," she said out loud. Without the possibility of failure there could be no sense of accomplishment.

She hiked down to her truck and called Monty on the cell phone.

"Sorry," she said.

"No problem," he said. "Catch any?"

"I caught them all," she said.

Monty laughed. "You didn't catch *me*."

"I'm not home yet," she said.

He said, "I think you're closer than before you left."

Flier's Club

Gillian Lunela Hartdog had felt increased amusement for her contacts with the general public as her career piled years on years. It was to the point where she could hardly wait to get in the truck every day and she missed it on her pass days, her days off. People were nuts and lead-pipe stupid, their antics wilder and more bewildering every year.

Not that she didn't sometimes overdose on people. She did at times. But she knew that when her tolerance was reaching saturation she could always drive up to the top of Brockway Mountain and breathe in the sunrise, take nature's new energy into her own soul and this would fix her for weeks to come.

Sunset was pretty, but represented an ending, a leaving. It was a time of negative energy and she imagined it drew off the day's sins and transgressions. But everyone liked sunsets and the public drove to the top of the mountain in droves to drink and gawk. Fewer people were early risers, and sunrises on Brockway were uncrowded and peaceful and serene as mornings ought to be, like the first smoke of the day and the first coffee. Morning was for thought and loin-girding or battle.

It was weird, she knew, but in her own mind she and those like her were green knights, Mother Nature's and the State of Michigan's good guys and gals in the bush.

Very first thing in the morning she used her Smartbook to check the National Oceanic and Atmospheric Administration website. NOAA Weather reports there tended to be more reliable than elsewhere, especially the stuff from cutesy and giddy TV chicks with the brain power of bricks. Not that weather predictions in the Keweenaw were ever easy in the common sense of the word. A rocky finger off the Upper Peninsula, the area seemed to catch shit from every frontal assault coming down from Canada, or up from the south.

This morning's forecast looked good. The two girls, Ellie and Kay-Kay, were in high school now, driving a beater Jeep and on their own getting themselves off to Calumet High School. The two were involved in everything, always busy and frantic, always on the dead run, but they had good grades and their menstrual meltdowns happened, but rarely, thank God. They were pleasant to be around and how could a mother ask for more?

Some of the girls' friends, different story. Many of them seemed to be drowning in some group psychosis of angst. *Don't think about that crap today,* Hartdog told herself. Today was for a pleasant patrol up to High Rock Bay at the far end of the Keweenaw peninsula, and a loop around the Mandan Road.

Her exact plan was to greet the day on top of Brockway Mountain, suck up maximum karmic energy, and get on with the day from there. A great part of this job was that she got to help people every day, even fools. She had learned early in her career, twenty-three years ago, that the job wasn't so much about writing tickets, but more about educating and assisting people and she was good at it, always calm in the face of chaos and disorder, a trait which had earned her the nickname of "Cool Hand Lu" from her DNR partners and colleagues. Even her husband Blick called her that, and sometimes her daughters would tell each other, "Better bounce that off Cool Hand."

"Babe," Blick said sleepily from the bed.

"See you at four, here," she said. "Make wood today."

"With you I could," he mumbled playfully.

"Knock it off, I've got work in the deep woods."

"Spoilsport," he said, plumping his pillow and rolling over.

"Girls," she said as she filled her morning thermos.

"Mom," they said in unison.

Blessed be those who can begin their day in peace, she thought, and walked out to her truck. Gas tank full, four-wheeler tank full, and the Honda in the Silverado's bed, chained in place, chalked in place, ready to roll. The Silverado's engine was nearly silent, the computer was on, and the Automatic Vehicle Locator System humming, there when and if she needed it. She hit a button and a box showed on the lower left of her screen, telling her exactly what conservation officers were on duty around the state.

As the lone officer for Keweenaw, her colleagues in south Houghton, Baraga, and Ontonagon would jump up into her area and help out by showing the flag. But they weren't on duty yet this morning and no surprise there. They were night folk.

"Station Twenty, One One Forty One is in Service." She loved it that her call number was the same as the main highway up the spine of the peninsula. Twenty was Lansing.

Just beyond Eagle River her personal cell phone chirped and the screen said, "Calumet High School."

"This is Gillian," she answered the phone.

"Yah, Gilly, Henry Miller here, where you at right now?"

"I just left home, just passed Eagle Harbor."

"Have your girls said anything about a flier's club?"

The balding vice principal had taught biology before moving into administration. Students called him Half Chrome not because of his monkish tonsure, but because the kids insisted he was a female in male clothing, a double X chromosome in an XY disguise. Kids could be so damn cruel. He was a good guy and a fine teacher and it amazed her how much her kids had to know in school versus what she had been saddled with. They were way beyond where she had been. They'd talked about cells and chromosomes in her time, but to make specific jokes out of them, not a chance. It was a different world, changing every day.

"Flier's Club?" she said. "Nope, don't know that term."

"Kids compete to see who can fly the farthest."

She had to think about this as the Military Road snaked north. "Like kites, rockets, model aircraft, like that?"

"No, they jump."

"Parachutes, homemade wings?"

"No Gilly, with nothing. They cliff-dive with no water below."

The conservation officer felt a chill. "Suicides?"

"There ya go. Suicides with a flair," the vice principal said. "Their friends videotape the event to post on YouTube."

"Why are you calling *me*, Henry?"

"I guessed you'd be out on patrol. Other cops are mostly running on complaints and such."

"Do you think my girls would be involved in this . . . *thing*?"

"Not as fliers, but your girls talk pretty openly with you, which makes you fairly different than most other parents."

"They haven't said anything, Henry."

"Well, I just thought you ought to know, Gilly."

She was immediately suspicious. "Why today?"

"Got a call from a colleague downstate, said they had some trouble with this thing and a few days ago there were rumors of some fliers headed to the U.P."

"To the Keweenaw?"

"No, to Pictured Rocks or to Lake of the Clouds."

Pictured Rocks was a national lakeshore and out of her range, way east in Alger County. Lake of the Clouds was in Ontonagon County in the Porcupine Mountains Wilderness State Park, not really close, but she knew that area well enough to patrol it when she was needed.

"Did the guy alert the state police?"

"He never said."

"Call him back, tell him to call the MSP as soon as you hang up. I'll alert COs in both areas."

She didn't know the Alger terrain at all, but she knew the Porkies and the escarpment overlooking Lake of the Clouds. It was a bit like Old Baldy in Yosemite, a dome-like slope not exactly made for smooth suicide leaps. The slope made it likely you'd skip your way down, banging rock faces all the way.

On the other hand, the Brockway precipices were tailor-made for teen madness. No sense trying to reach her girls. They would not answer their cell phones until they finished classes in the afternoon. She tapped in a text message. "Call me. Flier's Clubs? Love Mom."

Gillian Hartdog stopped at Esrey Park and had a coffee. The morning light was low but she could see two eagles in a snag, an adult and a juvenile. Various seabirds soared and hunted along the rocky coast and a flat Lake Superior. Several Caspian terns were performing their hover-maneuvers and straight-down dives to the lake's surface. The terns were strictly migrators this time of year.

Birds had air in their bones, could soar and float and glide and cheat gravity or use it, as they chose. Unadorned human bodies couldn't.

She was in a dead-phone zone when she tapped a text to the vice principal. "Flier Club, what school yr friend?"

She drove up Brockway Mountain Road from the west, would pop up to the summit, and work her way downhill to the east toward Copper Harbor and down the far side of the mountain.

No blue lights, no siren, but she felt her heart racing and she willed herself to calm down. This is just rumor, uncitable odds, like the lottery. Odds aside, her mind whispered that people do win lotteries, every day. Flier's clubs? How stupid could kids get? They could be so damn stupid. Where the hell did notions like this come from? YouTube? Good God.

Brockway Mountain Road was less than nine miles long and there were no posted speed limits. A county deputy had once told a reporter, "Speed itself is a self-correcting problem on the mountain." Lots of people laughed at that. She wasn't one of them.

Her phone sounded again as she hit the T on top of the mountain. She looked to her right. No vehicles on the loop on the very top. Good. She checked her message. "Empire County Day School. H.M."

She eased the truck to the left, looking downhill for pullovers and parked vehicles. Her phones began to chatter, her radios came to life as COs called to ask her if she had service. Brenda Lodge, the troop post commander from Calumet called. "You get the word on Flier Clubs, Gillian?"

"Yah, this morning. You?"

"One minute ago, direct from Lansing. What do you think, Alger or Onty?"

"Neither."

"You thinking Brockway instead?"

"I'm there now. Just checked the loop road on top, nobody there, headed downhill now. I'll work my way to the bottom and drive back up, keep running the route, just in case."

"Ounce of prevention," the state police officer said.

"You ever hear that term before this morning?"

"Never."

"Me either," Brenda Ledge said. "Youse keep me in the loop, eh?"

A Yooper raised in Carney in Menominee County, Ledge rarely revealed her roots in her speech. This thing had her shook and Brenda Ledge was not the sort of woman to shake easily.

One mile down from the summit, Hartdog saw a red Lexus SUV, an LX 570, not a kid's toy with a sticker price of seventy-five grand. The vehicle was empty. Hartdog slowed, pulled over and parked, grabbed her look-stick, a one-inch diameter, six-foot-long dowel with a GoPro camera mounted on the tip.

She eased out of her truck. The sticker on the back of the other vehicle said Crusaders, in red and white. Decades back in the Great Depression the WPA and CCC had built stone walls all along Brockway Mountain Drive. The kids were on the cliff-side of the flat-stone wall.

Clad in pricey top-of-the-line outdoor clothes, these were not Walmart girls: Ugg boots, eighty bucks a tootsie, kids from money, all girls. All four were looking at the valley between Brockway and Rock Ridge to the south on the other side of the valley.

Neither afraid of, nor attracted to severe heights, Hartdog stepped over the wall. "Morning ladies, who're the Crusaders?"

Four heads turned in unison. Eight semi-dark eyes staring at her. Dope? She hadn't smelled anything by the SUV, but had not gotten that close. Damn dope complicated things, sometimes made people more stupid than alcohol.

"Traverse City?" Hartdog suggested.

"Empire County Day School," one of the girls said.

"Ah Sleeping Bear."

"We live in Glen Arbor," one of the girls said in uplift, "but not public schools, see what I'm sayin?"

Twit. "You guys on vacation?"

"One does *not* holiday in Michigan," another of the girls said. "It's just not *done.*"

Bitch. "Well, this is a pretty overlook."

The girls nodded lethargically.

"Am I interrupting something?" Hartdog asked.

"Just looking," Miss No Holidaying in Michigan said.

"That's good. Don't blame you for wanting to see better, but why don't you guys step back over the wall. The winds up here are unpredictable. It can be calm one second and hit a gust of seventy the next, take you right off your feet and if you're at the wrong spot it will take you right off the mountain."

All but Miss No-Holiday crawled over the wall.

Hartdog heard a voice in her ear bud and triggered the microphone on her jacket.

"One, One Forty One, One Thirty Two, you up on the mountain? I got your message."

"Affirmative," she said quietly.

"Anything shaking?"

"Affirmative."

"Where you at?"

"Check AVL."

"I'm passing Mandan."

"Step on it, but come cold." Meaning no lights or siren.

"Thirty Two clear."

"You can like talk to people on that thing?" one of the girls asked.

"Yah. In fact it's hot now. Our entire conversation is going all over the state."

"Way cool," one of the girls said.

"What's up with the stick?" Miss No-Holiday asked.

The CO weighed what to say and quickly decided to be brutally direct. "Is this some sort of lame-ass flier club deal?"

"Dude," Miss No-Holiday said. "We like don't know nothing about no fly club."

The other three girls shook their heads, taking their cue from the fourth girl. Was No-Holiday their leader, or talking because she was the one out front? No way to know yet?

"What's ETD?" the CO asked.

All four girls stared dumbly at her. "Estimated time of departure. Like *takeoff*?"

The three giggled nervously.

No-Holiday said, "There isn't a schedule for fate."

"Fate? Since when is offing yourself fate?"

No-Holiday stiffened. "It is written."

"Nothing is written," Hartdog said.

"One cannot stop fate," No-Holiday declared.

"Why would I want to? What I want is to record this whole thing on my GoPro so I can put it up on the net."

"Like YouTube?" one of the girls asked.

Hartdog grinned. "Yoohoo, wake up people. YouTube won't take some retard's suicide vid."

No-Holiday stiffened. "Don't use that word, dude. It's like so rude."

Sore point. Good. "How about we just call it stupidcide?"

"Fate is eternal."

"So is ignorance."

"Are you trying to talk me out of this?" the girl asked.

"Oh hell no, I *want* you to jump. I want it on camera for other cops to see. I'll upload it to SpedDotCom see you as a wet spot on those rocks way down there."

"That's like gross," Miss No-Holiday said.

"Hey that site is real, and they pay serious money."

"No way," one of the other girls said. "Sped Dot Com?"

No-Holiday looked at the speaker. "You'd like sell a video of me?"

"Free market," one of the girls said.

"My act is not intended to be a commercial product," No-Holiday said in a strained, harsh voice.

"If you can sell it, that makes it commercial," the other girl said. "By definition."

"Totally unacceptable," No-Holiday said. "To fly is a beautiful thing, a gift from God for those who believe."

"It's a gift until the rocks kiss you," Hartdog said. "Five hundred feet. You jump, accelerate to thirty-two feet per second and gravity helps you by making a falling body speed up. First second you fall sixteen feet, by two seconds you're at sixty-four, three seconds you're at 144 and after three seconds you're already halfway to smashing down, 272 feet of five hundred gone, give or take. The whole damn thing happens simultaneously fast and excruciatingly slowly until impact."

"Not me," No-Holiday said.

"Sure you, why not? You've never killed yourself before so how could you know what's going to happen?"

"Well duh," No-Holiday said.

"Seriously, I clean up corpses all the time, I know about stupidcides. We get trained to deal with people like you, or how to clean up your remains. In fact, you jump I'll make your girlfriends scrape up the shit that's left."

"You're trained to talk me out of it."

"Hell no I'm not. I'm sick of the shit from your kind. *Jump*! I sell my vid and make money. Hell, all four of you can go at once, I'll be rich, a four-banger, I'm sure nobody got pictures of a four-banger before. C'mon, stop jawing and *do* it!"

No-Holiday glared at her. "You are sick, lady."

Hartdog saw One One Thirty Two, Gabe Raven, creeping along the other side of Mountain Drive, signaling with subtle hand gestures. Did she want him to cross over, or squat where he was? She put her left fist by her left thigh and he squatted and nodded.

"G'head, fly," she told No-Holiday.

"It's my decision," the girl said, raising her arms out from her shoulders.

"Don't fly with your arms out," Hartdog told the girl. "Don't you *know* shit? If you try to look like Jesus, you'll just piss off God."

"She might have a point," one of her companion girls offered.

"It's idolatry," yet another one said, "pretending to be Jesus."

"Don't start! I just want wings," No-Holiday said. "That's all."

Hartdog said, "You don't have wings now and you still won't after you blow your guts all over the rocks down there. God doesn't make angels out of dumbasses."

"God will protect me and welcome me."

"Really? You ever see a bird that's been sucked through a jet engine or a propeller? You think God protected the bird?"

"Birds aren't human."

"We are all God's creatures, all of us who are sentient, and he gave us free will. You decide to fuck yourself up flying, so be it. It's on you, not God."

The girl's arms came down to her sides.

"I want to be the first," No-Holiday said.

"To stupidcide yourself from up here? Dude, you're not even close."

The girl's shoulders slumped.

Hartdog spread the fingers of her left hand and made a subtle clawing motion. Her partner immediately began to crab-crawl across the roughly paved road.

"I'm going to fly," No-Holiday said in a flat voice.

"Fine, good. Let me get my camera closer, okay? Seeing some fool kill herself from start to finish ought to be worth a fortune. Step back six inches, I need the full view."

The girl edged back.

"Put your arms back behind your sides and swing them forward to streamline your jump, then go for it when you're ready."

The girl's arms went back. She said "Hey you guys," in a thin and reedy voice and she disappeared over the wall onto the road where Raven had snatched her and had her face down and in cuffs before she could react.

"Whose car?" Hartdog asked the three girls.

"Lena's," a girl said, pointing to the girl on the ground.

Hartdog went to the Lexus and took out the key. "Were you guys wanting to jump with her?"

"No Ma'am," they said.

"But you'd watch her kill herself?"

One of the trio said, "She'd never jump. She's a wuss. Is that Sped Dot Com thing like, for real?"

"It, like, should be," Hartdog said disgustedly. *Kids.*

"Put her in your truck," Hartdog told her partner. "One of the girls will drive the Lexus between our two trucks. We'll go down to Eagle River and get this squared away."

Gabe Raven came over to her; his eyes were popped out like golf balls. "You want to go *now*?"

"I can't," she whispered. "My legs are shaking so bad I don't think I can walk."

"Me too, Lu, but you? Unfucking believable. That was some majorly drastic shit. I can't even believe what I just saw and heard. How'd you think of GoPro?"

"I didn't. I just grabbed it from the truck."

"Holy shit."

When she finally calmed enough to get in her truck, Hartdog called Trooper Brenda Ledge. "We just got four girls from Empire County Day School."

"All jumpers?"

"Not sure yet. One looked like she would. You got units rolling this way?"

"Two."

"Tell them to work the mountain road east to west from on top. There could be more kids. Probably not, but let's assume the worst."

"Affirmative, let me know if you learn more."

It was late afternoon when she walked outside the jail for a break, and stretched. Stupid kids, no thought, herd animals. Hartdog texted her girls, asked their whereabouts, and got fast responses. Both were at home, one reading a book, the other one oiling her ball glove.

Teens lived a life apart, secret from adults and even secret from younger children. How the hell could you tell if one of them was suddenly turning stupid? She was still shaking when she went back inside the Eagle River jail.

Hard As Nails

"One, One Fifty Five, Station Twenty. We had a call from a woman in Ishpeming. She says her neighbor has taken in a fawn for a pet. The caller says the woman's son brought the animal to her."

Station Twenty was DNR HQ in Lansing, a room in the Mason Building filled with dedicated phone dispatchers who served as links between citizens and officers in the field. Dispatchers took complaints and calls and passed them to officers, 24/7.

"I'm almost home, Twenty." CO Prudie Fugasy was sun-burned, wind-burned and bone-tired. She had spent all day in her boat dealing with safety and licensing violations and issues, some fishing over-limit cases, and two nasty domestics in a campground, including the last one that turned into an all-out fight. She ended up lodging a drunk wanted on felonious assault warrants against a Detroit Metro police officer. And now, one minute from home get a call to turn around and drive fifteen miles to confiscate an illegally held fawn. *Well, shit.*

"One, One Fifty Five, One, One Forty Eight, I'm closer. I'll take that fawn call."

Fugasy radioed, "Thanks," and sighed. Her partner of three years, Dallas "D" Clay was simple, aggressive, and energetic. *Thank God.* Her plan for the night was to sit on the screened gazebo out back with a glass of red wine and read. Husband Sherm had taken the kids over to the Soo to see his parents, giving her a rare gift, time to herself. *Time alone, precious, silent, still, alone-time.*

She quickly changed into shorts and flip-flops, a T-shirt, no bra. It felt so damn good to be unencumbered by a load of equipment. To not worry about how she looked. She usually felt more pressure than some of the guys to look professional and attractive, and to fly the state flag for the public for the gray-green line. She desperately wanted a glass of merlot, but for reasons she couldn't enunciate, she delayed opening the bottle. COs were not always on call, but many of them felt like they were and that they could be called out at any time, which meant if she'd had any alcohol, she couldn't go.

Looking at her toenails she did not like what she saw. A game warden's feet were in some ways as important as her truck. She wiggled her toes. Can read later. I'll do my nails. She missed doing some girlie things, missed doing them on a regular basis, not on rare occasions when she happened to notice something. Missed pampering herself, *alone!*

Fugasy gathered the makings for her evening with no less focus than a priest before mass. Basin for her feet, towel under the basin, nail polish remover (which smelled suspiciously like the model airplane glue her dad used when she was growing up), nail undercoating, robin egg blue polish, nail strengthener. If her colleagues ever saw her polished toenails she'd never hear the end of it. Daughter Eula, seven, had gone gaga over robin egg blue, wanted it on everything. Three-year-old Samantha called it Robbers-Beg-Blue.

Ah, girl time. She toyed with switching off the phones but couldn't bring herself to do it. She got a bottle of Pepperwood Grove merlot out of the wine rack and put it on the counter. Under eight bucks, not bad at all. The label proclaimed "Groovy Green bottle." What the hell did that mean? She imagined hell as a place where sinners were made for eternity to scribble insipid promotional slogans and yell them at each other. How could you even look at yourself in the mirror if writing slogans was your job? Talk about your popcorn light work. She got out her personal wine glass and set it by the bottle.

Hubby Sherm called the wine Peckerwood, which made her laugh. Sherm was a beer guy, and she liked that. No pretenses. She was contemplating a long soak in the tub when the state cell phone clicked and coughed for attention.

"Fugasy."

"Prudie, D." His voice was hoarse. "I've got a ride-along in my truck."

"I'm just getting ready to pop the cork on a bottle of red. To indulge myself."

"What? No! Listen, Prudie, I've got a serious situation here."

"You're picking up a fawn. What situation?"

"The fawn." She could hear a catch in Dallas Clay's voice.

"I'm listening."

"The woman's son found the fawn and brought it home to mom."

"You have it?"

"I do."

"Drop it at the rehabber. Georgia Dizzo out in Lakewood already has several of this year's fawns."

"That's not the situation, Prudie. I know the damn drill."

"So why the yank and more to the point, why this phone call? I've checked out of service. This is Prudie time. Sherm took the girls to the Soo."

"I'm sorry, I'm so sorry, I'll owe you big time."

"Owe me for *what*?"

"The kid picked up the fawn in Wisconsin."

Fugasy said, "Fuck." Then, "You know what you have to do."

"I know, I know, but I have a ride-along."

"Somebody who wants to be a CO?"

"Yes," he whispered.

"Good, show him the seamy side of the work."

"Her, not him."

"No diff, D, male, female. This is reality. It'll do her good to embrace reality."

"I . . . just . . . can't."

Fugasy sat down. "Let me guess. She's hot."

"Mega."

"And you think she might be amenable to more than a truck ride."

"Distinct signals have been transmitted."

"I'm home, I'm stark naked, D."

"I know, I'm sorry, but you *got* to help me here."

"I do not *have* to." She toyed with telling him she had already started on the wine, but you couldn't lie to a partner, ever.

"I'm begging you, Prudie. Begging. I'll do anything."

"Where are you?"

"By the Monk highway."

"Okay start heading my way. I'll meet you at Yalmer Lane. Half hour."

She hung up. Should make him do this, not bail out his sorry ass. Stop your bellyaching, you said you'd do it, now get with it.

Yalmer Lane, truck behind truck, Fugasy met her partner and his ride-along. Hot *indeed*. She could feel heat coming off the woman from three feet away. Fugasy took the fawn from the girl. "I'm Prudie," she said.

"Jaymilla," the girl said. Twenty max, sweet voice and smile.

The animal was wrapped in a pink towel decorated with pale green leaves. "Got a rope?" she asked Dallas Clay.

"Don't *you*?"

She could see he was antsy, wanting to be shed of the fawn. She gave him the laser eye. "D."

"Yah, yah, I think I got something in my GoBox."

He went away. "You want to be a CO?" Prudie asked the girl.

"What's that?"

"Conservation officer."

"Oh yeah, for sure. I like really *adore* animals."

Clay came back with six feet of parachute cord and tied it to the fawn's neck.

"Hey Jaymilla," Prudie said. "You want to jump in with me and see what happens?"

Dallas Clay said, "Regulations dictate that she has to finish the ride-along with the officer she begins with."

"No problem," Fugasy said. "Just follow me."

"Can't," Dallas Clay said. "I'm out of hours and her vehicle's in Ishpeming."

Fugasy felt the desperation in her young partner. "Too bad. Another time, Jaymilla?"

"Cool, I'd love that," the girl said, "pleased to meet you ma'am."

Prudie walked her partner to his side of the truck. "You owe me, asshole. Don't throw your back out. I'm already handling your slack, bud."

"Thank you, thank you, Prudie."

"You even think about hugging or kissing me and I will inflate your stones to balloons."

Clay got in his truck and raced away.

The conservation officer had a cardboard box in back of her truck and put the animal in it and draped a towel over the top, leaving the little head with big eyes sticking out and staring at her.

"Do not even *look* at me," Fugasy told the fawn.

She pulled down a two-track about five miles from her place. Not the best spot because of nearby farms and houses, but it would have to do. She parked the truck, got a shovel, and quickly excavated a three-foot-deep oval.

She took the fawn from the truck, leading it by the cord around its neck. What a delicate, beautiful little creature. She'd like to find the jerkwad who caused this and kick his ignorant ass.

Chronic Wasting Disease had been found in deer in Western Wisconsin in 2002, and since then Michigan had a quarantine on all Wisconsin deer, dead and or alive. You could shoot one over there but it had to be deboned and butchered before you brought it back into the state.

Since 2002 the prevalence of CWD had risen in males and females and in all age groups in the stricken area. The disease was lethal to whitetails. All deer brought from Wisconsin had to be seized and destroyed. Officers had no other options.

Fugasy lay the animal in the hole and rubbed it until it curled into a ball. So warm, unafraid, its heartbeat quick but even. *Poor little bugger.*

She had her .38 snubby in hand, wrapped the towel around it, pressed the barrel to the creature's head and squeezed once.

The animal went limp and the officer wrapped the towel around it and filled the hole, covering the scar with leaves and pine duff. She took deep breaths to steady her emotions.

There were parts of this job the public did not need to know about, much less to witness. Dallas was right about that. Now she needed a hot shower to get the filth off her, a glass of wine and time to take care of her toenails.

Back at the house she looked at her toe supplies and began to laugh and cry at the same time. Her nail polish strengthener was made by Sally Hansen. It was called Hard As Nails.

Just One More Second

Yoo nevr hewp me whan dodie wend and I try at goon but it don't do no damm gud, I can't do dat, I can't doo noddin, Dodie she go die and I don't do noddin and what choice I got do somepin you no helup I ask you not tell me what do now Dodie gone and I all alone out here own hilltop owt from town, you say, girl?

"I didn't know."

Holy Petecrap. I got pud up sign say old shit feel shit, hep-hep-hep, need magical marriagedwana?

"I didn't know."

Can't say thet no moor ant now it don't matter shit I t'ink. Smalltown pipples spose look out each udder, tek care dem 'roun dem, not like I got done me, agknored.

"How could I possibly know, you know?"

So naou yookno, yookno, what you thing 'is ting was, eh, had mye gottdamm head go down yoo lapp now yoo lapp you tag gut loog I try yoo no gun waukt sloe down roed heavyday, hope dis it, did it, but neffer iss, neffer iss, I waukt when trees and flouers grooedd, butt nobutties seen old man waukt wid stick. Yoo cee my eyes, girl, yoo cee my eyes. Answer 'ere in eye's is mine nobuddy gift no shits old man tint dekache.

Nine-thirty in the morning, and Meghan Petryshen heard the dispatcher call out a fatal vehicle accident. She quickly processed the location in her mind: shit, not more than a half mile ahead of her, flipped on her blue lights, boogied straight at the situation, thinking, not this, not today. Winter was trying to roll in that morning with freezing rain and fog, and vehicle grills moved through it like it was gray Jell-O, nasty, nasty shit, visibility was down to yards at times with a mixture of sleet and snow and fog.

Petryshen saw an emergency light ahead, got to it, parked, left her engine running, stepped out, saw who it was, got a lump in her throat, went directly to the black truck, gluing her eyes only on Alicin Carmichael, ignoring all else.

The door was jammed but she managed to muscle it just enough to get it open.

Alicin was listing toward the open door. She was staring out, her eyes surrounded by dark red blood, almost black. Petryshen reached across the blockage in the front seat, popped the officer's seatbelt release, got her by the armpits, dragged her out, eased her down, propped her up.

"Al, Al it's Meghan."

Cee! same always yoo leaf mee here go off like when Dodie wend, nuddin les I speck, I speck. All dis tax monies nobody look me in eye say dis what it buy, for dose young buck, dose hold fart, wons lieg mhe.

"Alicin, can you stand?"

The conservation officer was standing on her own, but was unresponsive. "Al, if you're hearing me, nod your damn head." Petryshen looked up and saw the sheriff come pulsing up in his squad, jump out, and take over traffic control as EMS rolled up and went to the truck and one of them came over to them and said, "You ought sit down, officer, and let me take a look at you."

Carmichael seemed to come to life. "I already seen! Are you fricking people blind?"

Petryshen waved at the sheriff, got his attention. "I'm taking her home. I'll bring her to the hospital."

The sheriff was by the DNR truck, looking shaken and pale as death. He nodded without enthusiasm.

"Is that your blood, Al? Are you cut?"

"Not my fricking blood."

"Al, give me your sidearm."

"It's *my* gun!"

"I know that, give it to me."

"No."

"Don't be a fucking child. Give me your Sig."

Carmichael frowned, unsnapped the holster, and handed the pistol to her colleague, handle first.

"Okay now your radio and the rest of the firepower. I know you're packing a .45 slim-line under your tits in your vest, and you've got the state .38 snubby and a .32 hammerless snub somewhere. I want all of them."

The woman handed her partner her service vest and dug out weapons and handed them over.

"Jesus, you've got to be the most armed CO in the whole damn state."

"Wasn't worth a shit today, was it?" Carmichael said. "Meg?"

"What?"

"Meg?"

"I'm here."

"Am I here?"

"You are, Al, c'mon let's go, we're getting out of this place."

"Where he went you think, Meg?"

"Huh?"

"You know."

"You mean where are we going?"

"Yah, okay that."

"I'm taking you home to clean you up, take care of business."

"Got no business."

"Don't bust my balls, it's a figure of speech."

"Busted balls, yah I know," Carmichael said.

Go hed maggot jogs all cops stickemtites yooseeachudder, you cee my eye, I need you cee my eye, made you cee, you see, I kno you kno, had no choose, no hewp yoo, nobody and what Dodie do I don't kno.

Petryshen on her cell phone to Central. "One One Fifty Five has One One Fifty on board, transporting her to her residence and from there to the hospital."

"Fifty Five you want us to call Dutch?"

Dutch Carmichael, Alicin's husband. "Negative, I've got this, One One Fifty Five Clear."

"Central clear."

"You feel sick?" Petryshen asked her passenger.

"Nuh-uh."

"We'll get you cleaned up when we get to your place."

"My place? Dutch?"

"I'll talk to Dutch. We're going to your place to tidy you up some, and then we'll head for the hospital to get a blood draw, you understand, right?"

"Procedure, standard," the officer said. "SOP, right?"

"Right, going by the book now is in everybody's interest."

"I got to worry, you think?"

"Hush until we get some coffee in you, get you cleaned up."

"There, not there, Meg. I swear."

"Shut up Al. Don't talk."

Petryshen triggered Carmichael's home phone number. Husband Dutch answered right away.

"Dutch this is Meghan. Al had a little problem and I'm bringing her home. Listen to me, she's okay, all right? Dutch did you hear me? Answer me."

"Yah-sure, okay, she's okay."

"There in ten minutes, max."

"Okay then, what's going on?"

"I'll explain when I get there, but she is okay. Focus on that, Dutch."

An hour later in the hospital, blood being drawn to rule out alcohol, drugs, whatever, by the book. Al stared at the syringe, the needle in her arm, said nothing, looked almost disinterested at first before fixating on the blood filling the cylinder. Black, what's black blood mean? Alicin Carmichael asked the nurse.

"Your eyes are playing tricks," the nurse said. "It's red. All blood is red."

"Huh," the conservation officer said.

Cee, all blood same red, you blood, Dodie, my blood you cee my blood you cee my eye, I maked sure dat ok blood come there yoo-me.

Hansen arrived at the hospital, Michigan State Police lieutenant Eddie Hansen, Dutch Carmichael's hunting and fishing buddy, the two families owning a camp over in north Dickinson, together all the time when they weren't on duty. Why Hansen to lead the incident investigation? Why not bring in a stranger? This is already gonna be too fucking hard for everyone involved.

The giant lieutenant nodded at her. "You should have brought her directly here, Meg."

"Pardon me, El-Tee but you didn't see her, you didn't see it. You don't know dick at this point. I saw it, her, knew I had to get her out of there."

"I want this by the book, Officer Petryshen, you copy?"

"I copy, El-Tee. The tests will show nothing because there's nothing to find. She doesn't drink, won't even take prescriptions unless Dutch forces them down her damn throat. You *know* that."

"Put your emotions away," the troop said, "And back the fuck off, Meg. She's my friend and colleague too."

"Sorry, I know."

Hansen patted her shoulder. "No problem. We're all in shock. She's gonna need all her friends."

"You've been through this kind of thing personally?"

"I'm empathizing. Don't leave her alone."

"Not planning to."

"You picked her up at the crash site?"

"Worst thing I've ever seen, Ed. I focused solely on her face and her eyes, nothing more, didn't look at the rest of it, didn't need to. I saw her eyes and knew I had to get her out of there."

"You get her weapons?"

"First thing, radio too. Didn't want her hearing radio chatter about it."

"She carries more than two weapons."

"I got all four."

"Talk to Dutch, get *all* the guns out of their house. There's gonna be self-recrimination and it's gonna settle in quick-fast. We don't want her taking any stupid permanent solutions to temporary situations."

"It's not temporary for the vick."

"Meghan, that old fella is beyond our reach. Now we have to take care of those still with us. That will be difficult enough."

"Yes sir."

Petryshen called her sister. "Chris, Alicin hit a pedestrian about two hours ago. I'm going to stay with her and Dutch for a while. Grab my go-kit and bring it over to their place."

Anybody hurt bad?" her sister asked.

"Does dead count as bad?"

"Oh my God," Chris said. "I'll bring your stuff."

• • •

A week later, Alicin Carmichael was in Green Bay. Her lieutenant from Marquette had come by the house, not liked what he'd seen and heard. And one of the local judges arrived one morning, cancelled court, spent the day with her, just to provide company. It was the judge's idea for the counselor, and he told her "I know just the one." Dutch had to work. He had his own pulping business. When he didn't work, he didn't make money, her fault this, her fault that, everything her fault. Nightmare, every breath and second.

She drove to Green Bay alone.

The counselor's name was Ryderly, fiftyish, distinguished looking, pink skinned, veins in his nose, a voice like clicking gravel, an annoying kind of thing, yet unignorable. You had to deal with it. Him.

"Weather okay coming down?"

"That's all you've got?"

He smiled, held out his hands. "Okay, that was lame. Life sucks, right?"

"Only when you kill some old man."

"Want to tell me about it?"

"No, I don't."

"Not a problem. Want me to tell you about me?"

"Do I have a choice?"

"It's your dime—or the state's depending on how you look at it."

"My dime, no, state's dime sure, go ahead. You a shrink?"

"I am. My practice is almost all dealing with trauma cases, PTSD and such."

"That's me, PTSD?"

"I don't know. Is it? You driving much yet?"

"This is my first time in a vehicle to come down here. You know. Since?"

"Comfortable?"

"White-fucking knuckle every fucking mile. What's wrong with us living up here in such shit weather, snow, fog, crap?"

"These things also happen under blue skies and a bright sun. Don't blame the weather."

"Who do I blame?"

"Maybe nobody. I don't know the answer to that. Any self-harm thoughts?"

Carmichael made a puffing sound. "You mean like might I eat my gun? All the damn time."

"That's normal."

"Look," she said, "I had been up to Marquette for a trial the day before. I stayed with another CO that night, came home in the morning. Fog all the way. I'm driving along and the visbee is shitty but there's nothing in front of me and then there was. Bang."

"That's it, bang? Why that word?"

"I killed the man, might as well have shot him. Bang. Dead as a door-nail. You want to know if I was speeding?"

"Would that bring the victim back to life?"

"You know it wouldn't."

He said, "My backstory is this: I'm a cop in Madison, snowstorm, bunch of kids crossing from school in the afternoon. Could see them, saw them for a long distance, but I locked up my brakes, turned the squad into a dumb bomb, whole damn thing in slow motion, I still see it happening, and nothing I can do. I know it's coming and I can't do anything. I'm gonna hit kids with my patrol vehicle and I can't do anything and they aren't even looking, they're gonna get crushed and never even know what happens."

Carmichael looked over at the man. "You're making that up."

"You think so?"

She studied his eyes, could see pain. "No, I guess not. Sorry."

"It's okay, it's so fucking surreal nobody can take it on board first time they hear it."

"You hit them?"

"Four of them, all seven and eight, all dead on impact, nothing I could do. Turned out the brakes were faulty, a manufacturer design problem, not our maintenance not the operator, there were lawsuits for years, the county and the manufacturers all paid."

She had to think about this one. His vehicle had failed, not him. In her case, it was her failure.

"Visibility was bad," she said, "for me."

"You think that explains it?"

"No, I deal with bad weather all the time. We're game wardens and pay no attention to weather. It's totally irrelevant. We go and we do, no matter what, ever. It's up to me to handle it."

"You thinking about hanging it up?"

"Crossed my mind, I can tell you that."

"You love the job?"

"I guess," Carmichael said. "Is this how this thing is supposed to go, the two of us jawing about nothing?"

"Are we?"

"I was hoping for results."

"Which results?"

"I don't know. This whole thing was unnerving. Scary, you know?"

"Then how can you expect results?"

"Okay, I guess I really want to forget the whole thing."

"Do you think that's even possible?"

"Is it?"

"Hasn't been for me, but you're not me."

"Any of your patients able to forget terrible shit?"

"They don't forget, they work over it and through it, don't let it control them."

"I don't understand how they can do that. It's right in my frontal lobe every second, awake or asleep. I have day-mares, is that even possible?"

"You mean nightmares during the day?"

"I don't know if there's a word for them."

"Does it happen as you're trying to sleep or to wake up from sleep?"

"No, not then, right in the middle of the day, doing something, a day-dream, only awful."

The doctor looked at her, said nothing. "He talks to me," she said.

"He?"

"He, him, are you not paying *attention*?"

"I'm trying."

"The guy, the vick."

"Does he have a name?"

"I can't remember."

"Can't or don't want to?"

"Fellers, Charles James Fellers."

"Mister Fellers is talking to you?"

She rolled her eyes. "Not talk, not like a conversation. He's yelling at me. He's mad. You know?"

"Why?"

"I don't know?"

"He hasn't said?"

"Something about his eyes, seeing his eyes."

"His eyes?"

"I don't get it."

"Did you see his eyes?"

Carmichael stopped slumping in her chair and sat up. "I did."

"So you saw his eyes, the eyes of the man you killed."

"Yes, I saw them."

"And he's talking to you now."

"Not right now, but a lot, you know?"

"Telling you what."

"I saw his eyes and killed him."

"What vehicle were you driving?"

Carmichael stared at the doctor. "What's that got to do with anything? I was in my Silverado, my patrol truck."

"How big was the guy?"

"I don't know, not very. He was in his 90s, sort of bent over."

"You knew him?"

"There was an accident at his place a couple of years back. He turned in front of a motorcycle, killed the driver, put the dead man's wife in the hospital for six months. I came upon the situation on my way back into town, stopped to help the deputies with traffic that day."

"But didn't really know him?"

"No, not really. I only heard him say one thing."

"Which was?"

"He was pissed at the motorcycle driver because of the damage to his van."

The doctor raised an eyebrow. "This is the guy you hit?"

Carmichael nodded.

"And you didn't see him again until two weeks back?"

"Right, wrong. I saw in the local paper his wife of sixty years had died and I heard at the cop house he was despondent."

"When was that?"

"Earlier this fall, September?"

"Are you seeing some puzzle pieces here?" the doctor asked.

"Not really."

"What exactly does he say to you? When he talks?"

"It's mostly gibberish and about the only thing that comes through is that thing about his eyes."

"Is there a deer guard on your patrol truck?"

"Yes, I had my own made of steel, not that tube crap the state buys."

"What happened when you hit him?"

"I'm not sure I can go there," she said.

"Okay," Ryderly said.

"Foggy, sleety, one second it was clear, then thump."

"You drive over the body?"

She looked at the doctor. "No, he came all the way through the windshield. Into my lap." She looked down.

"Over your deer guard, across your hood, through the window, and into your lap? How did he get over the deer guard?"

"He just did."

"Have you hit deer, other animals?"

"Once in a while."

"Any of them come over the guard?"

"No."

"You ever think something might come over?"

She had to think about this. "Only way is if it was up in the air, toward the top, something tall, like a moose maybe?"

"But Mr. Fellers was small, right?"

"Yes, real small."

"And you saw his eyes?"

"Yes."

"He was looking at you when you hit him?"

"I guess."

"Why. Was he crossing the road?"

"We don't know, he isn't here to tell us."

"Why was he even out there?"

"Getting his mail is what the investigators think."

"Assuming he was moving across, even if he darted out, wouldn't you be seeing him from the side not facing him?"

"I looked right into his eyes."

"That doesn't strike you as a questionable eye witness fact?"

"I haven't thought about it."

"Maybe you should."

"Why?"

"I took the liberty of talking to one of the investigators. Mr. Fellers is well known by neighbors for causing vehicles to lock up their brakes, several times a week. He just walks out in front of vehicles, a lot, most of this behavior since his wife died."

"I haven't heard that."

"And you still haven't until the full investigation is done, but you need to know this guy's behavior was pretty odd and very questionable. The neighbors said he did this a lot, frequently, conclusion?"

"He didn't care what happened to him?"

"Reasonable to assume, but he never got hit, not once."

"I hit him."

"Bad visibility, same behavior from him."

"Suicide?"

"Alicin, you saw his eyes. The report says he was diminutive in size. He moved into your line so fast that you didn't see him coming, yet you did see his eyes," the psychiatrist said and paused. "He jumped up, Al, he came at you and jumped up and impact put him through your windshield. If he had been going sideways it would have been different. He had to have come at you."

"You're saying he charged me?"

"I guess that's an adequate description. It's the only one that seems to fit the facts."

"Why? I don't understand."

"Go back to the dreams, what did he tell you?"

"I don't know, like I said, ranting, gibberish." She closed her eyes. "Something about gun being not good."

"He was despondent, maybe he tried to end it with a gun, couldn't do it."

"God. How could I know that?"

Dr. Ryderly shrugged. "We know almost nothing about death, how a conscious mind shuts down, what happens to the soul, what a soul is, if there is one. We just don't know. But telling you about the eyes I think he was trying to tell you this was on him, not on you."

"Is that supposed to make me feel better?"

"It's supposed to make you try to take apart the experience with some of that objectivity and observation you use every day in your work."

"I don't know if I can do that. This is different."

"No, it's not. Life is life."

"This is death."

"Which is part of life."

Omaha! Blue!

Colonel Joe Romano had noticed her competence during her first tour and had her transferred from her guard unit to Speck Op HARAM FREYA, *Haram* meaning forbidden and Freya for Freya Stark, an eccentric Brit Arabist who had traveled alone all through the Arab world, speaking Arabic and Persian. Her last expedition had taken her into Afghanistan. One of a kind was Miss Stark, hugely simpatico to the plight of women in the Muslim world.

This was Major Meta Toucan's fifth deployment in ten years, two full one-year deals, two more six-monthers and this one of unspecified length, which unlike the others, had dropped out of the blue. The bosses in Lansing were not happy. They could barely tolerate National Guard service as part-time, but not as full-time, and ever since Rumsfeld had been running the Pentagon, all troops were treated as full-time Army. What could you do about it? Nothing.

And it was the same this time: Ten days after a call from Washington, here she was in Kabul, in Joe Romano's tiny office in a fortified building at the city's airport.

"How long have you been here?" she asked the colonel. "Do you *ever* rotate home?"

"Home is where my boots are," Romano said. "No wife, no kids and all I own fits in two duffle bags. Sorry about the hurry-up on this deal. I know it ruffled some feathers."

"It always ruffles feathers, no biggie." Toucan was a conservation officer in Hillsdale County, a job she truly loved. For the last year she had been trying to get into the Wildlife Resource Protection Unit, an undercover operation, to no avail. Her friends thought it was because she was a woman, but she was sure it was all the war deployments. Being a woman could be a barrier, but not to all things. She was a woman here and the Army showed no qualms of any kind about using her skills and knowledge. "Why such a yank this time, Colonel?"

Romano handed her a small manila envelope. She cupped it open, dumped the contents into her hand. She saw an 18-carat gold button, decorated with a half moon. She felt her heart race. "Where is she?"

"Not Kabul," the colonel said.

"How'd you find her?"

"Pure chance, a Goatsucker op in Kandahar."

She doubted it was pure chance. Sima Firoozi operated far outside the laws of chance. Goatsucker was the term for snatch-and-grab missions targeting enemy leadership and potential high value intelligence sources. Special Ops were going all the time, every night, all year long.

"Was she the target?"

"We didn't even know she was there. The team made entry and she popped up with an AK, whacking ECs. Our team killed three other men. She dropped the weapon, held up her hands and yelled 'Omaha! Blue!' The team nearly shit their pants," Romano said with a smirk.

Omaha was a signal some professional football quarterbacks used to tell teammates the play clock was nearly out. Blue meant extreme emergency and I can't talk. Toucan had adopted the OB code for her agents and operatives. It was rarely used.

"What happened after they snatched her up?"

"Everything by the book. They treated her as an EC detainee, hogtied her, hooded her, threw her on the chopper. Treated her as an enemy combatant all the way, disappeared into the Kandahar night and checked her into IC Hugh."

IC stood for interview/interrogation center. Hugh was the facility's name, one she'd never heard before, meaning it was new since she'd last been in the country. "New?"

"Very."

"Anyone talk to her?"

"No ma'am, we all went by the book you wrote on agents. She important?"

Romano was West Point lite, hated arbitrary procedures, red tape, ring-knockers, spit-and-polish, ass-lickers and vain-glorious office soldiers. His code was simple: Know the job you're gonna do and do the job you know. He was the best leader she had ever known.

"Could be huge, Joe."

The bearded, long-haired man nodded. "Say when you want to flip the switch."

"Let's do it now," she said. "Everything at the IC has to look gold standard authentic. She in a burka?"

Romano nodded.

"I need a ruck with a carton of smokes, an ashtray and a pint of Jack Daniels. Clean room. No cameras, no mikes, no witnesses, I want her alone, just her and me. And a plate of fresh fruit."

"Don't let the door hit you in the ass," Romano said. "Get some! Your bird is on the roof. Elevator up. Jap-made and man is that fucker smooth." The colonel had an inexplicable interest in elevators, could ramble for hours on their history, models, you name it, he knew it.

"Call-up duration?" she asked from the doorway.

"Long as it takes to do what you gotta do. You're all one when done is done. This a big league deal. Meta?"

"Could be ginormous, Joe."

"I loathe that word. Get your ass up to and off my roof, Major."

• • •

It was a bumpy two-hour ride and she slept poorly, awakening as the chopper let down on another roof and as she got out, she saw mountains all around them, but not close. Armed guards waved her at a door and opened it for her. Inside the door a soldier handed her a ruck. "Fruit coming as soon as you get in your room, Major."

She nodded and went down the narrow, poured concrete stairs, which opened onto a floor. A soldier said, "Major Toucan?" and she nodded and he said, "This way," and she followed him to a narrow, surgically sterile all-white room. It was sparse. One bed, a prayer rug, a table and chair, a metal water jug. A black figure rose from the bed, came to her, said, "*Allah akbar*. You took *your* time. Are we green?"

"Negative. You'll be escorted to another room."

"*Salam alaikum.*"

"*Ensha allah.*"

The soldier took her to a new room, all white but much larger, one table, two chairs, no windows.

As soon as her escort left, Sima Firoozi said, "Now?"

"Green light."

The woman ripped her way out of her heavy dress, shed down to panties and bra. "I would so love to burn all that stuff," Firoozi complained. The woman was thin, blonde, forty, brown-eyed with tawny apricot skin. Born in Teheran, raised in the US, West Point grad, now a major and destined to move up, but this was her third year undercover in Ira Pakigan, Toucan's term for Iran-Pakistan and Afghanistan. Firoozi had cojones the size of truck hubs, more lives than a dozen cats, perfect in Pashto, Dari, and a dozen regional dialects.

"How'd you get goatsuckered?" Toucan asked.

"Planned it, rather, created conditions for it. I had six bozos looking for martyr fame in the jihad, low-level soldiers, my personal security escort and my being a woman they didn't exactly take the mission seriously. Along the way I talked to a little bird who talked to a bigger bird, and like that, result: goatsuckers blowing doors and charging the room."

"Risky plan."

"If I didn't take this chance, I would be dead in place, which is why I'm here and not there. They bring you all the way from the States?"

"Just flew in today. The ultimate hurry-up, quick-fast track." She noticed Firoozi's hand shaking.

Knock on the door: Toucan opened it, a soldier brought in a basket of fresh fruit, put it on the table, about-faced, and departed.

"Your hand," Toucan said, opening her rug, ripping open the cigarette carton. She tossed a pack to Firoozi, who tore it open.

Toucan handed her a lighter.

Firoozi lit up and inhaled deeply. "Goat is great. The locals smoke dry goat dung."

"No they don't."

Firoozi smiled. "It tastes like it." She inhaled again. "Beautiful. Exquisite."

Firoozi's cover was that of a teacher of girls and women. The Taliban forbade any schooling for girls, and at the same time maintained secret madrasas solely for girls. They were taught the Qur'an and science. Only a few people understood the purpose of these schools. It had been Firoozi who learned about them and sought to penetrate one of the operations.

"Your hand is still shaking."

"You should see my soul. We broke the bank, Meta, grabbed the brass ring, bull by the horns, tiger's tail, all that good stuff."

Vague rumors suggested a woman ran the madrasas for girls. They'd heard this for years. "The Head Mistress?"

Firoozi leered. "Herself. I was in Helmond Province, teaching."

The whole idea was for the operative to attract attention, meet people, serve as bait for big Taliban or Al Qaeda fish, though the latter's big shot had mostly run for the hills, literally. "You on the Head Mistress's BFF list now?"

The undercover sighed. "She was 'impressed' by my zeal and my knowledge of *The Book*. She recruited me to create a program where I was. Last year she came back and pulled me out, made me part of her personal security team."

"You've been travelling *with* the Head Mistress?"

"It's awful duty. She covers a lot of ground, moves all the time, on foot or by mule, never in a vehicle. She's afraid of IEDs, can you believe it?"

"Where is she now?"

"Not important where she is. What's important is where she's coming, which is Kabul." Firoozi paused and snorted. "God that sounds like the title to a second-rate Broadway musical, Coming to Kabul!"

"Headed to Kabul for what?"

"Kaboom in Kabul is what for," Firoozi said. "To coincide with US troop withdrawals, destabilize the government's authority, affect public opinion."

"Against us?"

"No, against Afghans only. Karzai's people can't find a hole in a doughnut. They won't get a sniff of the Head Mistress until she's long gone."

"Can we steer the Afghans?"

"You can't steer incompetence and what secret stays thus in this country? Neither the ANP nor the ANSF can be trusted with anything. Largely shit national unit doesn't erase tribal and clan underpinnings."

"Does the Head Mistress know what happened to you?"

"There's no way to know what she knows. You know how information moves in this country. What I hoped she'd see was that I was snatched in a routine raid."

"Your escorts are all dead."

"That may be a better scenario. One woman with five escorts. It would make sense to grab the woman if you killed all the escorts, just to find out why she was there. I'm hoping that's how it gets read."

Toucan needed to think. Speck Ops ran missions every night and rarely announced results, the only exception being high value targets.

Firoozi took a deep drag on a cigarette. "I can't go back, Meta. I'm done with that undercover shit. It's not in me to pull it off anymore."

"Have you got tactical details on what's coming?"

"No, somebody needs to replace me."

Meta Toucan stared at her colleague and friend. "No way I could pull this off."

"Don't play the girl and undersell yourself," Firoozi said. "You can do this. You have to."

"I wouldn't know where to begin."

"But I do and I'll draw the map. I have the key to the Head Mistress."

"You do?"

"Damn right I do."

"I can't even pretend to be a teacher of Islam."

"That's not your mission."

The women looked at each other.

"You want the key?" Firoozi asked.

"She have an organization?"

"No and that's her strength *and* her weakness, just her and three security escorts, all women. Low footprint. Sometimes they also have Taliban escorts, but usually they go and do all on their own. This country makes most women invisible and they don't really need elaborate extra security. Less is more."

"Why any security at all?"

"That's a great question," Firoozi said. "You ever hear of a MacGuffin?"

"Golden Arches offering?"

"A plot device for movie writers. You point everything at finding the MacGuffin to the exclusion of all other things."

"That's supposed to be the key?"

"The key is, there is no MacGuffin."

"The Head Mistress is the MacGuffin, is that what you're saying?"

"Three-card Monte, find the red queen. My BFF security girl is the Head Mistress, but she pretends to be just one of the girls. The others are decoys, one of them wrapped in a suicide vest with my girl carrying the trigger."

"That makes for a tough get," Toucan said. "They make you wear the vest?"

"They all take turns."

"That sucks, makes her ungettable."

Firoozi shrugged. "Irrelevant. We kill her, her shit ends there. All her little girl-bombers will boogie. From what I saw and managed to learn, the Head Mistress wants only mentally challenged kids, no older than nine. She tells them they're helping their families, and leaves God and martyrdom out of it. The Head Mistress is smart. She knows you have to deal differently with women than with men. Unlike men, girls rarely kill for ideology."

"Is there a pipeline of bombers?"

"She claims it, but the kids she wants are damn few and far between. If she disappears I think the threat disappears."

"What I hear you saying is that there's no point in my replacing you if we can take out the Head Mistress in Kabul. How?"

"The wonderful world of human incendiary devices. Light her own personal candle."

"Is she turnable?"

"Negative. She's a total whack job, Meta. End of story."

"Seems like she'd jack up security coming into Kabul."

"She thinks Kabul is clown camp and Karzai the head clown, a total tool and fool. She's convinced she's invisible and to those few who might recognize her, the vest deters."

"Is the Head Mistress vested?"

"Are you *kidding*? She wants no part of meeting Allah. She's interested only in killing infidels."

"And you know where she'll enter the city."

"I did. I'm supposed to meet her."

"She won't suspect something?"

"She might, but like I said, escort dead, woman found, it makes sense they'd take me away and then release me after they figured I had nothing to do with the dead guys. I think I'm okay on this."

"Where's she coming in?"

"The riverbed, coming up from the southwest."

Toucan knew that the Kabul River this time of year was reduced to a series of meager, pestilential pools and puddles. The walled river in the city served as a dumping ground for garbage, trash, human waste, and bodies. "I'll probably have to take this up the line. We're saying we want to whack, not detain the Head Mistress."

"Unless you want to try to replace me."

"No way I can cut it. I'll take this to Romano."

"You want an argument? Here it is. Where will it stop? The Head Mistress is hardcore. She gets off on killing."

Toucan cringed. Some Afghan men joked female suicide was the devil's work, a form of getting off because most women couldn't get enough earthly sex, which is why they had to be hidden to keep from inadvertently lighting male fires. "Joe needs to know," Toucan said. "He'll know how high to take it."

Firoozi yawned, and lit another cigarette.

"What size are you these days?" Toucan asked. "I think you used to be a six."

"Still am, I think."

She watched her friend put on her burka again and left her in the room. She asked to see the IC Hugh's duty officer, who turned out to be a captain. "I need a secure phone."

The captain took her to a room with a phone and she called Colonel Romano and reported the whole thing.

"You ever do anything like this before?"

"No sir."

"I can send a Spec Ops team. You guys ID, they hit."

"Less chance they'll make just the two of us."

"Probably a better chance they'll wax your fannies, too. Firoozi's a psycho, three years undercover, in this fucking place? God almighty. You need a ride?"

"Tonight, after dark, her and me, full uniform for her, size six."

"Boots?"

"Her sizes should be somewhere in the system. Small also six, maybe seven."

"Done. I'm not taking this up the line until I talk to the both of you, understood?"

"Yes sir, tonight."

Toucan explained to the other major what lay ahead.

"The shit I had to do out there," Firoozi said wistfully. "I'm done."

• • •

A hood for Firoozi on egress, in case anyone was watching. In Afghanistan it made sense to assume eyes and ears were everywhere and invisible, which they were. Mostly they didn't need fancy electronics. Tribal societies were adept at reading behaviors in order to ascertain intent. This ability was impressive. And scary.

Firoozi changed into BDUs on the chopper, said, "These feel *so* good!"

"Boots when we get there," Toucan said. "Or tomorrow."

Romano listened without interruption. Firoozi did most of the talking.

"How did you get under my radar without me knowing you were there?" he asked when she was done.

Toucan said, "NTK, sir."

"I didn't *need* to know this?" the colonel asked incredulously.

"No sir, you didn't. But we want you to make an announcement."

"What is it?"

"Six ECs killed in a raid, a suspected high value female captured, but escaped three days ago, reward for information, the usual boilerplate."

"We're not taking this upstairs," Colonel Romano said. "Topside didn't find the Head Mistress, didn't even know for sure she existed. You found her, you take her out."

• • •

All night before the event she is remembering a meeting in Gaylord. Toucan alone on one side of the table, the field captain and the Wildlife

Resource Protection Unit lieutenant on the other side, the questioning muted, unenthusiastic, and she read between the lines, the decision already made before she even walked into the room. She wasn't in the running. It was her gift to be able to read people and it was a double-edged sword. Had she gotten the job, she would not be in Kabul again. They would have pressured her to resign from the Guard. Firoozi would be out there alone. Everything in life had a reason, even when we couldn't see it.

The mission plan was devoid of subtlety. Make contact, kill the Head Mistress and her entourage, don't even think about prisoners. Kill the main target first, hope she wasn't hooked to some sort of deadman's switch detonator.

The stench of the riverbed was at its highest. There were women in burkas all along the trickle of water, a kaleidoscope of blues and blacks and reds, all masked and invisible.

Green plastic bin ahead of them. Firoozi said, "Three women, all black."

"You're sure?"

"One wears red shoes. Vanity dies hard. That's her." Firoozi touched her face screen and the three figures immediately rushed toward her, red shoe in the lead.

The two soldiers pulled FN SCAR STD rifles with 13-inch barrels from slits in the folds of their dresses and opened up.

They had practiced for days, now spent three rounds each on target one, two each on the other two, the whole thing rolling out in Slo-Mo and Toucan saw women behind the targets scrambling for cover. Three down, Major Meta Toucan took a C-4 charge with a timing detonator set for one minute, dropped it on the body with red shoes.

The two women ran hard, counting in their heads and suddenly dropped face down as the explosive went, and in igniting the vest on one of the women stimulated an even bigger bang. They doubled back. The hole was four feet deep, a dozen feet across. Nothing left but rag scraps floating.

Four days later, both women left Kabul in a Medevac flight headed for Ramstein AB, near Kaiserslautern, Germany.

• • •

"This work can be dangerous," a lieutenant colonel told them. They were in a nondescript building at the air base. Had come in the night before, housed in the BOQ, fetched to a meeting this morning.

Firoozi remained for more debriefings prior to reassignment.

Toucan caught a flight back to the World.

• • •

Gaylord again, another meeting in the regional office with the WRPU lieutenant and the captain. Toucan's body was still somewhere between Kabul and the world, and she had been asked to attend a brief meeting at the airport in Washington D.C. on the way back. "That was a faster than normal deployment. Glad you're back," the captain said. "We wanted to talk about your application for the detective position."

The lieutenant took over. "Not everyone is built psychologically to work off the grid. It may look romantic from a distance, but not so much when you're in the soup. The reality is unsettling to most people."

Were these fools for real? "Most people. Does that mean most men and women or most men, or just most women?"

The lieutenant looked warily at her. "Men and women."

"And you know this how?"

"Beg your pardon?" the lieutenant said.

"How many women have served as detectives in your unit? Ever?"

"Uh."

"None," she said. "Shame on you guys."

"There will be other openings," the lieutenant said.

"Not for me. I can read tea leaves better than most people."

"You shouldn't assume."

"I'm not assuming or waiting. I'm retiring."

"To do what?"

"The Feds have recruited me."

"What Feds?" the captain asked.

(The offer made in D.C. had made her laugh out loud and she had accepted on the spot.) "Sorry sir, NTK, Need To Know. I'm not at liberty to say."

"Have you thought this through?" the lieutenant asked.

"Thoroughly."

"What if we offered you the detective job right now, today?"

"I'd ask if I get to kill bad guys and you two would hem and haw and I'd say no thanks. Omaha. Blue."

"What the devil does that mean?" the captain asked. "Omaha what?"

"Time's up," she said, getting to her feet.

Dogskin, the Olympian

"Mom, Dad?" No response. *Where's the dog? And what's with the house temperature? It's fricking sweltering in here.*

Conservation Officer Cindy Poquette had stopped by while on patrol, hoping to score a bowl of soup and check in with her folks. They were in their seventies now, and exhaustingly busy. Where do they find such energy?

She checked the thermostat. Eighty-one! Jesus, this costs them big time. *What is with those two?* She was tempted to reduce the heat on principle, but her eccentric parents usually had reasons for everything they did, reasons she as their daughter and only child invariably found wanting.

Eccentric? Was that the right word? Weird, actually. Dad had changed his name from Harry to Dogskin in the sixties. Her mother Annalee had been know as Dancing Tulip in those days. They had boxes and albums filled with photographs. Annalee unabashedly adored her husband. Every time he came into a room she'd sigh and fan herself with her hand, say, "Oh Lord God the testosterone surf is up." As their daughter she had to force herself not to heave or gag. *How can I be so fricking normal and they so . . . not?*

The names alone made her cringe. Dogskin because her father was hirsute to the nth degree, as hairy as a German shepherd in its winter coat. Even dad's shoulders were hairy, covered entirely by what looked like hand-hooked needlework. "Source of his power," her mother would whisper. She had no idea what her mother meant; didn't want to know. *I'm thirty-eight and this is my quandary, not that age has anything to do with it, causatively or correlatively. It was just that I expected to be more comfortable with the whole thing by now. But no, not even close, and this has been bothering me for my entire life.*

Leave or look around? Mom and Dad never left without telling her first so that she could watch over their lake cabin. In winter she drove in with her snowmobile to make sure there were no break-ins. They went down to Arkansas in winter, to fish for trout, they said. Both of them were crazy about trout.

What if one of the local whackadoodles have busted in on them? *This is Iron Mountain after all. It might not be Motown, but we have our own black tar heroin, weed, rock cocaine, speed, homemade crank, the whole menu for fucked-up stew. Doesn't look like they're gone, but where are they?*

Upstairs a screaming, drawn-out shriek was followed by a bellowing yell and then an elongated, ululating wolf-howl, like a dog losing its mind and all of this just up the stairs, which she flew up as the screaming continued from their bedroom. "Mommy, Dad!" The screaming and howling continued. She tried the door handle. Locked. Odd. She pulled her Sig Sauer from its holster with her right hand and crushed the door open with her left shoulder, stepping into the room with the semi-automatic up and ready, the old axiom, never look where you aren't pointing your weapon.

She looked at the bed, saw both of her parents nude and on top of the covers, her mother astride her father, both of them shiny with sweat. Their dog, Butch Cassidy, ran over to her to be petted.

"Mom? Jesus!" she said. "I mean . . . *Jesus.*"

"We're doing nothing wrong, immoral, unethical or illegal," her father said as her mother rolled off him and lay beside him.

"Good God," their daughter said. "Cover yourselves. You had the dog so upset he was howling. I mean why is Butch even *in* here?"

"Butch is our timer," her father barked happily at her. "What the hell is wrong with you, girl?"

"*Me? What's wrong with ME?*"

"There's no need for that tone, or volume," her mother said calmly. "It's Butch's job," her mother concluded in her sweetest estrogenic voice.

"His job, the *dog* has a job? Since when?" They are *certifiable*. *They are. BOTH of them.*

"He times us and howls every forty-five minutes," Annalee said. "Why don't you go downstairs, sugar plum, and I'll come down and make your favorite grilled cheese Sammy. I have a fresh batch of corn chowder I can warm up."

"Good grief," Cindy said.

"Sex is our gig, our thing," her father said. "Always was, always will be. With luck we'll *die quasi cuniculorum fornicatione.*"

"Sex is *not* a gig, not a thing," Cindy argued.

"We'll have to agree to disagree, sugar plum," her mother said.

"I should go, I'm sorry I interrupted your . . . I should go."

"No, stay," her dad said. "Please?"

Her father was annoying as hell, irritating, self-assured, a real ass. He had been a paratrooper in Vietnam and a hippie after his discharge. He never said anything about combat, though she had found a Silver Star in a box once. All he would talk about were the screwed up logistics. "FUBAR," he'd yelp. "Fucked Up Beyond All Recognition." In the early seventies her dad opened a military surplus store in Warren, near Detroit, and the business had grown to twenty-five cities. He'd sold the business ten years back and media had reported the sale price at an estimated $200 million, but she didn't know exactly how much. Her folks paid no attention to money, never talked about it, lived a simple life in a simple house, drove a Ford. Dad's hobby had been militaria and over the years he had collected enough to fill a thirty-thousand-square-foot pole building. The collection was being added to on a regular basis and there was a man named Sam who was their on-site appraiser. Her dad had left high school in the eleventh grade, but loved Latin, which he tended to spout when he was overstimulated, happy, sad, or mad.

She went downstairs, took off her duty belt, and hung it over a chair back. She sat at the kitchen table trying to calm herself, saw the five-gallon jug in the corner, still full of half-dollar coins. Those quarters had made her rich during elementary school at St. Skosh. Several times a week her dad would grab a hand full of the coins, walk out on the back porch, fling them into the woods and yell, "Coin hunt!" and she would scramble out to search for them, never stopping until she found all twenty of them, which made for a five-dollar reward, huge for a kid. But sometimes she found them quickly and went back up on the porch and found the door locked and she'd yell and yell and nobody would open it and finally she learned to take a seat and wait until somebody remembered her and opened the door again. She'd tried the front door a couple of times, but that was always closed too. Weird, but lucrative, and she liked to think that her ability to find the half-dollar coins had in some way helped her be more observant and helped her to develop the skills she needed for a career as a conservation officer.

Her mother came downstairs in a diaphanous kimono and red mules

"*Mom!*"

"What?"

"You two need to act your age."

"We are. We're the new forty."

"You're pushing the old eighty."

"Oh honey, you've always been such a horrible prude. Not that we would demean you for that. We love our little girl."

"Your little girl is thirty-eight now."

"We still love you."

Her father joined them. "Your mother's right, our little prude. It was always well . . . cute. Honestly we thought you'd grow out of it and be more like us in your full womanhood."

"You two! Do you have any idea what the neighbors think of such goings-on?"

Mother Annalee said, "Of course I know what they think. Ginny, Karla, Judy, Brenda, Ruth, they all want to know what I feed your dad, and they all want the recipes."

She reached for her duty belt.

"Stay stay," her dad implored with his hangdog look. "It was time for a break. We're between sets."

Arching an eyebrow at her father. "Sets, what kind of sets?"

"You know, two-a-day training."

Mulling this, she asked, "You mean . . . you . . . have sex twice a day?"

"No," her mother said. "We make love a lot more than that, but in two two-hour sessions a day. It's fun and healthy."

Felt her jaw drop as her mother rambled on. "Well it's always been twice a day, hasn't it, when you were growing up, unless Dogskin could get home for a nooner. We *loved* our nooners in those days."

"Don't forget after-schools," the father said. "Those were the *best*."

"After-schools?"

Her mother looked from her daughter to the big glass jar and squealed, "Coin hunt!"

She felt nauseous. "That was about *sex*?"

"You never figured it out?" her mother asked.

"Training for what?"

"You attitude is just why we haven't told you," her mother said. "We knew you'd be upset. We're training for the senior world sex games."

Her father added, "For Branson, next May, it's a huge deal. It's not open to anyone. You have to qualify."

Mommy said, "It's like ice-dancing, you know, without the ice?"

I don't want to hear this, she told herself. Then, *yes I do*. "I don't get it."

"You have to perform at a sanctioned qualifying meet," her father said.

"Qualify, like compete for a score?"

"Oh yes," her mother said, "and the style judges are very exacting."

"We're ranked number one in the Eight Decade Class," her father said, "but the judges are talking about elevating us up to the championship flight to compete for the overall gold."

She had to think this through, calmly. My mother and father . . . "People . . . uh . . . watch . . . uh you . . ."

Her mother said, "Fucking? Of course, sugar plum. How else could they judge our style?"

Am I really having this conversation with these people. With my parents. If they are my parents? "Do you like, send them a video?"

Her mother laughed. "No honeybunch, it's a live competition and timed on a sanctioned competition bed."

She hefted her duty belt and buckled it in place around her hips. She stumbled toward the back door trying not to break down in tears.

Her father followed her outside in his skivvies and L. L. Bean moose-hide slippers. "When God gives you a gift," he said, "you have to use it or lose it, *deus autem dat gratiam te ute vel perdiderit.*"

She looked back at him from her truck, a gaunt skeleton of a man matted in dark hair, Sasquatch on the back porch. "You are not *my* parents," she said out loud, threw the truck in gear, stomped the accelerator, and burned rubber racing away from the house.

Game for Names

"Norge, your name is Norge?" The probie was a tall drink of water, not the slightest bit gangly, but snake-eyed, cold snake eyes.

"Right, Norge, Margethe, they call me Mossa."

"Do snakker norsk giordu?"

"I barely speak English," Norge said, shaking her head. "I know people who speak Norwegian, but never had the urge myself."

Rule out Norwegian heritage as common ground. "Yut-yut, Didi Kort," the woman said. "Your field training officer."

"They told me I'd have Kenny Kander for Phase Three. I had him in the first go around."

"Yut, plans do sometimes change. The Viper got tagged by Lansing for something more important, and they assigned you to me. You can think of me as Kenny if it makes you happy."

"Doesn't matter who, I guess. Do I address you as FTO?"

"Only if you want to really annoy me. Just call me Didi. Phase Three, you understand the rules?"

Norge nodded. "I have the principal responsibility to do the job and you observe and step in only to save my butt, which is why you're in civvies."

"Are you feeling nervous?" Kort asked. The recruit looked like she'd never been nervous about anything.

"I don't think so."

"You're either nervous or you're not. Nervous is like pregnant."

"I guess I'm not nervous."

"Listen Norge, I'm going to give it to you straight. The truth is that you're a controversial figure. Great skills, maybe even unmatched at this stage, but you're a loner and that's put the serious bother on everyone in Lansing. You're a serious, no-mix, no-blend, no-help loner. You ring all their alarm bells."

"No help?"

"Other recruits say you don't step in. No initiative, no teamwork."

"I thought the idea was to graduate on our own merits to establish we can each carry the load."

"Well, I guess that's right, but what about all the officers who haven't been to the academy. Will you assume they don't need your help?"

"I haven't assumed anything. They made a big issue about weeding out people who can't do the job and most of the things we do down there are scored individually, not with other cadets."

Kort, fifteen years in uniform and not a DNR Academy graduate thought: *A bit of emotion in that response. I just touched something. Promising.*

"The job requires self-starting, initiative," Norge said.

"Yut-yut, but it's more than that. You have to be there for others and they have to be there for you. That's the bottom line for all of us. It's like marriage without sex. Tell me what happened with Bailyn."

Norge shrugged, didn't answer right away.

"I'm not the Inquisition," Kort said. "Just curious. It's getting a head up toward a legend. A woman kicks a male cadet's ass and then he resigns. That shit just does *not* happen."

Norge sighed. "They had us boxing. Bailyn came up one bracket and me up the other. I watched him crush his opponents, knew he was a lot stronger than me. I went right at him, put a shot on his Adam's apple, one to his guts and an uppercut to his jaw, and over and down he went."

"Out cold, the story goes."

"Yes."

"The story is you cheated."

Norge frowned. "There's no cheating in a street fight. There's win fast or get murdered, nothing in between."

"Nobody knew you boxed professionally."

"Only eight fights."

"All of which you won by knockouts we subsequently learned. You never mentioned professional boxing during interviews. It came right out of left field and it's left people wondering what the hell else you've kept back. Trust is at stake in this, Norge."

"I needed money. I used another name. My friends, family, nobody knew. I fought in Illinois, near Chicago."

"Why the secret?"

"It was personal."

"You could have kept on fighting?"

"I fought enough, made the purse money I needed. I was done. Is this a problem?"

"Is it?"

"I did nothing illegal, immoral or unethical."

"You never told anyone about it when you were supposed to lay out your entire background during interviews."

"I never told the interviewer about the first blowjob I gave my boyfriend either, so obviously there must be some sort of reasonable limit in what one must reveal."

Kort couldn't help chuckling. "Point taken. You married?"

"No."

"Ever?"

"Never."

"Boyfriend?"

"None of your business."

"Ah a girlfriend then."

"Same answer, what the hell is going on?"

Kort thought. Direct and tightly wound. The report she got was that Norge was near the top of the class in everything, physical and mental, and on those parameters she looked topnotch, but everyone around her and above her questioned her group commitment. Won't or can't play with others, the report said. Stayed on her own on weekends, never mixed with others at night, kept her nose in the books. Twenty-seven years old, four-year Army vet, college grad with a 3.8 GPA and a major in criminal justice, all-conference basketball player three years, 170 pounds of sinew and muscle. Perfect on paper, but she gave off vibes that kept people at a distance. She feels okay to me.

Captain Pete Kalvelidge called her two days ago. "We're putting you in for Kander."

"What's wrong with him?"

"Nothing, but you're a tougher FTO and we need this probie under the microscope, see if she can handle the job. My guess is that she'll fold the first time the feces fly. Push her hard, no mercy. She either measures up, or she doesn't."

Kort had hung up and opened a beer. Kalvelidge's attitude is a solid mark in Norge's favor. The captain is a douchebag, a conference room warden with minimal field experience. He earned quick promotions because he was glib by half and unusually facile with numbers. Kort couldn't stand to be in the same room with the man, and to most officers with their boots in the dirt every day, he was less than dirt, totally lacking their respect as a person. Only his rank got respect, and that for order and nothing else.

"Fall," Kort said. "We ought to find something shaking."

"We? I thought you're along just in spy mode."

Whew, sharp, fast tongue, weak filter maybe. "Figure of speech, Norge."

"Kings are in and on their redds," Norge said.

"And you know this how?"

"I checked rivers on my way up here yesterday to meet you."

Good initiative. "Where should we go?"

"Slapback River."

"You looked there? Most people don't even know about that one."

"I heard talk in Lansing."

"You looked at the Slapback? That's usually last to catch king runs."

"They're in thick now."

"Where, by the parking area?"

"No. They're downstream about a half mile in all those S-curves, just upstream of the Old Fed Book School."

"Why there?"

"It's a long hike from parking, and there's no easy way to cut off escape. The snaggers'll be drinking and doping and tired when they get back to their rides."

Impressive. "We call that Batboy Bend, a real magnet for outlaws. Hit them after dark?"

"No, in broad daylight when we can see best. They'll be there."

"They'll have watchers."

"Not on the other side of the river."

"Too deep to cross."

"Not if you know the area."

"How the hell would you know?"

"Had a friend in college. We used to come over here to fish for trout and hunt birds. Her grandfather has a camp not far from the S-curves, on the far side."

"This too never came out in an interview," Kort said.

"Well mea fuckin' culpa," Norge said. "I'm also skeptical about God. That didn't come out either. So what?"

• • •

Three hours and they watched three different crews, and Norge was about to move in and take fish when Kort saw a new crew wander up the river, herking and jerking away with leaded hooks. "Fuck," she whispered. "Bryce Hoff."

"Who is?"

"Suspect in a Houghton murder. He disappeared about six months ago," Kort explained, squeezing her probie's arm. "Hoff's one sick puppy, a very dangerous dude. He looks like Howdy-Doody and has the heart of Charlie Manson. There's an officer warning on him. Approach with no fewer than three badges."

"Are you telling me we should bypass this jerk simply because a paper says we need another officer?"

"What do you think?"

"I think the woods and rivers are our house, Didi. This asshole's wanted for murder, not ganking hubcaps. I say we take down his ass. I checked the duty list earlier today. Logan's on right now, up county a bit. I'll call him and ask him to roll down here to back us up. He can meet us in the parking area."

"Why there? Hoff is here."

"My show, right?"

Kort wasn't all that certain. Hoff in the mix changes everything. Doesn't it?

"Uh, okay."

"We take him in the parking lot as he goes to get into his vehicle. If we try grab him on the river or in the woods and we miss, we'll have a hell of a time finding him. We'd need a dog and a lot of manpower. But if we wait and converge on him in the parking lot, let him get almost to his vehicle, he's contained, and all his chances and options are reduced."

"He'll be armed."

"We assume," Norge said.

"No, we *know*. This asshole is always armed. Always."

"You know him?"

"Pinch him several times, illegal bear, illegal deer, timber theft, he always fights and he's always packing at least a knife or two. Take a damn good look at him," Kort told her partner.

"He's a big guy ," Norge said.

"The further one goes north the bigger the mammals grow," Kort said. "Do not let that piece of shit get hold of you. He's unpredictable and erratic and his temper is downright bloody."

"The plan sounds all right to you?"

She's asking for input? This is good. "Well, other than having to deal with Mr. Bryce Hoff, it seems good. Yut-yut, let's do it."

Norge used her 800 mhz to call Logan, who immediately agreed to help them.

Hoff had a spinning rod and was flinging lead fifty yards at a gulp, tearing up fish he hooked in the sides as he reefed on the rod, bending it double, hooking the fish with muscular twitches making the leaded hook shoot along the bottom. They could hear the line swishing out on the cast, the reel barking, the squealing against the drag when a fish was on and being dragged.

"Quick," Norge told her FTO. "There's two trails, one along the river and a less distinct one further inland. You take the close one and I'll take the other and we'll meet in the parking area by the road. Your trail hits a pile of boulders, but get off the trail there, and circle around in the water to the trail on the other side. Too easy to get surprised in the rocks."

"You really *do* know this place," Kort said. "Our boy's busy—behind us."

"Go around the rocks in the river. You said this guy is erratic and we don't know for sure where he is right now."

Cautious, maybe too much so. Need to keep an eye on this. Could be the first sign of cracking. Some candidates looked fine in training, but melted in reality.

Norge showed Kort the shallow ford and they hurried across. Norge kept going inland and Kort turned on the riverside trail.

• • •

There was a black state CO truck pulled up on the road near the parking area. Norge moved on the truck. Logan was called Logjam by other officers for reasons unknown. *This juvenile fixation on nicknames rubbed her entirely wrong, more evidence of a frat-house culture suffusing the largely male conservation officer corps. Nicknames. How lame.*

"Kort's on the river trail," she told Logan. She'd met him briefly twice before.

"Whachyouses got going?"

"Bryce Hoff snagging down at Badboy Bend."

Logan said, "That makes my day complete. That *asshole*. Why aren't we downstream?"

"Grab him at his vehicle, limit his options, hem him in. Too much space for him to run on the river or in the woods."

Norge activated her radio. "Two One Sixty, Two One Forty, copy?"

No answer. She felt hairs go up on her arms and the back of her neck.

Logan stared at her. "Call backup," she said.

Logan was immediately on the radio, requesting help.

Norge cut through the parking lot to a row of pickups nearest the river trail. All but one was pointed downstream, only one truck backed in and pointed out. The exception was a rusty white Jeep Grand Cherokee. The Jeep had a red rear pull-up door, and a brown driver's door.

She was surprised by Kort's silence, and worried. She toyed with calling again, but decided against it. She took a post near the back of the Jeep and listened on her radio as county deputies began streaming toward the area.

She looked down the trail and saw nothing and a moment later saw Bryce Hoff. He had Kort by the neck and was dragging her, her toes bouncing off the ground.

Norge said into her radio, "One, One Forty has a visual on One, One Sixty. The suspect has her. Tell all vehicles to come in quiet, no lights or music."

"One One Fifty Eight clear."

She heard the calls going out from the county dispatcher to deps as she watched Hoff moving with Kort toward the truck.

Kort's hair and face are bloody. Her body is bent like a rag doll and she's not resisting, which suggests she's stunned, her brain not hitting on all cylinders. Get back into cover and take a knee. The giant Hoff went right in front of her and grabbed at the rear door, slapped Kort several times, and chucked her in back. He's laughing. Whoa. Move deliberately, don't let your temper go.

She moved on him as the man tried to get into the driver's seat. He had Kort's pistol and she was somewhere in back. Norge caught him with a punch in the temple, but he somehow slid on down into the seat, got the key in the ignition and started engine. She had hold of him through the driver's window and kept punching him over and over and over, all to the side of his head, but the Jeep surged forward and the door was still open and she got her left arm hooked on the window frame and kept punching up at the man's throat with her right fist as the vehicle veered and she nearly let go, but he shot out onto the gravel road and accelerated. When he steadied the Jeep, he reached over and tried to mash her left hand and she got a punch into his nose sideways and blood shot out and then they were fishtailing and she was sure they were dead, but Hoff somehow righted the vehicle on the gravel until he hit something hard and the vehicle bucked into the air and she was hanging on, knowing if he shed her she was going to get hurt bad. Hang on, don't let go, look for an opportunity. Focus on him, nothing else.

The Jeep was semi-airborne and swerving. Her mind was clear, all life now in the slowest of motion. She managed to bend her right knee up to her chest and get her backup .38 out of her boot holster as Hoff slashed at her with a huge knife, and she yelled "Conservation officer, stop!" He kept driving, she yelled again and then calmly pulled the trigger. Pulled it twice. The Jeep hit some sort of obstacle and flipped onto the passenger side, slid through a marsh area, and no matter how hard she tried to get inside or to let go, she seemed attached to the damn thing. This is not so good, was her final thought.

• • •

Ambulances, EMT vehicles, state police cruisers, deputies in SUVs, the dull day illuminated red, white and blue. Norge and Kort were slumped on the lip of an EMT truck. Norge's back hurt like hell, both of her legs were torn up by the dragging, and a med tech was picking gravel out of her right knee and shin. Her right hand was bandaged.

"Knife cut," the EMT said. "Not serious. It'll stitch fine."

"Okay," Kort said in a business-as-usual tone. "Critique for Day One, Phase Three: Get to your partner sooner and if you have to shoot another asshole like Hoff, blow his fucking head off."

"I was aiming for his head when we hit that last bump," Norge said.

"Don't make excuses."

"How'd I grade out on being there for others?" Norge asked.

Kort said, "What do those assholes in Lansing know. You all right Mossa?"

"Been better, Didi."

"Can't do no better than come home alive at the end of your shift," Kort said.

Logan stood with them, listening, looking worried and relieved. "Balls," he said.

"Beg your pardon?" Norge said.

"Your new name, it's Balls."

"I like the one my folks gave me better."

"This one you had to earn," Logjam said.

She smiled inwardly. Maybe this nickname thing isn't so juvenile after all.

Two-riffic

"You'd write Jesus a ticket for fishing without a license," Brother John said with a pained yelp.

"What's your point?"

John had legally changed his name at age eighteen to Turk and started his own church, the Church of Christian Compassion in the Here and Now. He had gotten a minister's license over the Internet. Jerrilyn Virtue thought Turk an odd name for a Christian minister, but Brother John was not one for hearing criticism or suggestions, especially from women. He saw his mission and job as directing, steering, and whipsawing the unenlightened, a category that included his eldest sister, the cop (yuck).

Despite his holier-than-thou superiority and her pushiness, Jerrilyn loved him. All right, it seemed dumb, but Turk was an actual and ardent believer in the achievability of world peace, forgiveness, golden rules and all that other goody two-shoes stuff. It rankled Turk that his sister was in law enforcement, carried a handgun, pepper stray, a taser, baton, and cuffs. What rankled him most, she suspected, was that she could arrest and charge lawbreakers and he could only rail at those outside his rules. Sheer envy, she thought, which made it funnier. And sadder. Poor Turk.

"'Member, sis, compassion. We are all God's creations, all his children. Not every lawbreaker is a criminal. Most of us innocently make mistakes. Even the dishonest make honest mistakes."

"Love the mistake-maker, hate the mistake, right?"

"Amen, Sis. Go forth with forgiveness in your heart."

And my ticket book close by, she thought. Some people did make innocent mistakes, but these were easy to identify. Many others, however, knew exactly what they were doing and some days it was so many more than many, approaching the extreme wall of all, every damn contact she had would be way off the reservation and by steely-eye choice, not chance, accident, or serendipity.

Today was supposed to be a marine patrol day, all day in her boat on the big lake, but it was raining a soft warm rain and she knew the worm dunkers would be drowning garden hackle in pursuit of fat brook trout in the cricks, and so it was she spent her day looking for trout-cheaters and arranged her day's route so as to arrive tonight at a moose marsh she had found last fall, and had been watching for the last month.

There was a huge bull in the area. She'd seen him a half dozen times in the month, always at the break of dark into night. Last night she had walked out closer to the marsh and bumped into a shooting shack erected on a four-foot berm to give the shooter a full look at the open marsh, the perfect view, a shack situated by someone who knew what he was doing.

It wasn't enough that all the local rabbit and bird hunters hated wolves because they feared for their hounds and dogs, but those same people considered area moose to be community pets.

To whack moose in these parts was akin to homicide. Local and summer folk alike treated the odiferous creatures as royalty, even to the point of naming them. Pearlie. Big Horns, Betty Luna and her calves Ulrich and Uta. It was insane. Names for moose, for God's sake. Ridiculous.

Over in Thwart Lakes, Ronette Pare of Hot Ron's Pasty Post had a three-county wall map covered with acetate. Every morning Ron and the locals met to mark the locations of sighted moose. They were tracking twenty different animals and every morning over coffee you could get great directions to see one of the giant animals.

Tourists and summer people could be a pain in the ass. Over a dozen years she had gotten pretty good at predicting the behavior of certain locals, not all of them and not all the time, but enough that it became a deterrent by putting them off balance. Locals had reasons for doing things, but tourists and summer folk were prone to just doing, on the spur of the moment, pure impulse creatures, they were often trouble. There was no way to predict them.

It was as if crossing into the Upper Peninsula sucked out peoples' brains. She sometimes fantasized having a huge cinderblock building on US 2 outside St. Ignace with a sign, Visitor Brain Storage Service Here. Rates by Day, Week, or Month.

Nobody had been in the shooting shack last night, but today was Saturday and she guessed the would-be wrong-doers might indeed be installed. The blind itself was new, homemade, but beautifully engineered, she guessed it could be popped up in five minutes or less and it was substantial. Best camo job she'd ever seen, designed to make it look like cattails, both spectacular and effective. Blind on a moose marsh, definitely a place to sit on Saturday night.

Might just be a photographer, but her gut said no.

• • •

Bad skeets tonight. It was August now and they should be mostly gone, but this was a wet summer and there had been an unpredicted, unexpected second hatch, and this crowd seemed particularly pesky and carnivorous. Still, it was summer and not February, drowning in a three-hundred-inch snow accumulation, the kind of weather that caused snowmobilers to check their tiny brains before mounting their high-speed toys.

Virtue stashed her truck a half-mile from her destination and made her way across a massive beaver dam flooding and halfway across she came nose to nose with a pair of wolves, who turned tail and ghosted away from her, looking back now and then. This was prime wolf rendezvous country where the packs taught cubs to kill by starting them on beaver.

Nice and dark when she reached the blind, and it surprised her to see a handicapped van with a hydraulic lift door/entrance. The front had a small bench seat and the steering wheel in the center of the dash, not on the left side. *Geez. How much did this kind of engineering cost? Geezohpete.* Two large rifle cases were open on the floor behind the driver's seat.

Felt her heart rate pick up. What had Turk said, that even the dishonest could make honest mistakes? The mistake this bozo made was coming into *her* area. Virtue whispered into her 800 mhz radio and ran the plate, which came back to a two-year-old Hummer, not a new Ford van. The owner's name was Galway Twist out of Ann Arbor.

Two rifles likely meant two people. Hard to predict any more than that. Virtue ducked into a cedar line that terminated near the blind, plopped herself on the ground against a tree, and nibbled a strawberry cereal bar.

The blind was not twenty feet away from her and it was eerily quiet. Most people made some kind of sound, even when they were trying to be still, but not tonight. Dead silence. Weird. And also pretty impressive. She didn't have to like what someone was up to in order to begrudgingly admire and respect skills. Virtue and her colleagues trained year-round, man-tracking, hand-to-hand fighting, shooting various weapons, using a boat as an offensive weapon, various drive schools. Conservation officers were defined by so many skills it was hard to squeeze them into an application form. Summer survival, winter survival, first aid, trapping, wilderness survival, all the skills based on what the job required and hammered home by constant unrelenting practice until she could walk into a situation and pluck forth the exact skill she needed.

Still silent in the blind, too much so. Had the shooters bypassed it for another shack located elsewhere? Damn. Get closer, look and listen.

Had on her NVG goggles, which turned the world a sickly green, evanescent, surreal.

The large blind struck her as too large. She fingered a Velcroed flap, eased it open, looked ahead, saw nothing, hunched to enter.

"You're half in," a voice said.

"Half-out," another voice chirped.

"Be of one mind and decide, like a big girl," the first voice said.

"Or not, and hang in the balance, neither in," this from voice two.

"Nor out," said voice one.

"A whisper between within," said voice two.

"And without," voice one concluded.

Jerrilyn Virtue stepped inside, looked left and felt herself blinking wildly, the person before her barely five feet tall, four legs, four arms, an octopus-like thing, two of the arms gripping rifles with night scopes, long tubular silencers, futuristic stuff, like biathlon firearms.

And two heads sort of pressed together.

"Nice weapons," the CO said. "DNR, put your weapons down. Now."

"Name is Sally," said voice one, which Virtue now thought of as Head One.

"I'm Ally," voice two, head two remarked.

This was making her feel badly disoriented, vertiginous . . . need to steady yourself. Get down on one knee, look out on the marsh, ignore the . . . whatever it was. "I don't understand," she said.

"Like relativity," said Sally.

"And evolution," Ally said.

Sally: "We're neither plausible."

Ally: "Nor probable."

Sally: "Biologically feasible, of course."

Ally: "We're the pudding."

Sally: "Of the proof within."

Ally: "Here, not caged in a freak show, free and at large."

Sally: "Like free-range chickens, thanks to Dear Old Daddy."

Ally: "Bless his dearly departed soul."

Sally: "He's with Mum now."

Ally: "In hell, I'd allow."

Sally: "Is God perfect?"

Ally: "As some declare."

Sally: "Or a bungling meddler?"

Ally: "Bunkum peddler."

Sally: "The OB told our Mum."

Ally: "This here thing you've wrought."

Sally: "Is a million to one."

Ally: "'Craniopagus', the doctor said."

Sally: "One in a couple million."

Ally: "Others like us is mostly most severely deceased."

Sally: "Neither Ally nor Sally nosiree."

Virtue was mesmerized. What in the hell is this? Who is this person . . . no, these people . . . oh God help me.

Sally: "We keep on living, whoopee!"

Ally: "They shipped us to Harvard, let it be known."

Sally: "To hoist our petard."

Ally: "Alas and alack, the docs to us did swarm."

Sally: "Yellow Holy Cow! And yowzer, here's a new life-form."

Ally: "Way, way outside the acceptable norm."

Sally: "One in a couple million."

Ally: "Might be a gazillion."

Sally: "They enrolled us on the spot."

Ally: "Without debate or Tommyrot."

Sally: "Told us to study what we will and what we want."

Ally: "Mi casa, su casa, our nurturing haunt."

Sally: "And so we settled in."

Ally: "Academics only, not a hint of sin."

Sally then said as an aside, "Even fantasizing sex."

"Was a great big hex," Ally added.

Sally explained, "Instead of sex we elected to hunt."

Ally said, "Shoot 'em all, big and tall."

The officer shook her head, felt an ache starting to pound just above her forehead. *Need to check those damn weapons, but can't get it together, don't dare move. Girl/girls, joined at the head, good god.* Finally managed to mumble, "I need to see hunting and operator's licenses."

"Why?" Sally asked indignantly.

Ally said, "Seems odd and targeted, aimed at Craniopagate twins specifically, talk about profiling. Not fair, not fair."

"You know we're not identical," Sally announced.

"Yet not entirely different either," Ally said.

"We share a mind," this from Sally.

"Thalamic bridge," Ally explained. "One brain two minds."

"Think," said Sally, "of a circuit board blinking and winking."

"When we say we feel for you," Ally said. "It's physiological."

"Not imagined empathy," Sally pointed out.

"Feel free to stare," Ally said. "Join the crowd."

Sally said, "You'll find us neither cranky nor cowed."

"Licenses, ladies. Please," the officer said.

"It's not as if we have to put up with this intrusion," Sally said.

"We Wags claim Fifty-Six."

"Explain," the CO said to them.

"Amendments Five and Six," Sally wag said.

"Refuse self-incrimination and we shall want a lawyer," Ally said.

"This is not our fault," Sally weighed in, fidgeting and grinning weirdly.

"We're hebephrenics," Ally said. "Schizoids with one personality coming apart. See our giggles and grins, our nervous tics, drool down our chinny chin-chins?"

"Personaliteeze," Sally said. "Two not one."

"If she must second guess," her sister said, "I think we're done."

Sally said, "She always calls us one and knows we're two," turned her eyes to Ally's side, stated, "I am exceptionally very, very, disappointed in you."

Virtue said, "Ladies?"

"*What*?" Sally snapped. "Who raised *you* rude?"

Expounded Ally: "When we get the lawyer we're owed, you can expect to be sued."

"You can't prove we were hunting," Sally pronounced.

Virtue picked up the rifles, unloaded them and sniffed the barrels. Looked through the scopes. She put them out the door opening. The rifles were feather lights, almost weightless.

"Never shot," Sally said.

"Even the breeze," Ally added.

"Much less the moon," Sally said.

"You're both in possession of a firearm without a license. Hunting at night. Illegal night sniper scopes and silencers. The Feds will get on your case for these."

"We say again, Fifty-Six," Sally said.

"That declared, we're done talking," Ally said.

"I don't like all this balking," Virtue said.

The twins grinned Cheshire cat grins.

"How did you plan to harvest a moose?"

The girls were giggling and pinching each other.

"Stop that," Sally cried, "when you pinch me you pinch yourself."

"Such a sham," Ally said. "When you show pain I only feign to feel, my reaction is fake not real."

"Bitch," said Sally.

"Ditto," Ally said.

"Sally and Ally, the Sisters Wag," Virtue said. "You're under arrest, this business here is not a gag."

Sally told the conservation officer, "Now look and see what you've gone and done and all me and Ally wanted was some Saturday night fun."

"The law's the law," Virtue said. "I don't make them, I only enforce them."

Ally said, "The very same thing those Nazis said in Nuremberg, following orders."

"We're the victims," Sally said. "Biology and chance in evolution's dance, a new life form which one day will be good form and the new norm."

"The slings and arrows of outrageous fortune," Ally added.

Virtue asked for Baraga County's assistance, and no deputies were available, but a cop from the Keweenaw Bay Indian Community heard the traffic and rolled in. His name was C. J. Drew, thirtyish, morose, but exceptionally patient in loading the cumbersome Wag sisters into his Tahoe.

The conservation officer got the girls' rifle cases from the van, locked their vehicle and trekked back to her vehicle, stopping to light a cigarette along the way. Her first in a month. It helped calm her. What had Turk said, "We're all God's creations?"

Maybe so, she thought. But sometimes it was a stretch to get to that conclusion.

• • •

Virtue got to the county jail in L'Anse, expecting the sisters to be well into in-processing, but they weren't there, nobody had seen them or the tribal cop. Virtue got on her radio and called, but Drew didn't answer. Had something happened to him, them? She began to worry. An accident?

She drove back out to the site, this time heading to where the van was parked.

No van, no shooting shack, no nothing, everything gone.

"I'll be damned," she said out loud and dialed the tribal police chief.

"C. J. picked up two prisoners for me. He and they never made it to the jail."

"I know," the chief said. "He released them."

"They were my *prisoners*."

"Illegally, you were on tribal land."

"That's bullshit and you know it."

"Doesn't matter Jerri. You push, and the Tribe pushes back, tees it up in mumbojumboland."

She'd been down the tribal legal road before. It rarely went in her favor. "Why, Chief?"

"Them girls is all alone, one of a kind. You'd have to be a tribal to understand."

"They were attempting to kill a moose."

"Did they?"

"No."

"You can't litigate intent or a non-act," the police chief said. "Even under tribal law."

"Night sniper scopes, silencers, no licenses."

"Did you ask to see their tribal cards?"

"Why would I do that?"

"They're Soo Tribe."

"That's bullshit, Chief."

"C. J. says they're real smart cookies, those girls to be like that, and all on their own. You have their rifles?"

She saw where this was going to go. "What rifles?"

"I see," the chief said. "I'll have to have a powwow with your lieutenant in Marquette."

"Knock yourself out."

• • •

Turk was watching *Duck Dynasty* when she got home. "Interesting day, Sis?"

"Same old," she said and went to change out of her uniform.

Facings

Sheer terror had a real face and an intensity that spewed out of the eyes, the lower jaw hanging down, gasping hyperventilation often wracking the victim.

This afternoon CO Steffi Darlecky had dealt with five clear cases of terror, each victim rambling incoherently about "things" in the woods on the county line near Bald Mountain. All five vics had been referred to her by county deputies and she had talked with each one at the sheriff's office in L'Anse.

The five all came from an aging hippie crowd at a compound they called the Happy Valley Association of Free Humans. Darlecky had met several individuals from the compound, and found them so saccharine, just talking to them made her teeth hurt. Worse, they all seemed otherworldly to the extreme state of absolute cluelessness. They schooled their own children, grew their own food, heated with wood, had no electricity and no running water, much less indoor privies. Their water came from two wellheads.

The conservation officer had never been inside the actual compound, had always met the Free Humans wandering elsewhere, almost always disoriented or totally lost and she had seen them back to their gate and gone about her business, no thank yous, no how about a cup of coffee (Free Humans avoided stimulants—of course they did). They marched through the gate and that was that.

She, like deps and local state troopers called them the Creepy Peeps and now she had met five of them, all at the jail, and tried her best to interview them as they sobbed and shook and stared off into the distance with sunken eyes.

Some of this was to be expected from witnesses in any situation: But this time there was so much jugheaded crap and only one point of agreement, that each of them, she eventually concluded, believed they had come face to face with the unspeakable countenance of a monstrosity, which might or might not be humanoid, and was certainly and emphatically in their views, not a candidate for Free Humanhood.

Deputy Clare Charles sat through the interviews with her and afterwards remarked, "You gonna look into it?"

Clare was a nice woman and solid cop. "I make it a point to never look for monsters. They show up often enough on their own."

"What monsters?" Darlecky shot back.

"You didn't hear what those folks were saying?"

"What I heard was a lot of fear and jumbled mumbo jumbo."

"You want to look for evil, it's all yours," Clare said. "Me, my job takes me down other roads."

"You afraid of the dark, Clare?"

"Not afraid, but I don't have a vampire's love for it either."

Vampires? "*Clare.*"

"Just sayin'," the dep said. "You like crawling around in the night, it's all yours."

Ten minutes later Darlecky got cornered by County Board Chairman Theodore Nathaniel Thinnes, who went by TNT. "Jeepers, Darlecky, you gonna let monsters be scaring the pants off our citizens?"

Darlecky knew a lot of female citizens of the county who'd willingly lose their pants over a lot of things before fear.

"I'll drive out that way and take a look-see," she told him.

"Tell you now, girl, I bump one in the woods, it'll get six rounds of 44 mag."

Darlecky rolled her eyes. "Yah, that's smart."

"You need to shoot 'em all, catch 'em in a barrel trap, whatever it takes. You get paid good to protect citizens from this kind of thing."

"For God's sake, we don't even know what this is, or even *if* it is, TNT."

Where did monsters fit into state fish and game laws? She had no clue.

"Just do your job," TNT said, "and if you don't handle it, you can bet I'll be on the horn to your El-Tee in Marquette."

"I would not recommend that call," Darlecky said.

"Why not?" TNT asked.

"Because Lieutenant Tubbs thinks you are a pompous blowhard. He's always telling his officers that if he has to deal with you face to face . . . well, he never says what exactly he'll do, but I'm sure you've heard stories of his temper."

"I heard. Thought it was the usual bull you DNRs spin to keep folks on edge."

"Give Lew that call, find out for yourself."

"You call your superior officer Lew?"

"I was his field training officer. He's like my younger brother."

"Just do something to make the problem go away," TNT said, and sashayed away.

As soon as Darlecky reached her truck, her state cell phone clicked and clucked. "Darlecky," she answered.

"Spike Phillips. Heard you're organizing a monster hunt."

Phillips, who had no known given name, only the initials C. S., was the L'Anse post commander for the Michigan State Police. "There's no such thing as monsters, Spike."

"Not even Tim McVeigh and Charlie Manson?"

"Criminals, not monsters," she countered.

"I guess we can agree to disagree."

"What the hell do you *want*, Spike? I'm busy."

"Just bustin' your balls, Darlecky."

She closed the phone to his laugh and drove out toward the area of the sightings. All five had been seen in the evening over the last two days, all of them on the north slope of a mountain, near the mouth of the Little Huron River, which was two or three miles from the Free Humans compound.

No point guessing what might have stimulated the weird reports. As a cop you learned early in your career to keep your imagination in check, and to deal with reality as it revealed itself. The complicating factor in this was night. She was sure of that. She still found it remarkable how many people were scared out of their wits by the night. She had never been afraid, which put her in a very small minority. Even some other conservation officers were creeped out by the dark and some wouldn't work nights unless forced to.

Whenever she mentioned this phenomenon, most people objected until she ticked off her list of evidence of mankind's dislike for dark: twenty-four-hour street lights, nightlights in every room, vehicle headlights you couldn't turn off, cabinets and trucks filled with flashlights, closets of kerosene lanterns and candles, houses and farms in the country with twenty-four-hour spotlights. Dark was an enemy to be pushed back by light. Just listen to your minister or read the Bible. The dark was where the wild and untamed ruled.

Ridiculous.

Huron Road would take her to the mouth, but it was soft sugar sand and with snowmelt still in the rivers, the Huron would be too deep and swift to wade. Instead she took a two-track down the other side of the Huron to Lake Superior, parked and locked the truck, got her field pack and headed up hill into the woods to look around. Still plenty of light left which would make it easy to look for sign.

Sign of what? What exactly kind of marks did a monster leave in its wake?

Can't believe I'm out here doing this. The crap COs are expected to do.

• • •

Several strenuous hours and no sign of anything unusual, not even any deer sign to speak of and before she knew it, night was coming in fast. Recent rains left the forest floor damp and quiet. Darlecky sat on a rock overlooking a small vale and ate her sandwich, venison meatloaf on Huron Mountain Indian Bread. When dark fell, she thought about angling directly back to her truck, but in for a dime. It would make more sense to play this out, loop around Bald Mountain to a two-track running south and walk that back to the truck.

She was skirting an area of tamaracks when she heard muted voices and slowly made her way toward them, wondering who the heck was in the woods tonight. Not mushroom hunters, not in the dark.

A muffled voice said, "You *can* do this."

"Can't."

"Can."

"Can't if I can't move my damn legs. I'm froze in place here."

"Deep breaths, Paul. Control your breathing. This is just dark, nothing more."

"I don't want to."

"I don't believe you. It's all you talked about driving up here."

"I was whistling in the graveyard."

"This is not a graveyard, Paul."

"In your head, maybe."

"C'mon, give it a try."

Darlecky kept listening and inching forward, closing in.

"Okay, one more time and if I can't, I can't."

"You can."

"Don't push me, Tank."

"I'm encouraging, not pushing."

"It feels pushy. Perception is reality."

The CO knelt and listened, heard no more voices, thought she heard the vague sound of boots pushing wet leaves, an occasional twig popping. No flashlight from the voices and no sound, damn impressive sound suppression.

Several times she got on her knees and shone her red penlight to find where leaves had been ruffled. They were quiet all right, but not trying to hide their trail. *Got you,* she thought. She moved ahead, picking up her pace.

Their sign led her over a ridge and down into the bottom where it cut directly east, and they must've hurried on because she heard no sound and picked up her speed until she heard faint voices again, found the leaf trail leaving the two-track up into some rocks.

She was easing between two boulders when a bright light lit her up and stopped her like a deer, wide-eyed, mouth hanging open.

"Who the hell is dogging us?" a voice demanded.

"Get your light out of her face. She has a badge, Tank."

"Badge? Who the hell are you?" the first voice challenged.

"I heard your voices and wondered who was out here. Conservation Officer Darlecky, Michigan Department of Natural Resources."

The gruff voice. "Outside our wire we get followed by a girl game warden in full battle rattle and we never hear shit until she's on top of us. If she's Muj, we'd have been meat."

The light was still in her face. "I'm sorry, guys," Darlecky said. "How about you get the light off me and we talk?" As soon as they turned off their light, she turned on her SureFire and put it right in their eyes.

"Hey!" the gruff one barked.

"Turnabout. Want to see who I'm dealing with."

Having said that, she found it hard to keep the light steady, and finally clicked it off. She had just seen something so horrible, so unimagined she could hardly describe it to herself.

The three stood in darkness. "We're not supposed to be out here?" the less gruff voice asked. The one called Paul, she thought, guessing.

"Not at all, you guys are cool. This is state land."

"So why you want to red-ass us," gruff voice asked.

"Just doing my job," Darlecky said.

"Give it a break, Tank," the other voice said.

"Are you guys lost?" she asked.

"Do we *look* lost?" This the voice she now identified as Tank.

"You guys camping out this way?" she asked, changing subjects.

"Camp RFC," the one called Paul said. "Got up here two days ago."

She'd never heard of a Camp RFC. "Just the two of you?"

"Ten of us," Paul said.

"Nine, ass-wire," Tank grumbled. "Harlan ain't makin' it."

"If you fellows don't need directions, I'll be on my way."

"You work a lot in the dark?" Paul asked.

"My name's Steffi," she said. "We work at night all the time during certain times of the year."

"*This* time of the year?" the second voice asked and added, "I'm Paul, he's Tank."

"Not so much this time of year."

"So why you out here?" Tank asked.

"Had several reports of unusual activity out this way."

"Fuckin' screamers camp," Tank complained.

Paul said, "We encountered some people over the last two nights and we musta scared them some."

Tank said. "They run off screaming like maniacs."

"We're just out working on some issues in our rehab," Paul said.

"Rehab?"

"Army," Paul said. "We come out to the woods to readjust to darkness."

"Vets?"

"We're housed in a trauma unit in Dayton," Paul said. "Some of us have been under reconstruction for four years."

"You saw our faces," Tank said. "We're in what the sawbones call the close-enough stage."

She was at a loss for words and decided to mostly listen. "So you're up here."

"Mostly it's a little R&R," Paul said. "Fish, consume some brain grenades. You want some coffee?"

"Wouldn't mind. You got a thermos?"

"Back at camp, not with us."

"Sure," she said, thinking, Ohmygod. She had never seen such disfigurement before, not ever. It was beyond imagination.

• • •

Their faces might be wrecked, but the men were in impressive physical condition, their camp two miles from where she'd encountered them, a nice cabin on a feeder creek, not a hundred yards from where it dumped into the East Branch of the Huron River. Rocky country, with terrible footing, a hair off the grid and great for brook trout, if you were willing to make the wading effort.

The men introduced themselves, stared her in the eye and she did her best to do the same, but it was really hard. Felt almost like they wanted to make her flinch and look away. But she refused to let herself. Paul and Tank reintroduced themselves in the light. Then Garrett, Ratface, Noseguard, Looselip, Alexander, Barak, and Toejam.

"Barak?" she asked the one man.

"Yah, sounds like the Prez, but I didn't get the same pigment gene."

"He's a Jewboy," Tank said. "Ignore his shit."

The men's faces were horribly disfigured, some much more severely than others, but all bad, none of them looking like anything other than a primitive mask. For some reason they reminded her of the floppy bug-eyed faces of newborn birds, all nasty, distended fleshy angles and splotchy blotches of discolored flesh.

"You guys serve together?" she asked, immediately sorry. It was a stupid question.

Paul said, "No, we met in various rehab units along the way. Most of us will get back to active duty if we can get our heads on straight after the surgeons finish. We're the lucky fuckers. So many guys with no arms, no hands, legs, feet, dicks, you name it. We all just got whoomped by the ugly stick."

"Sandbags," Tank said. "Some guys just sacks of sand."

"Shutup, Tank," one of the men said.

It all settled after awhile. They gave her coffee and Darlecky stepped outside with Paul. "Those people you guys ran into, what happened?"

"Not much. They walked up on us in low light and freaked out. I can't blame them."

"You're not offended?"

"No, we see this crap all the time, every time we leave our ward or base and we get it from people who should know better too, including doctors. We just didn't expect it in the north woods," he said with a laugh.

"Lot of people out looking for morels," she told him.

"We don't want to be a bother."

"You're not."

"If we're going to freak out the locals, we'll need to stay deep in our property."

"Baloney," Darlecky said.

Paul stared at her with owly eyes.

"You game to try something?" she asked him.

"Try *what*?

"Work on issues," she said.

• • •

The auditorium of L'Anse High School was full. In two days, Darlecky had drummed up major community and media interest in the monster sightings and she announced a Friday night press conference to reveal her findings.

She looked at the wall clock. It was 7 p.m. She walked across the stage to a lectern and said, "Okay, everybody, I guess it's time." TV lights came on.

Someone in the rear of the auditorium yelled, "It's about damn time!"

Darlecky stared out at the audience. "Do you believe in monsters?"

They responded with applause and some foot-stomping.

Another voice yelled, "Stop jacking us around and get *on* with it!"

Darlecky went over to the side door on the stage and opened it. Nine men in various military clothing filed out and stood in a line behind the lectern.

She introduced them left to right, by name, by rank, by where they had served, and where they had been wounded.

Not a sound came from the audience. A cough now and then, labored breathing, someone sobbing.

My Perfect Italian

Dating? Seriously? He was nice enough to look at, polite, full-haired, straight white teeth, trimmed and manicured nails, a lawyer, well traveled, worldly and experienced, charming, everything a woman could want. And she couldn't remember his name. He had hit on her meekly but relentlessly for weeks and finally she had caved to the pressure, and here they were and she had no clue to his name. None, it was gone, blank, lost in a void.

Nametags should be mandatory on dates, she told herself.

What's his face is holding his menu, looking over at her. "What will you have? Do you like fish?"

"Only sole, only plain."

"Nothing else?" he asks.

"Just sole, that's all."

"But you must try other things. Life requires risk," says he.

Risk? She was a conservation officer. Her life was risk, nearly every minute of every workday. "With my food, I want no risk. I know what I like and I know when I'm hungry."

"Are you hungry now?"

"Not particularly."

"What about wine?" he asks.

"What about it?"

"Do you like it?"

"Some of it. I know what I like."

"And nothing more?" his voice is tinny.

"No."

He orders a Pouilly Fuisse, same price as a box of ought-six ammo. This sort of spending offends her sense of propriety and frugality, what she calls the art of living thin.

But he pushes the issue in a tender way and this amuses her and to some extent, astonishes her. The wine is good, very good.

"You like it?" he asks.

"Yes, it's very nice."

"Would you have it another time?"

"No."

"No?"

"It might not be as good next time and that would disappoint me. I'd rather remember this time and how good it was."

He has a foie gras starter, followed by fricasseed lobster in a thick white sauce, with steamed vegetables and fresh warm bread.

She has sole, plain, grilled, alone, the way she likes it, no frills on the side.

No desserts. Both of them work hard to maintain their figures and condition. Superfluous calories are enemies.

"A nightcap at Gagnon's?" he asks as they await the check.

"No, too many drunk college kids and the wait-staff treats you badly."

"I know a quiet little place in Negaunee. Very quiet, not filled with beery kids, almost like a club. They will treat us respectfully."

"If not," she says, "we will go elsewhere."

The place is small and dark, a half dozen tables, intimate, faded furniture, a little dusty, she likes it immediately.

They are seated by an elderly woman. "What will you have?" she asks.

"Irish coffee," she says.

She toys with the cream-berg on top when the drink is delivered. There is music coming out of the walls or ceiling.

"Do you have a boyfriend?" he asks.

They always ask, sooner or later. "Not at present."

"You like, live alone?"

Ah one of the like-folk. She hates this speech convention. "Yes, of course."

"Do you like living alone?"

"It's what I do and how it is. Yes, of course, I like it very much."

"What about vacations?"

"What about them?

"Do you take holidays?"

"Of course."

"Do you go anywhere special?"

"Sometimes."

"Downstate?"

"To Italy, in the south. I can't abide the north."

"What do you do there?"

"I walk in the hills."

"And you walk a lot in your job?"

"Yes, a great deal, but in Italy there are stone steps up to remote villages, the sort of places where you don't have to see other tourists. Children in the village crowded around me, made me feel special."

"You like children?"

"Sometimes, not always."

"You walk, that's all?"

"Sometimes I go down the hills to the sea and get wet and dry myself on a large flat rock."

"You're a sun-worshipper," he asserts with a smirk.

"Not at all. I use the sun only to dry me."

"Do you wear a bathing suit?"

"Never. Once in Sicily a man came to the rock and looked at me for a long time. He was short with dark skin and black curly hair. His teeth were bad. He had a shotgun on a rope sling."

"Were you afraid?"

"I rather liked it, but he went away."

"Did you cover up?"

"No, I wanted him to look, to see. He was only looking. A lot of men are like that."

"What sort of man do you want in your life?"

"I don't know. I met an Italian guy in college, seven years older than me, an instructor. He was good to me, very kind and generous. He gave and he gave, and I took and I took. He was the best of all of them."

"All? How many is that?"

"I don't know. Must there be a number?"

He ignores the question. "What happened to your Italian?"

"His contract was up. He went back home."

"Did he ask you to go with him?"

"He begged me, but I said no. I had just gotten my own apartment, just begun to be on my own. I wanted independence. I think I will never know another man like him."

"If it were now, would you go?"

"In an instant."

"But you had that chance."

"No, I had not had my independence yet, and I didn't want to give that up before I knew what it was."

"Relationships require sacrifice," nameless date says.

"Not for me."

"But aren't you lonely?"

"No, I am alone. That's not the same as lonely."

"Do you want to remain alone?"

"I don't know. That's the way it is, isn't it? There have been men, all bad except my Italian."

"When you go to Italy, are you looking for him?"

"Never."

"What made the others bad?"

"They took."

"But you took from your Italian, took and took, you told me about it."

"Only from the Italian. He knew I needed that. The others didn't know what I needed."

"Which is?"

"To be alone," she says. *Is he thick?*

"You can't be *with* someone *and* alone."

"I have. Lovers should live apart, not spend all their time together."

"I don't understand what made the Italian so special," he says.

"He allowed me to be whimsical, to play the radio and stereo as loud as I wanted. I read, only pre-1900, but even before that time, there are many bad writers to be discarded."

"TV, movies? You don't strike me as a reader," he says.

"Because I'm a cop?"

"Not that. I don't know why. What exactly do you read?"

"Dostoyevsky, Nietzsche, he's much maligned you know."

"Do you cook?"

"Only waffles. I hate to cook. The stove is my enemy."

"What do you do at night?"

"When not on patrol? I read, but if my day is too long, I get over-stimulated. Then I can't sleep."

"When you can't sleep, what do you do about it?"

"Nothing. I lie there and fret about it."

"What about exercise?"

"That only stimulates me more. My Italian knew how to calm me. He lived close by. We lived together apart. I would call him and he would come and put me to sleep."

"But no boyfriend currently."

"There was one not long ago, but I sacked him. He was no good."

"In what way?"

"In all ways."

"How old was he?"

"Forty-seven."

"That's too old for you, too great an age gap."

"Not at all. At twenty-four I had a lover sixty-two. It was okay."

"Do you know *what* you want in a man?"

"To let me be me, to allow me my whimsy, to know what I need without being told. He must be a good dancer and to come to me when I cannot sleep. To take me to dinner but not order for me."

"What about marrying for love?" he asks.

"It's better to marry for companionship."

"Why?"

"Passionate love and mystery evaporate if you're together all the time. It's better to marry a companion, have your sex and passion with others."

He looks totally bollixed and she tells him, "I don't know how to take care of a man, not really."

"What do you mean?"

"My hand, my mouth, I don't know how to do all that, don't know what a man wants or expects. I don't need orgasms to enjoy sex," she discloses, looking at him eye to eye.

No kiss good night, no hug, no promises of a call or another date. "I had fun," is all he says.

She smiles, lets him walk away. Sighs with relief.

Talk about an ordeal.

• • •

Next day, she partners with CO Halifax Shopsovitch, and he asks right away, "You have your date with that guy?"

"Yes."

"Go okay?"

"It's over," she says. "Done."

"Give him the Italian bit?"

"Both barrels."

"Think he'll be bugging you any more?"

"Don't think so," thirty-year-old Sicilia Turberville said. "How come you asked about the guy and didn't use his name?"

"I can't remember it," her partner admitted. He was the best partner, always had her back, lifted her when she was down, calmed her when she got hyped, allowed her whimsy to run free.

She chuckles. "Me neither."

"Last night you couldn't remember?"

"Total blank, not even after I got home. It went bye bye, I guess."

"Why go through the agony of dating if you're not interested?" Shopsovitch asks.

She shrugs. "You never know."

Printed in the USA
CPSIA information can be obtained
at www.ICGtesting.com
LVHW080258051123
761582LV00038B/319